D0336557

THE THREE
DAY AFFAIR

MICHAEL KARDOS is the author of the award-winning story collection, *One Last Good Time*. He is assistant professor of English and co-director of the creative writing program at Mississippi State University. This is his first novel.

MICHAEL KARDOS

THE THREE DAY AFFAIR

BAINTE DEN STOC

WITHDRAWN FROM DÚN LAOGHAIRE

A Mysterious Press Book
for Head of Zeus

First published in 2012 by Mysterious Press,
an imprint of Grove/Atlantic, New York.

This edition first published in the UK in 2013 by Head of Zeus Ltd.

Copyright © Michael Kardos, 2012

The moral right of Michael Kardos to be identified as the author of this work has
been asserted in accordance with the Copyright, Designs and Patents Act of 1988.

All rights reserved. No part of this publication may be reproduced, stored in
a retrieval system, or transmitted in any form or by any means, electronic,
mechanical, photocopying, recording, or otherwise, without the prior permission
of both the copyright owner and the above publisher of this book.

This is a work of fiction. All characters, organizations, and events portrayed in
this novel are either products of the author's imagination or are used fictitiously.

9 7 5 3 1 2 4 6 8

A CIP catalogue record for this book is available from the British Library.

ISBN (HB): 9781781850817
ISBN (TPB): 9781781850824
ISBN (E): 9781781852002

DUN LAOGHAIRE-RATHDOWN LIBRARIES	
DLR20001014801	
BERTRAMS	22/02/2013
	£15.99
BR	

For my family

PROLOGUE

Six years ago, my band's bassist was shot dead in a New York nightclub. Her name was Gwen Dalton, and she'd only been with the band a few months when she was killed.

Our original bassist, Andy, had surprised us all when he decided to move to Los Angeles with his girlfriend. We were annoyed that he would leave New York just when the band was finally creating a stir. High Noon had been together for five years, and we'd worked hard to build up a following. We were finally packing the Wetlands and CBGB, and a small indie record label was talking to us about recording a CD. So how can you leave us now? we asked him. How can you do that to us?

"I'm doing it for love," he explained.

And how do you argue with that?

We held auditions at Fred McPhee's apartment in the East Village. Fred was the band's guitarist and lead vocalist. I was the drummer. We'd already heard half a dozen players stumble their way through our songs when Gwen showed up.

In all the years I'd played in rock groups, starting at the age of fourteen, I hadn't ever been bandmates with a woman before, and for a brief moment I was doubtful. Then Gwen lifted the instrument out of its case, and I saw that it was a custom-made, six-string Fodera—four grand easy. As she tuned up, her fingers ran nimbly up and down the fretboard. Underneath her spiky hair and pink lipstick was a delicate face, but her fingers were stubby and callused. A musician's fingers. We taught her one of our tunes, which she picked up immediately. The second time through, she was already adding licks that Andy couldn't have played. By then we were all loosened up. She was smiling to herself, head tilted in concentration, and it was obvious that we'd found our new bassist.

All that fall we played shows throughout New York and Connecticut and New Jersey. Gwen had infused our jangly rock sound with a hint of funk and looked good doing it. But on Sunday morning, December 5, 1999, at 2:10 AM, while we were packing up our equipment after a gig at the Cobra Club near the Columbia University campus, somebody fired a gun outside on the street. The bullet passed through a window and struck Gwen just above her right cheekbone. She had been talking to me at the time. I was standing less than three feet away. When she got hit, her head jerked to the side a little, as if an invisible hand had slapped her. She stood there for the next few seconds, and I stood watching her and wondering why she'd suddenly stopped talking.

The shooting was a drive-by, the intended target somebody out on the street who fled the scene. It had nothing to do with us. No one was ever caught. Gwen died two days later at St. Luke's Hospital. I was there in the critical care unit at the time, pacing outside her room. I remember looking in and seeing the nurses moving their hands and a doctor shaking his head and the setting sun absurdly bathing her parents' faces in the prettiest orange light.

That night, I told Fred that I wouldn't be playing the drums anytime soon.

My wife, Cynthia, and I had always thought of ourselves as city people. She was from Philadelphia. I had grown up in Bayonne, and lived in Greenwich Village since graduating from college. But now my heart would lurch with every sudden noise. I'd spend most nights wired on coffee, sitting by the window of our third-story walk-up and staring out at shadows. I felt wholly unable to protect either myself or my new bride from any of a thousand brutal deaths. One day during the week before Christmas, we went exploring on the Jersey side of the Holland Tunnel and kept driving until the traffic lightened, the trees became plentiful, and we had ourselves a good, quiet suburb.

Besides playing in the band, I had been working part-time in a midtown recording studio. I told my boss that I wouldn't be back. Cynthia hired a headhunter to find her a new public relations job in Jersey. By the new year, we had packed our things into a U-Haul and were gone.

We knew the suburbs would be less exciting than the city, but really that was the appeal. We chose the town of Newfield, where the people we talked to assured us that any criminal activity was limited to Halloween and involved nothing more than toilet paper and eggs. The public schools, we learned, were top rated. We planned to have children someday, maybe soon, and Newfield felt like the right place to raise them.

And yet the adjustment to Newfield was hard, the silence itself unnerving. The calm we'd sought away from the city made it too easy for me to become preoccupied by my own thoughts. Eventually I found work at a small recording studio not far from home. The hours and pay were lousy, but it was a job I knew how to do, one that put me in contact with other musicians and demanded my full attention. And in time, I found myself able to sleep through the night again.

If our lives weren't exciting, they were nonetheless filled with happy moments. Husband-and-wife moments. Nights-out moments. Christmases-by-the-fire moments. By the time the Twin

Towers fell nearly two years later, our lives were far enough removed from New York City that our horror held no special currency.

I wasn't making music anymore, but I was helping others to make it. Cynthia got promoted several times at the PR firm. And when we found out she was pregnant, we were glad. Three years had passed since our move to Newfield, and we felt ready for this child in our lives. By then, violent crime was about the furthest thing from my mind, until the night when I helped one of my best friends kidnap a young woman.

PART ONE

CHAPTER 1

I T ALMOST DIDN'T HAPPEN—the kidnapping and everything after. That's the part that gets me, even now.

The phone call came early Sunday morning, waking me out of a dead sleep.

"You're going to have to count me out, man," he said, before identifying himself.

"Who is this?" I'd had to fumble for the telephone in the pitch-black bedroom.

"I should stay in California."

"Jeffrey?"

"Guilty as charged," he said. "And completely and utterly in hell."

He would talk this way sometimes, full of woe and melo-drama, back in college. But college was a long time ago. "What's going on?" I asked. "Is everybody okay?"

Cynthia was awake beside me then, hand on my arm. I glanced at the clock on my bedside table: 4:55 AM.

"Oh, crap," Jeffrey said, "you were asleep, weren't you?"

"Forget it. Just tell me what's the matter."

"Wish I could," he said. "I really do. But I shouldn't even be . . ." His voice dropped off; the sudden silence frightened me.

"Jeffrey?"

"Ah, shit," he said.

"*What?*"

"Nothing. My glass fell over."

It occurred to me that it was 2 AM in California and that Jeffrey was slurring his words. "Where are you?" I asked.

"Me? I'm at home."

"Is Sara with you?"

"She's upstairs sleeping. She doesn't know I'm calling."

"Why *are* you calling?"

"Trust me," he said, "you don't want to know."

Of course I did. After all these years, I was glad that Jeffrey still saw me as someone he could reach out to in the middle of the night with a problem—even if the problem was that he'd been drinking and needed an old friend to dial up, to remind himself he still had old friends to dial up.

"Try me," I said.

"No, I shouldn't have called. Sorry to bother you—but I'm serious about the trip. You don't want me there." He was due to arrive in just a few days, along with Nolan and Evan, my other two best college buddies. "I'm not in a good place. I should really call the airline right now and cancel. I'm serious."

I sat up a little in bed and tried to sound more awake. "Listen to me—we're your friends. We want to see you, even if you're feeling like shit. It'll be good for you. So forget about canceling, all right?"

Outside my window, a single car drove by, its headlights briefly casting light on the bedroom shades. I watched the window darken again, thinking that Jeffrey might have fallen asleep at the other end of the line. But then, as if remembering his manners: "So how are you and Cynthia doing?"

Classic Jeffrey. I told him we were doing fine, and that I looked forward to giving him the complete update when I saw him in a few days. "Seriously, though, are you okay?"

I heard him yawn into the phone. "Sorry," he said. "I think I'm a little tired."

"If you want, we can talk tomorrow, when we're both a little more awake."

Another pause. Then: "Yeah, that's a good idea. You always were the smart one." His voice was fading fast. "Okay, good night, Will."

When I awoke again a few hours later, the call already felt like a half-forgotten dream. Except, when I checked my e-mail that afternoon, I had this message:

Hey, Will—

Wow. I'm really sorry to have woken you up like that. And to have been so melodramatic. God, I'm a jerk. A lot of that was the gin. I'm really okay. Anyway, you're a good friend. (Okay, the best.) And you were right—of course I'll be there. A return to Jersey? No way am I missing that.

Looking forward to seeing you and the guys soon.

Your friend,
Jeffrey

Neither of us mentioned the call again. I assumed he was probably embarrassed by it, and I knew there'd be plenty of time for us to talk when we saw each other in just a few days. So I waited.

But there it was. He was going to cancel his trip, and I had talked him out of it.

9

• • •

They arrived on Friday.

I'd spent the morning and early afternoon in the recording studio with a band called The Fixtures. Teenage bands could be a headache, but these kids had talent to match their ambition. We were having a productive session, but by three o'clock I had to call it quits and rush everyone out before the traffic leaving New York would clog all the westbound roads, making the drive back to Newfield unbearable.

Walking to the car, I called Cynthia at the house and learned that Nolan had just arrived from Kansas City.

"Tell him I'm on my way," I said.

"I'll tell him," she said, "but don't drive like a maniac, okay? We're fine over here."

I headed home. Though only a dozen miles from the studio, Newfield was like another world, where you heard more birds than cars and the strongest smell was the cypress mulch that people lovingly laid at the base of their shrubs. Our street was lined with neatly pruned maple trees, and at the end of it stood a brick elementary school. Each morning, small children walked past our front yard, chattering like squirrels and lugging their huge knapsacks.

Our craftsman cottage was the smallest house on the block and only a rental, but buying a home would have meant living someplace cheaper, less desirable, less safe. And safety was key. It was the whole point.

The day before, I'd mowed and edged the lawn. Pulling up to the house now, I admired my work. Those were the kinds of things I noticed then: a freshly cut yard. Daisies in terra-cotta flowerpots lining the walkway.

Across the street, Dr. Ferguson was hosing off his Lexus. Sudsy water streamed down his driveway. He waved. I waved back and went inside. Through the kitchen window, I saw Cynthia and Nolan in the backyard kneeling over our empty garden plot, where in a few weeks we would be planting tomatoes and peppers and summer squash. I went out to greet them.

Seeing me approach, Nolan stood and then helped Cynthia up. She was starting to show. I liked how she stood differently now, shifting her weight to accommodate the changing center of gravity.

"Hands off the wife," I told him.

"Take it easy, killer," Nolan said. "She's only been showing me her dirt."

Cynthia and I had both grown up in neighborhoods of brick and concrete, where tall buildings blocked out the sun. We couldn't get enough of our grassy yard. One of our photo albums was full of pictures from our first summer in the house: Cynthia in her cutoffs and Velvet Underground T-shirt, gathering up twigs from the grass. Me mowing the lawn, shirtless and grinning from behind mirrored sunglasses as if our small rectangle of land were a thousand-acre stake.

"It's good to see you, buddy," Nolan said. We hadn't seen each other since our last golf weekend a year earlier. We hugged.

He stood six feet and three inches tall with unlined skin and a full head of black hair—not a speck of gray—that he kept neatly trimmed. At Princeton he'd rowed crew for a year, until it got in the way of his studies, but he still kept himself in shape. When we'd get together, even after a night of drinking, he'd wake up at dawn to run a few miles before breakfast.

"You're looking good," I said, though truthfully his eyes looked tired. I'd been receiving his e-newsletter, *From the Campaign Trail,* since January, when he declared his candidacy for the U.S. House of Representatives. But I gathered that the trail was weedier and windier than the newsletter was letting on. "You're also looking like you could use a beer."

11

We went inside, where I got two beers out of the refrigerator and a bottle of spring water for Cynthia.

"I'll take mine for the road," she said. "I'm going to get caught in traffic as it is."

"You can stay," I said. "Honest."

She cocked an eyebrow at me.

I hadn't asked her to clear out for the weekend. But she understood that for my friends and me, these annual reunions were an important tradition. And she figured it would be a good chance to visit her sister, who lived in Philadelphia with her boyfriend and three-year-old daughter.

"Not a chance," she said. "The estrogen is leaving the building. Just do me a favor and don't get into too much trouble while I'm gone." As if this were going to be a wild bachelor party instead of old friends catching up. Playing a few rounds of golf. A little poker. "And maybe carry my suitcase for me."

I brought her bag to her car, asked if the tank was full, if the cell phone was charged. "Call me before you go to bed," I said. We kissed, and my fingertips brushed the small of her back as she bent down to get in the car. I stood on the front lawn, squinting in the sunlight, as she backed out of the driveway, waved her pretty fingers, and drove away.

Back in the kitchen, Nolan tossed me an Albright-for-Congress baseball cap. I stuck it on my head.

"Wear it everywhere," he said. "By the way, Cynthia looks hot."

"Thanks," I said. "And very classy."

"How far along is she?"

"Almost five months."

"This is a pretty sweet life you're leading," he said. This was good form, I knew, rather than honest sentiment. Nolan had no wife, no kids, and was content. "I mean it," he went on, "the house,

12

the garden, great wife, kid on the way . . . I'm glad to see things are going so well for you."

For a while I'd hesitated before asking my friends to come visit me here in Newfield. In the nine years since college, Nolan, Evan, and Jeffrey had all become remarkably successful. And as long as I'd been a struggling New York musician, I believed that my world made sense to them. They understood risk taking if the rewards were big enough. But I couldn't help feeling uneasy about them coming here to the suburbs and seeing my current life through the lenses of their own.

I felt ashamed, suddenly, for feeling this way. Friends understood. It was what made them friends.

"I'm a lucky guy," I said.

"Glad you know it." Then Nolan clapped his hands once and leaned forward in his chair at the kitchen table. "All right—so talk. What's the big mystery?"

I'd asked him to arrive in town before the others because I wanted to discuss something important.

I opened my beer and took a sip. "No big mystery. I've been kicking around a business idea and wanted to run it by you."

"I'm listening," he said.

I had done a lot more than kick the idea around, so I launched right into it: I wanted to start a small record label. The vital parts of a record company were the ability to make a great record and to promote it. I knew how to make a great-sounding record. And Cynthia was the best PR person I knew.

I explained that the owner of the studio where I worked had already agreed to let me record there off-hours for utility costs and a percentage of sales. For fifty thousand dollars, I figured, we could record and promote our first two CDs.

"I know some great musicians out there," I said. "All they need is some exposure."

"How much money have you raised so far?" Nolan asked.

"Raised?" I shook my head. "We've been able to put a few thousand into savings. But now with the baby coming, we wanted to see if we could move things along."

"So you're asking me to invest?"

I didn't like asking Nolan for money. Jeffrey, actually, was the wealthiest of my friends—but Nolan owed me. During his first run for state senate, I'd moved to Missouri for the last four weeks of his campaign. I'd given him my time, because that was all I had.

"Ten thousand," I said, then quickly added, "I know it's a lot. But you'd be part owner, of course."

"That'd be interesting, owning part of a record company." He sipped his beer, set it back down on the table. He looked at the label for a moment. At last he said, "But I won't invest ten thousand dollars. I'm sorry."

So much for that.

"It's okay," I said. "I understand."

He frowned. "Do you?" He drank from his beer, set it down again. "You're going to run into costs you never expected. That's how business works. So if you think you'll need fifty thousand, then you ought to be raising a hundred. So no, I won't invest ten thousand. But I'll invest twenty."

He finished his beer, got two more from the refrigerator, opened them, and handed me one.

"You're joking," I said.

He laughed. "You're my friend and a talented guy. I believe in you. Why on earth *wouldn't* I invest?"

I had no answer. "So twenty thousand, just like that?"

He snapped his fingers. "Just like that." He grinned. "Now, if we can get twenty grand each out of Jeffrey and Evan, that'd go a long way toward getting those first two records off the ground, wouldn't it?"

It sure would. And maybe I'd mention it to Evan at some point over the next few days. But Jeffrey clearly needed a vacation, and I intended to give him one without hitting him up for cash.

The majority of Newfield's citizens commuted to New York City, where for eight or ten hours they pushed and pulled the levers that made America run. Newfield Station was at the center of town. I parked the car, and Nolan and I waited for Jeffrey and Evan to arrive on the 4:12.

In the past, we'd met up in Palm Springs, Hilton Head Island, Bermuda. Once a year, I didn't mind splurging. But now I was trying to save, and so back in January I'd asked them all to consider coming here. My friends worked long and hard, and I didn't like asking them to downgrade their vacation on my account. Yet without a single complaint, they'd all agreed to forgo an exotic locale for a weekend in Jersey.

At least the weather was cooperating. The forecast called for a sunny, mild weekend. The sky was currently a deep blue, with only the thinnest rim of gray on the western horizon.

I'd reserved tee times at two courses about thirty miles to the northwest, in the Kittatinny Mountains, an area I hadn't been to for years. Back when I was a Boy Scout I'd camped there a couple of times but had found the woods frightening. I was a city kid, not used to nature or silence. By high school these same woods had become a place of escape, somewhere to hike around with friends and drink· beer. You could forget you were in New Jersey, walking for hours without coming across a single irritated, short-tempered soul.

Tomorrow we'd warm up with the easier course, one with wide fairways and few hazards. Then on Sunday we'd play the top-rated public course in the state, a heavily wooded eighteen holes in a secluded valley, where supposedly it was common to spot eagles overhead.

15

"You can't imagine how much I've been looking forward to this," Nolan said, when I described the courses to him. "Campaigning can wear you down."

"I remember," I said.

"Nah, that was only a statewide election," he said. "This is a whole different ball game."

I'd wondered whether Nolan would have time for us this year. But when I'd e-mailed him a few weeks earlier, asking if he was sure his campaign could do without him for a weekend, he fired back a philosophical reply: *If I can't take a weekend off to see my closest friends, then what the hell is it all for?*

The train arrived and spat out dozens of businessmen and women, well dressed but rumpled in the aftershock of their workweek. Jeffrey teetered off the train, suitcase in one hand, golf bag in the other. Seeing us standing by my car, he set the suitcase on the ground and waved. We went over to greet him.

"I didn't see Evan on the train," Jeffrey said by way of greeting. He'd boarded at Newark Airport. Evan was supposed to have boarded the same train earlier in New York.

Just then my cell phone rang, cutting the mystery short.

"Don't even try to imagine all the fucking work that got dumped on me today," Evan said into my ear.

He was a year away from making partner at his law firm. The way he explained it, to make partner at a major New York firm you couldn't simply work eighty-hour weeks. You had to work eighty-hour weeks and ask for more.

When I got off the phone, Nolan and Jeffrey were both looking incredulous. I confirmed their suspicions. "He's tied up."

"Tied up?" Jeffrey said. "What the hell does that mean?"

I shrugged. "Lawyer stuff."

"Oh, for Pete's sake," Nolan said. "Jeffrey made it. *I* made it. . . ."

"He said he'll be here tomorrow morning," I told them. "He

16

promised to be on the first train." I picked up Jeffrey's golf bag and headed to the car. "Come on—you guys must be starving."

They were. We decided on an early dinner. Afterward, we'd go to the golf range and hit practice balls. Then we'd head back to the house for a drink on the porch.

"I bought a bottle of Scotch and some cigars," I said as I lowered Jeffrey's luggage into the trunk.

"None for me," Jeffrey said. I figured, given how drunk he'd obviously been last weekend, that he meant the Scotch, until he added, "I've quit smoking."

"So have I," I said. "Cigarettes, anyway." It'd been a month since my last cigarette. Not easy considering where I worked— where there was no ventilation and the carpet reeked so badly it seemed to have been woven *from* smoke. "But I've got a baby coming. What's your excuse?"

"Same as yours," he said. We looked at him, confused. "Sara's pregnant."

"Well, I'll be damned," Nolan said.

Jeffrey and Sara had been married for eight years with no children.

"Congrats, man," I said. "That's terrific news."

"Yeah, I guess so," he said listlessly, and I couldn't help wondering just what the hell he wasn't telling.

Antonello's was a favorite restaurant of Cynthia's and mine for special occasions. I returned from the restroom to find antipasto on the table and Nolan engaged in a full-on sales pitch.

"I told Will it sounded like a great idea," he was saying to Jeffrey, "and that he should count me in for twenty. So what about you?"

I sat down, torn between interrupting the conversation and hearing what Jeffrey had to say. He shrugged. "I'll have to think it over."

"Forget it," I said. "We can talk about this some other time." Then, to Nolan: "I'd rather hear about your campaign."

"Think what over?" Nolan said. "Come on, we're talking about a twenty-grand investment. It's a no-brainer."

"Look, guys," I said, "I don't want anyone feeling pressure over this."

I wondered, though, if I was being completely honest. Jeffrey lived two blocks from San Francisco Bay. He had joined an Internet start-up at the beginning of the boom. When the company went public, it took him five beers over dinner to admit to us that his stake in the company was "hovering around thirty million dollars." This was at another of our golf weekends, in Palm Springs, and I remember him trembling when he told us. He could have been confessing a crime. He had just turned twenty-five.

I'd been staggered. Playing the drums was earning me fifteen thousand dollars a year. The trip to Palm Springs was costing me close to a month's pay.

There were a few follow-up questions, but soon enough conversation returned to the old standbys: stories from college, highlights from the day's round. The fact of a twenty-foot putt was more real to us than thirty million dollars. After dinner we played low-stakes poker long into the night and finished off a case of beer. We were laughing again. A lightness to the evening had settled in. By morning, I'd done my best to put Jeffrey's wealth out of my mind. I think everyone had. We never talked about it again.

I hadn't planned to ask anyone other than Nolan for money this weekend. But now that the matter was on the table, I couldn't help weighing Jeffrey's enormous wealth against the relatively small investment Nolan was asking him to make. Okay, so Jeffrey was feeling a little gloomy lately. But still. If our situations had been reversed, I liked to think I would've opened my checkbook without any hesitation.

"But this is a solid plan." Nolan dipped a corner of bread in a plate of olive oil and used it to point at Jeffrey while he talked. "It's solid, and Will needs for this to happen. You're not even going to help him get it off the ground?"

"The music business is risky," Jeffrey said.

"So take a risk." Nolan tilted his head, as if just noticing something. "You seem really down. Are you down?"

Jeffrey smiled. "Good work, detective."

"Okay, so tell us what the fuck's the matter."

I had planned to share a golf cart tomorrow with Jeffrey, see if he felt like talking. Nolan was always a little more direct.

"Oh, a lot of things." He took a sip of water. "I don't mean to be mysterious. I just don't feel like getting into it now."

"You're in a rut, aren't you?" When Jeffrey didn't respond right away, he said, "Of course you are. You just turned thirty, you've got a baby coming, and you're looking at the rest of your long, boring life and freaking out. Am I right?"

"I guess it's something like that," Jeffrey said, though his face was uncharacteristically hard to read.

"Piece of cake," Nolan said. "Know what you need to do?"

"I give up."

"Do something unexpected. Surprise yourself. That's why guys are always skydiving and swimming the English Channel and shit. You need a shock to the system, something to remind yourself that you're alive." He poured himself some more wine. "And for starters, you can become a record company executive."

"Or," I cut in, "we can table the whole discussion about making records until later." The waiter was setting a vast tray of food on a stand beside our table. "How about we just eat until we can't move. How does that sound?"

Jeffrey managed a smile. "I think I can do that."

Nolan laughed suddenly.

19

"What?" I asked.

"There's a girl over there"—he nodded somewhere behind me—"who looks just like that fifteen-year-old you asked out at the Quakerbridge Mall. You remember?"

"Fuck off," I said, not bothering to glance over my shoulder. "She looked a lot older. And she said she went to Trenton State."

"Yeah, and with her mother right there, overhearing the whole thing."

Jeffrey glanced over at the girl. He shook his head, then refilled his wine as Nolan and I recounted this anecdote we all already knew, one of the many we told and retold over the years.

When we stopped speaking, Jeffrey took a sip of wine. "So, Will, have you thought of a name?"

I explained that Cynthia and I had decided ahead of time not to find out the sex of the baby. "So our list is getting pretty long."

"No, I mean a name for the record company."

"Oh." I smiled, having decided this long ago. "Long-Shot Records."

"Good name." The combination of wine and shared memories seemed to relax him. His face warmed. It was good to see. His moods could be as erratic as his golf game. Some days he had the touch of a pro, and other days he'd psych himself out and miss every three-foot putt. You never knew exactly which Jeffrey you were going to get. "All right," he said at last. "I surrender. Count me in for twenty grand."

"Glad to hear it." Nolan smiled, but then his smile faded away. "Seriously, though—do something bold. Surprise yourself. And for God's sake, don't buy a sports car."

Sometimes Cynthia asked me what we talked about when we got together and played our rounds of golf. She must have imagined us on the course baring our souls, the game primarily an occasion for the talk of old friends. But it wasn't that way. We talked, but mostly we golfed. Conversation tended to center around the previous shot, the next hole. Which club to use, which way the green might break. At night, over steaks, we'd reminisce. We had a deep well of stories from which to draw. But weightier conversation felt almost like an intrusion, business to be gotten through.

And yet tonight, as I ate my chicken cacciatore and drank my wine, I was thinking that even long-standing friendships required periodic injections of the now. At one time, we had all taken classes together and lived in the same dormitories, drunk from the same kegs and vomited on the same lawns. Our lives were led in close proximity, and we knew one another as only friends living together do. And while we liked to believe that our shared past was the anchor from which we could drift only so far, the truth was that each of us had changed. Maybe even a lot. And this should have been cause for celebration. It meant that we'd grown up. But to acknowledge this, to announce, "Look at me! Look who I've become!" would have been to disappoint everyone somehow, to destroy the illusion that we knew one another as well now as we once did.

The funny thing was, Cynthia wouldn't have liked me when I was twenty. Twenty-year-old Will was too raw, too desperate for everything: love, success, and confirmation that all his choices were the right ones. Probably we were all a little wiser now, a little more complicated. All of which is to say, I felt grateful for our new business partnership. Our friendships were secure to the degree that we all trusted in the past's strong anchor. But here, finally, was something new to bind us together, something in the present that had us looking to the future.

I proposed a toast.

"To what?" Jeffrey asked.

"To your fat pregnant wives," Nolan said. "And to Will's new business."

I raised my glass. "To old friends."

Leaving the restaurant, full from dinner, I thought about the phone call I'd make on Monday to Fred McPhee, my ex-bandmate, offering his new band a record contract. I loved knowing that I could help him reach a level of success that we—High Noon—might have had, if it hadn't been for Gwen's death. And for a moment, I could imagine it was all already happening: the record was made, rave reviews were being published. Songs I'd recorded and Cynthia had promoted were being bought and reviewed and downloaded and talked about.

And maybe—to continue the fantasy—we'd make enough money where, after some time, Cynthia and I could buy a home after all, a slightly larger place where we would raise our child.

Nolan asked me if I planned to give Cynthia the news about Long-Shot Records on the phone tonight or surprise her with it on Sunday. But this was no decision at all: I would tell her as soon as I heard her voice.

Looking back, I'm glad I allowed myself that fantasy. Glad to have indulged in that much hope—because within the hour, everything would change.

It started at the golf range, where the three of us stood on adjacent AstroTurf mats, driving our golf balls into the dark, misty field. Despite the earlier sun, it'd begun to drizzle, and thunder rumbled in the distance as we settled into the rhythm of our swings. After hitting a dozen or so balls, I happened to glance up at Jeffrey, who was standing to my left. I'm a lefty, and Jeffrey's a righty, so we were facing each other. He stood over his ball as if he were about to take a swing. But the backswing didn't come. He just stood there, head down, holding the club. At some point he must have sensed me watching him, because he looked up.

"Hey, Will?" he said quietly.

I raised my eyebrows in response.

More silence. Then, in the careful voice of a physician making a grave diagnosis, he said, "She's cheating on me again."

Before I could think of a suitable reply, he looked down, brought his club back, and swung. The ball went so high that I lost it in the grayness overhead. To my eyes, never good at twilight, it simply shrank into the sky and was gone.

On the drive home, Jeffrey was being very quiet. But as we approached the little shopping center across from the entrance to my neighborhood, he said, "Pull in there." He wanted to buy antacids at the Milk-n-Bread. "My stomach's been killing me lately. Stress."

"Stress?" Nolan said. "It was the clams."

In a few hours Newfield would be placid again, but at 7:15 the Friday rush was still in full swing and traffic in the westbound lane was bumper to bumper. "For real?" I asked.

"Trust me—you need to stop."

I put on my left blinker and, seeing a small opening in front of an SUV, raced across the lane of cars. I pulled into a parking space and Jeffrey got out.

"Wait here," he said. "I'll be back in a minute." He went into the Milk-n-Bread.

Nolan clicked the radio on and immediately started fiddling with the dial. "He shouldn't have given you such a hard time back at the restaurant," he said, settling on a Van Morrison song.

"It's his money. He can decide what to do with it."

"Bullshit. He's just being negative. I love him, Will, you know that. But he can be such a downer sometimes."

23

Maybe so, but Nolan's observation was based on incomplete information. He didn't know about Jeffrey's marital problems, and it wasn't my place to tell him. And so with Jeffrey inside the Milk-n-Bread changing all of our lives forever, Nolan and I sat in the car quietly and listened to the radio, while the drizzle turned to the kind of soupy rain that was good for vegetable gardens but bad for golf. The forecast was turning out to be wrong, and I hoped that our round tomorrow wouldn't get rained out.

A white-haired woman left the store using a magazine for an umbrella. She hurried to her car and drove away.

The song ended. Another began. Daylight savings wasn't for another week, and now that the sun had set night was coming on quickly.

When the next song ended, Nolan unbuckled his seat belt. "Oh, hell," he said, "I'll go and see what—"

Just then the door to the store swung open and Jeffrey came outside. But not alone. He was holding on to the arm of a young woman who was wearing the tan pants and red shirt of a Milk-n-Bread employee. They hurried toward us as if she were a young movie star and he her bodyguard, helping her quickly past the paparazzi.

Jeffrey opened the back door and half guided, half pushed her into the car. He climbed in beside her and yanked the door shut. And before I could ask a single thing, he shouted: "Drive!"

That one word, and my mouth went completely dry. All I could imagine was that the cashier had been injured. Another young woman was going to die, and I was about to watch it happen. It felt, suddenly, preordained, as if my life these past three years had been nothing but limbo, a long wait for this exact moment.

"Hurry up, Will! Go!"

"What's wrong with her?" I managed to ask. "What is it?"

"Just fucking drive!"

What do you do when your longtime friend tells you to drive? You drive. So I did. I fucking drove, stamping on the gas, gunning the car out of the parking lot, and hanging a right onto Lincoln Avenue.

My heart raced, but unlike Jeffrey I wasn't panicking: I knew exactly where I was going. Ever since Gwen's death, it'd become a compulsion of mine always to know how to get to the nearest hospital. My house was 5.8 miles from Mountainside. The recording studio was 3.5 miles from Valley Regional. Wherever I was, whatever I was doing, some part of my mind was always quietly mapping routes.

We needed to go six miles—fortunately to the east, where the lane was all clear. I sped up and checked the rearview mirror. The young cashier looked left and right, eyes wide. She was either breathing quickly or shivering. It was dark in the car. Was she bleeding?

"What happened to her?" I asked.

No response.

"Jeffrey!"

"Just keep driving." His voice quavered.

"I can have us at Mountainside Hospital in ten minutes," I said.

"Hospital?" Jeffrey said. "Why there?"

"What are you talking about?"

"Forget it. Go somewhere else."

Now I was utterly confused. "Go *where*?"

We were at least a mile down the road, leaving Newfield now, passing storefronts and a supermarket and a car dealership. Another driver might have sized up the situation differently, maybe more accurately, but all we had was me behind the wheel. Only me, with my particular history and my refusal ever again to wait around impotently for an ambulance to arrive. It simply hadn't occurred to me, yet, that this could be anything other than a second chance for me to save a young woman's life.

The oncoming lane was at a standstill, but we were flying. I sped through the next intersection toward Mountainside Hospital and waited for answers as the road widened to four lanes.

"Oh, for Christ's sake," Nolan said, his voice louder than before. "Will somebody explain what the fuck's going on? Honey, take a deep breath and tell me what's the matter."

"Really?" The girl looked at me, then Nolan. Maybe she saw the bafflement in our faces. "He just—" She took a deep breath, and another. Jeffrey was looking down at his lap. "He just—" But then she began to hyperventilate and couldn't get out another word.

CHAPTER 2

O NCE I BEGAN TO understand the key facts—there were no grave injuries; this was no mad dash to the hospital after all—my first feeling, however fleeting, was relief. I was at the wheel of my trusty Cutlass Ciera with my old friends and, yes, this young cashier, but the radio was on and I was driving the well-worn roads of my daily life. These were facts I could cling to. Whatever the girl thought might have happened, she must be mistaken. This was Jeffrey. All hundred and forty pounds of him. He was not a threat. A little moody? Sure. But not a mean bone.

When he finally spoke, only a few more seconds had gone by, but we'd traveled another full block. "I didn't mean to take her."

Take her. Those two words, despite all the immediate evidence, hit me like a knockout punch.

The girl lurched for the door—foolish, since we were going more than forty miles an hour. "Hey, be careful," Jeffrey said, grabbing at her hands. "You'll hurt yourself."

"Don't touch me!" She yanked her hands away.

"Take it easy," Nolan said. "Nobody's going to hurt you."

"You *kidnapped* me!" Her eyes were wild. I couldn't stop looking into the rearview mirror. A car blared its horn at me for drifting into the oncoming lane.

"Jeffrey," Nolan said, "what in God's name—"

"I had to take her," Jeffrey said. "I swear—now wait a minute. Just listen to me for a second. Just listen. The thing is, I'm flat broke."

This was either a brazen lie or an astonishing revelation. Either way, I couldn't have cared less.

"What's your point?" Nolan asked.

"My point?" Jeffrey sounded offended. "Didn't you hear me? I lost it all! You can't imagine—"

"The girl," Nolan said. "Connect this to *her.*"

"Connect?"

"Why is she in our fucking car?"

"She would've called the police," Jeffrey said, as if this made perfect—or any—sense.

"What am I missing?" Nolan asked.

Jeffrey sighed. "I sort of robbed the place."

"No, you didn't." Nolan shook his head. "Tell me you fucking didn't. Holy Jesus Christ."

I tried to imagine Jeffrey committing a crime. What had he said? Did he have a weapon? But the details would have to wait. What mattered right now was the girl in the backseat. Through the rearview I could see that she had a small nose, freckles, thin lips. I might have seen her before, working at the Milk-n-Bread. I'd probably flirted with her a little at the register, just to convince myself that I was still young enough to flirt with someone her age, even though I knew I wasn't.

"What's your name?" I asked.

She met my eyes through the rearview. "Are you insane? I'm not telling you anything."

"Well, I'm going to take you back to the store now."

"Don't you dare turn this car around." Nolan's voice was almost calm, as if he'd made a decision and already come to terms with it.

"Nolan."

"Think about it. Robbery, kidnapping . . . it doesn't matter how *long* we kept her. No one will care about that."

I shook my head. "You're only saying that because of the election." It was easy to imagine the headlines. The scandal. Even if we let her go and Jeffrey were somehow able to take the heat alone, Nolan was still ruined. That much seemed obvious. "You're afraid of bad press. That's why you're thinking—"

"Bad press? You don't get it—if you stop this car, the three of us are going to prison. Trust me on that."

Jeffrey groaned. "I think I'm going to be sick." The girl scooted farther away from him.

I could better comprehend vomiting than kidnapping. Cynthia and I had just finished paying off the car. And the prospect of Jeffrey getting sick in it was what finally made this unreal moment all too real, leaving me with a new set of facts.

We had been driving for almost five minutes.

We were already several miles away from the Milk-n-Bread.

We had not yet returned the girl.

The radio played on. Rain smacked the windshield. My hands were sweating on the steering wheel as the tang of panic rose higher in my throat.

"We have to take her back," I said, "or go to the police ourselves to explain." But I was already in the next town and had no idea where the police station might be. Mapping police stations had never been my compulsion.

"Wrong," Nolan said. "We need to go someplace—Will, shut the goddamn radio off."

29

I shut it off.

"We need to go someplace," he repeated, "where we can talk this thing through. Work out a solution."

"We've only gone a few miles," I said.

"Wake up, man! Look at what's just happened. Three men in their thirties just took a teenager against her will and *drove away with her*. Do you think the police will care how far we went?"

"I thought she was injured! I was heading to the hospital."

"Liar!" screamed the girl, who'd clearly had enough. "You all planned this—I mean, you're driving a *getaway* car!" She glared at me again through the rearview.

"See?" Nolan said. "Nobody's going to give a shit what we say." His voice lowered, sounding grave. "Get this through your head, Will: Jeffrey robbed that fucking store, and *she's* right. You're driving the getaway car. It happened. It's happening. The minute we let her go, she's running to the police." He looked over at her. "And don't even pretend you aren't."

"Damn right I am."

Nolan shook his head. "Will, buddy, I know you don't know what to do, so I'm telling you. Drive someplace safe where we can think for a few minutes and figure this out. You need to trust me. That's what you need to do right now."

I wanted to argue with him, but there was no time to think. That was the maddening part. I looked at the clock: 7:22—now seven minutes had passed. Everything was happening too fast. Buildings and streetlamps were flying past us, and every second that I didn't make a decision, a decision was being made for us, because we were getting farther and farther away from the Milk-n-Bread with no easy way back. The traffic in the fucking westbound lane was at a standstill. I'd been caught in Friday rush before. If I turned the car around right now, it would be forty minutes, easy, before we were back at the store. And with the rain? More like an hour.

I couldn't bear the thought of her being in my car that long, and I was searching desperately for something to say or do when Nolan added, "Mark my word. If you stop this car, you're going to miss out on a lot of your kid growing up."

His words made my gut squeeze and my eyes lose focus. The streetlights along the road dimmed for a moment, and I was afraid I might pass out. I'd always believed in Nolan, trusted his instincts. For as long as I'd known him, he was the guy who wanted—and deserved—the ball with ten seconds left. I gripped the wheel tighter and my vision returned. The car was still slowing down—my foot had been off the gas for the last quarter mile—but it didn't seem to matter. Nolan was already on to other things.

"This'll work out just fine for you," he was saying to the girl now, his voice less dire. "So don't sweat it for a second. We'll have you home in no time. You have my word. This'll be just fine."

It turned out that those words, directed toward the backseat, were what I most needed to hear. Jeffrey had lost his head, but now we'd set things right. Nobody was injured—thank God for that—and nobody had meant anyone any harm; therefore, I told myself, everything could be fixed. All we needed, as Nolan said, was a little time to work out a solution.

Trust Nolan, I kept telling myself—a simple, comforting mantra. *Nolan will know what to do.* I gently placed my foot back on the gas. We passed the army/navy store and the Lincoln Diner.

"He's right," I said to her, forcing myself to sound calm and reassuring. "Don't you worry about a thing."

"*You're* the one who should worry," she said.

She was a young, frightened girl trying to sound tough, but I didn't doubt her willingness to make our lives immeasurably harder. She'd never allow us to walk away from this. Not unless we convinced her.

31

"We should go to your house," Jeffrey said to me. "The house is empty, right? So that's where we need to go."

"With all that traffic?" Nolan said. "We'd never get there."

"So we drive around awhile first until the traffic lightens."

"No," I said. "I know where I'm going." Home was out of the question. And to get to the hospital, I'd have had to turn off this road a mile back. Then I realized that for the last minute or so, I'd already been heading away from the hospital and toward the safest place I knew.

CHAPTER 3

THE DAY CYNTHIA AND I moved into our house in Newfield was one of muted celebration. The stillness of our house unnerved me. I slept fitfully that night and awoke in the morning with heavy limbs and a need to stay in bed all day. And the next day. And the next. I passed the hours not reading, not watching television, sleeping the occasional hour in the afternoon and then lying awake all night.

Even the fear I'd felt in our SoHo apartment, following the shooting, began to seem preferable to this nothingness, endless hours marked by the movement of shadows on the bedroom wall, punctuated by birds or kids outside flaunting their cheerfulness. Yet I felt unable to do anything to relieve this private, ugly grief that I couldn't explain to Cynthia. The truth was that I had fallen, a little, for Gwen. She and I had been partners, drums and bass, night after night making music and sweating together under the same hot lights. After she died, my feelings of genuine sadness were undercut—polluted—by the selfish wish that Gwen were still alive just so I could prove my faithfulness to my wife.

Mostly, I wanted to lie in bed and not think about Gwen or the shooting. I didn't want to think or feel anything, or even exist.

When Cynthia tried to talk to me, I answered in monosyllables. Or I didn't answer at all.

Get up, I'd think. *Say something. You're hurting the woman you love.*

When she suggested that I get professional help, it took every bit of energy I had just to refuse.

I'd hear Cynthia unpacking our things, stacking dishes in cabinets, and running loads of laundry. I would sleep during the day, and at night I would lie in bed awake while Cynthia slept. Sometimes I'd get up in the middle of the night and sit in the kitchen with the lights off, returning to bed with the first hint of daylight.

After three weeks, Cynthia got around to tough love.

"Will," she said one morning, her hair wet from the shower. She sat on the bed and shook me to be sure I was awake. "Will, today you're leaving the house. I'm going out to run errands. I'll be gone an hour or two. When I come home, I don't expect to see you here."

When I got around to opening my eyes, I saw that she'd left on the bed the Help Wanted section from the newspaper and a county map. I wanted to remind her about my heavy limbs, but she was already gone.

I showered for the first time in too long, and on my way to the kitchen for juice I took a good look around. While I'd been sleeping, Cynthia had made the house ours. Our pictures on the walls. Our books in the shelves.

Rather than look at the help-wanted ads or the map, I got in the car and drove. Drove for hours, getting myself lost, and then more lost. Midafternoon, on my way back home, I found myself on the main street of some run-down, slightly urban area, and I remember feeling a strange comfort in having found a neighborhood reminiscent of the one I had just fled. Seeing a weathered sign for Snakepit Recording Studio, I pulled over to the curb. The building stood between an antique furniture store and a nail salon that appeared to be out of business, its glass door cracked. The studio's entrance was around back. The door was shut but unlocked, so I went in. The dark, musty hallway reeked of stale beer and cigarettes, and I felt thankful for the familiar, acrid smell. I didn't hear any activity, though, and I was about to leave when a man's voice called out from someplace deep inside the studio: "What do you want now, for fuck's sake?"

My eyes slowly adjusted to the dim light as I went farther down the hallway, past a restroom, past the darkened recording room, to the control room. Sitting behind the sound console was a man of around sixty with a messy white beard and a pair of wet, resigned eyes that suggested he was world-weary, drunk, or a little of both.

"Sorry," he said, "I thought you were that homeless guy. He wanders in here if the door doesn't latch shut."

"No," I said, "I have a home." The man was paging through a copy of *Hustler*. "This your studio?" I asked.

"Proud owner since eighty-six. Bought and mostly paid for."

I introduced myself.

"Joey Pitts," he said, and we shook hands. "So what can I do for you?"

"You don't by any chance need an extra recording engineer, do you, Joey?"

He sized me up. "You have any studio experience?"

I told him the name of the New York studio where I worked and, briefly, why I left.

"Are you into any hard drugs?" he asked.

"No," I said.

"Are you a douchebag?"

I told him I wasn't.

He nodded. "I could actually use a little help. I got a band coming in an hour. You want, you can stick around and assist. Like an audition."

35

I called home and left a message telling Cynthia where I was. That I'd be home late.

"Okay," Joey said, shutting the magazine and setting it on the console. "Have a seat. Let's talk."

At eleven that night, after the band left, Joey hired me on a trial basis. We negotiated a salary (that is, Joey proposed one; I agreed). We shook hands and left the studio together.

The street was quiet except for a streetlight buzzing at the end of the block. On the curb beneath it stood an old man in torn pants and a gray hooded sweatshirt, rocking from foot to foot. Seeing us, he started to come our way.

"And here we go," Joey said. "You work here, you'll be seeing a lot of this one."

The man asked us for a dollar. "For protecting your car," he said.

"Ignore him," Joey said, "or he'll be your friend for life."

I couldn't ignore him. My father spent his professional life helping just such people. He was licensed in clinical social work and directed Hudson County Coalition, an organization that oversaw local shelters and soup kitchens and, when there were funds, did some occupation training. Back in high school I volunteered there sometimes. My interest had more to do with helping out my father than the homeless, but ever since then I'd never been able to ignore a panhandler. At least I had that check mark on the merit side of God's scorecard.

I reached into my pocket and pulled out two quarters. In the months and years that followed, I'd drop countless quarters into that same hopeful hand.

The man stuffed the change into the pocket of his sweatshirt, which was several sizes too large for his small frame.

"You seen my dog?" The man had the veiny nose of a longtime drinker and the fragile eyes of somebody who'd disappointed his share of well-meaning counselors.

I told him I hadn't seen any dogs. "What kind is it?"

"Man, you know my dog."

"Sorry, I don't," I said, concluding that the dog in question probably had never romped anyplace other than this man's imagination.

"How about you?" he asked Joey. "You seen him?"

"I told you a hundred times already, I haven't seen your dog. I see him, you'll be the first to know."

Through with us, the man went back to his spot beneath the streetlight and sat down on the curb. Joey and I kept walking. When we were out of earshot, Joey said, "I don't care much for that guy, but I kinda liked his dog. Real well behaved. Last week I saw it on the side of the street, about a mile from here. Road pizza." He shook his head. "Well, good night."

I got in my car and turned on the radio but didn't drive anywhere. Joey beeped his horn as he rode past. When he was out of sight, I got out of my car again and walked to the sub shop a half block down the road. Chairs were stacked in the window, and a lone employee wearing a sauce-splattered apron was sweeping the floor, but the neon sign overhead claimed open for business. I bought a cup of coffee and a footlong Italian sub. Extra tomatoes, no hot peppers, exactly the way I liked it. When I left the shop five minutes later, the neon sign was dark.

"I'll keep an eye out for your dog," I said, and handed the man his dinner.

When I began to work at the studio, the equipment—and the other engineers—were all in states of dysfunction. Joey knew I could help him. I was dependable and competent, and lacked the sort of ambition that would have me leaving him suddenly for a better studio and stealing his clients away.

Almost immediately, he began to give me more responsibility. Rather than work the sound console himself, he preferred to drop by and shoot the bull with the bands. The studio was his own small kingdom where he could come and feel welcomed. Otherwise, he wasn't too interested in the day-to-day business of the studio, and in six months I was in charge. I fired the incompetents and lobbied Joey to overhaul the main console, which he had bought used when he first opened the studio.

This became my life, working at a third-rate recording studio in the middle of New Jersey, spending the bulk of my days with musicians of questionable talent, and then coming home to our house in the burbs. Cynthia and I were living the middle-class dream, only we weren't middle-class, and I needed to figure out if this bothered me. And if it didn't, why not.

Yet I must not have been entirely without ambition, because after about a year at the studio I began to toy with the idea of starting up a small record company. At first I kept it to myself. I began to save a little, and convinced Joey to throw some money into fixing the studio's worst atrocities.

When I finally told Cynthia about my idea, I remember being bothered by her instant enthusiasm. It was August, and we were sitting on the back porch having breakfast. The porch was my favorite part of the house. Our little yard felt private, its perimeter lined on the sides with burning bushes and in the rear with forsythia hedges that, come fall, would turn a brilliant yellow.

"It isn't a terrific plan," I told her. "It's risky as all hell."

"Maybe so," she said, "but I love the idea of our working together on something. And anyway, you need this. I know you do."

I hadn't been any fun at all for quite some time. That was putting it mildly. Not that I walked around sulking. But I had accepted unhappiness as a small price to pay for a life filled with most of the things I wanted.

"There are other remedies for depression," I said, "besides throwing our money into a risky business."

"Such as?"

"I don't know. Prozac? Therapy?"

Cynthia took my hand and began to rub it. And trying to sound nonchalant, she said, "Why not all three?"

A year and a half had passed since the shooting and our flight from the city. And now, rather than the heavy exhaustion following our move to Newfield, I felt tired of mourning. Tired of being tired. Tired of sadness. It was enough already.

And after a few more months, and with a little help from both Dr. Shelling, PhD, and Pfizer Inc., I felt myself finally coming out of something I hadn't even known I was still so deeply in.

Cynthia and I began to laugh a little more, make love more often. We began to talk about the future: not only the record company, but us. Being together. Starting a family. We even started thinking of names.

CHAPTER 4

N OW, THREE YEARS AFTER Snakepit Recording Studio had first saved
me, I was counting on it to save me again.

I parked the car behind the studio, where it wouldn't be seen
from the street, and went in ahead of the others. Nobody was
scheduled in the studio until my session with The Fixtures on
Monday evening.

The lights were all off. "Hello?" I called out. No reply.

I went outside again.

The sky had fully opened, and thunder was cracking fiercely. I
trudged through puddles to the car and waved them in.

Jeffrey got out first. He stood in the lot looking toward the
street, making sure no other car was coming. Nolan went around
to the backseat, opened the girl's door, and guided her toward the
studio. She had warned us in the car that her grandmother would
be calling the police the minute she didn't arrive home; we immediately used this information against her, making her swear on
her grandmother's life that she wouldn't run away or scream.

Screaming wouldn't have helped anyway. There was the over-
powering sound of the rain. There was the thunder. But also, in
the moment just after I waved them in, an ambulance went by, its

siren blaring. The coincidence was uncanny. If there was a moment when we could have still undone everything, that siren cut it short. It fired us into action, and fifteen seconds later the four of us were drenched but safely inside the studio. I locked the door behind us.

Off the hallway was the studio's main recording room. Inside, along the walls, were two much smaller rooms, A and B. The doors to each room were made of glass so that musicians could see one another while recording.

Room A used to be a storage closet and locked from the outside. The girl sat on the floor. She had left her purse in a locker back at the Milk-n-Bread and had sworn—again, on her grandmother's life—that she didn't have a cell phone on her. We took her at her word; no one was going to search her.

Nolan, Jeffrey, and I sat in the control room staring at one another. Their hair was wet and their faces looked ghostly in the studio's dim light. Looking at Nolan now—running his hand through his hair, squeezing his eyes shut—I knew there was no plan. He'd asked for the ball because that had always been his instinct, and I'd given it to him because that had always been mine. But the game was already over.

He opened his eyes and, seeing me, seemed to know what I was thinking. "She'd have gone to the police," he said.

"Of course she would've. But this is making things worse."

He ran a hand through his hair again, and asked Jeffrey the obvious: "What the fuck were you thinking?"

Jeffrey shook his head. "I tried to tell you, I'm broke. And we were promising Will all that money at dinner. And I just . . . I don't know. Panicked, I guess."

"Wow." Nolan glared at him. "I mean, that really is the stupidest thing I ever heard. So how much did you steal?"

41

Jeffrey reached into his front pocket and pulled out a wad of bills. We watched him count it. "A hundred and eighty dollars," he said, not looking at either of us, and put the money back in his pocket.

"You lose millions," Nolan said, "and so you steal a hundred and eighty dollars and . . . you *took* somebody." He closed his eyes, took a deep breath. "I mean, how could you?"

Jeffrey sighed. "It all happened so fast. Nobody else was in the store, just the two of us, and I know this might sound crazy but it just didn't feel like that big of a *deal* until the second after she'd handed me the money. It didn't even feel real. But then I pictured Sara and the baby, and the police coming after me, and . . . it just happened." He glanced over in the girl's direction, then away again. "I know that I did it, but it felt like an accident. Like I didn't mean it at all. Do you understand what I'm saying?"

"Not even a little." Nolan punched a fist into his palm. He used to do this in college during debates and later during his early campaign speeches. Since then, he'd learned to tame the gesture. "Robbery isn't an accident. Kidnapping isn't an accident. Nobody in the history of the world has ever kidnapped somebody by accident."

"Well, I did."

More hand punching. "Well, fuck you then."

"No, fuck you, Nolan. I didn't intend—"

"You didn't intend what?"

"I didn't—"

"You didn't what?"

"Let me *talk*! Okay? You never let me talk. Will you let me talk?"

Rain drummed steadily on the roof. The building was well insulated and soundproofed, and I tried to remember if I'd ever heard police sirens from in here.

"Well? Talk!"

"Don't rush me," Jeffrey said.

Nolan pulled his chair closer to Jeffrey's. "Let me explain something. You and Will and I are in the deepest of shit. Do you understand? You robbed a convenience store and kidnapped the clerk, and unless we figure something out fast, the three of us are going to pay for it. The police are probably on their way already. They might be here in ten minutes. They might ransack Will's house first and buy us an hour or two. Either way, there's, you know, a good reason to hurry things along."

The thought of Cynthia returning from Philadelphia to find our house ransacked made me sadder, in a way, than the thought of her returning to find me in custody.

"She looks cold," Jeffrey said. She was sitting on the rug, arms around knees, head down. Shivering, maybe crying.

"I'll be right back," I said.

"Where are you going?" Nolan said.

I ignored him and went into the main recording room and turned up the thermostat. Then I knelt in front of the bass drum and pulled out the blanket that I kept in there to dampen the drumhead. The blanket was stiff and musty.

"Back up a little bit, okay?" I called through the thick door.

She scooted backward. Her hair was dripping.

I unlocked the door and opened it just enough to hand her the blanket. She took it and immediately wrapped it around herself.

"So can I please call you by a name?" I asked, and she looked at me. But I didn't know what else to say. I wondered who she was, this girl of the Milk-n-Bread. Did she work there to save money for college? To help support her family? Did she have a boyfriend? What were her ambitions?

I wanted her to understand that this was all a mistake. But I couldn't think of a way to explain, and there was no time. I started to close the door.

43

"Wait!" she said. The door remained a few inches open. "This is scary, you know?"

"I know it is."

"The police are probably already on their way."

"It's possible."

"You really didn't know this was going to happen?"

"Scout's honor."

"That guy's your friend?"

I nodded. "He's all right, once you get to know him."

Her shivering had subsided a little. "Marie. That's my name."

I knew it was my turn, and lying seemed pointless. "I'm Will."

"Is that your real name?"

"Yes. Is Marie yours?"

Her answer was a sneeze. For the first time, I really looked at her. The freckles at the base of her nose said tomboy, and yet she had smooth, feminine skin, the look of someone who could make herself glamorous if she wanted to. I'd been wrong about seeing her before in the Milk-n-Bread. That wasn't why she looked familiar.

"My nana is sick," she said. "She doesn't have anyone else. It's just me and her. My shift ends at eight o'clock, and I'm supposed to go home after."

Of course she had a grandmother depending on her. "We're going to do everything we can to get you home on time. I promise."

"Will?" she said.

"What is it?"

"Please don't let anyone . . . hurt me."

I looked away and saw the nicked-up wooden floor. The rotted ceiling tiles. Microphone stands and cables lining the wall. One of Joey's posters of Pamela Anderson, circa 1995, for the musicians to ogle.

This was Joey's studio, but it was my turf. Jeffrey might have grabbed the girl, and Nolan might have ordered me to drive. But I had taken us here. I was responsible, and she seemed to know it, and she was letting me know that she knew it.

What if I told her to leave right then, just run as fast as she could out into the street? Would anybody stop her? And why wasn't I giving her that chance?

Optimism is a strange word, given the situation, but I believe that's what kept me from letting her go right then, before everything else that happened happened. I was as frightened as I'd ever been, yet alongside my fear was a trace of optimism, because I knew what this girl didn't: We meant her no harm. Together, Nolan, Jeffrey, and I would solve the problem, fix the damage that'd been done. All we needed was a little time.

"Nobody's going to hurt you," I said. "We're going to get you home really soon. In the meantime, try to warm up." I clicked the door shut.

When I returned to the control room, Jeffrey and Nolan were looking at me too expectantly. I didn't like being looked to for answers. All I'd done was produce a lousy blanket. Yet I'd also made a discovery.

"It's because she looks like Sara, isn't it?" I asked Jeffrey.

"No, she doesn't," he said. "Why would you say that?"

"She does," I insisted. "She looks like your wife. And if Sara's been cheating on you—"

"She has?" Nolan said.

Jeffrey shot me a look, but maintaining his confidence had dropped on my list of priorities.

"And then you run into this cashier," I said, "who happens to look like her. . . ."

45

"Wait a goddamn minute." Nolan looked over toward Marie, but her head was buried in her arms. "Let me get this straight. So to get even with your wife for fucking some other guy, you kidnap an innocent teenager?"

Jeffrey shook his head. "That isn't why I did it."

"Okay, then why?" Nolan asked.

"I already told you why, she was going to call the—"

Nolan waved Jeffrey's words away. "Why would you rob the fucking store in the first place?"

"We're all ears," I said.

Jeffrey sighed. "Maybe it's like . . . you know, what we were talking about at dinner. Why guys go skydiving or whatever."

"Now *this* I don't need to hear," Nolan said.

"Look, you're the one who said, 'Surprise yourself.'"

Nolan stood there, shaking his head. Almost any explanation would've been better than that. But what did we expect to hear? Some secret chamber to Jeffrey's heart revealed? No. People committed self-destructive acts every hour of every day. There had been days in my own not-too-distant past when I felt about as bad as a person could feel. The only difference was that Jeffrey had acted on those feelings and taken us along for the ride.

"Well, has it worked?" Nolan forced a laugh. "Do you feel alive? We'd all sure like to know."

Jeffrey looked down at the floor. "I don't—"

"*You don't know, you don't know*—we heard you!" Nolan lowered his voice. "But do you *know* that our lives are ruined because of you? Do you *know* that we're all probably headed to prison because of this?" When Jeffrey didn't answer, he murmured, "Fucking lunatic."

"Okay, here's an answer you might understand," Jeffrey said. "Maybe I *was* feeling depressed, and she did look a little like Sara, okay? And so I panicked. And when we panic, we do stupid things."

46

Nolan's eyes narrowed. "What do you mean, 'I might understand?'"

"Nothing. I don't mean anything. Just that . . . as someone who has also *done things* that maybe you shouldn't have—"

"What things? Huh?"

"Forget it. It doesn't matter."

"No, I really want to know."

"I said forget it."

"All I know is, I never decided to fuck over my friends. Jesus. Next time you panic, do us all a favor and just kill yourself."

"Shut the fuck up, Nolan," I said. My departure from Dr. Shelling and her prescriptions for Zoloft were too recent for that sort of crack.

Marie shifted positions and seemed to be watching us now. Waiting for our next move.

"She thinks we're going to do something awful to her," I said.

We all looked at her. When Nolan spoke again, his voice was calmer. "Jeffrey. I'm sorry, okay? I didn't mean that."

"Glad to hear it."

"All I'm saying is, you feel depressed, you deal with it. Like Will did. You get help. You don't do . . . *this*."

Sensing the shift in mood, Jeffrey said, "I'll take full responsibility."

My own anger flared. "What planet do you live on?"

"I will. I'll tell the police—"

"You'll tell them what? That you somehow forced Nolan and me to help you commit a felony? What could you possibly say that would make things any better?"

"No, I mean, I could . . ." But he was out of ideas.

"And anyway, we aren't innocent, are we? I drove the car. Nolan said not to return her to the Milk-n-Bread. I listened to him. Now we're all here. And I don't see any of us rushing to set her free. So

47

that means we're all in this." Nobody contradicted me. "So what do we do?"

"We let her go," Jeffrey said. "What else *can* we do?"

Nolan shook his head. "Money."

"Come on," I said. "She'll take the money and turn us in anyway. We fucking kidnapped her."

"Yes, Will. We fucking kidnapped her. I think that's already been established. You and Jeffrey and I all kidnapped that girl over there. So stop saying it already. Please. I'm begging you."

"I don't think," I said, my words more measured, "that a bribe will work."

"Have you tried? Do you have another suggestion?" His voice lowered. "Do you want to *kill her*? Because we could always do that." He looked at each of us. "No? I didn't think so. There, we've ruled out murder. See? Progress."

"I guess we could offer her some money." I was feeling the particular exhaustion that comes from having only bad options.

"That's right," Nolan said. "Everyone has a price."

"That's a cliché," I said. "It isn't even true."

But Jeffrey seemed to cling to the idea. "How much should we offer?"

"Two hundred and forty-six dollars," Nolan said. "How the hell should I know? You think I've done this before?" He sighed. "Let's say a thousand."

"You think that's enough?" Jeffrey asked. "That probably isn't enough. You should ask her what she wants."

"She works at a Milk-n-Bread."

"Still . . ."

"Jeffrey, I'm not particularly interested in your judgment right now. A thousand dollars is plenty. Agreed, Will?"

"Might as well give it a try," I said. Actually, the plan seemed terrible, but it was all we had. And a bribe seemed like small potatoes compared to robbery and kidnapping. "But who do you think ought to—"

"I'll talk to her," Nolan said.

Good. I didn't want that job. "She told me her name's Marie."

"And you believed her?" He shook his head. "Forget it. It doesn't matter."

"Maybe I should be the one," Jeffrey said, "since it was me who, you know . . ."

"*You?*" Nolan said. "You go in there, you'll end up accidentally raping her."

"Fuck you," Jeffrey said.

When Nolan stood and left the control room, Marie's eyes widened. She hugged herself tighter.

CHAPTER 5

People assume that to get accepted into a school like Princeton, one needs to be an exceptionally well-rounded student. This is false.

In high school, near the end of my junior year, my guidance counselor called me into her office one afternoon and told me that my grades and test scores gave me a shot at a top college, but that I ought to sign up for more extracurricular activities. Maybe run for class office. Volunteer at a hospital. I decided to do none of those things, because I was more interested in my rock band. We called ourselves Burn, and our logo had flames, and we practiced at high decibels every afternoon in Ronnie Martinez's unfinished basement. The way I saw it, Burn was the only extracurricular activity I ever needed.

When I arrived at Princeton, I quickly learned that my guidance counselor was wrong. Top schools don't want well-rounded individuals. They want a well-rounded class. For that, they need kids who are especially *unrounded*—ones who are exceptional at physics or the cello or the writing of poems, kids who solve complicated math proofs or pilot airplanes or start up foundations to promote literacy or fight diseases in remote parts of the globe. Put them all together, there's your class of Ivy Leaguers.

I hadn't done anything remotely exceptional even though others thought I had. During my senior year, for the annual science fair I designed a lens for our high school's old telescope that filtered out most of the spectral frequencies of light pollution. Later, I'd learn that this type of lens already existed. Still, it was new to me, and apparently to everyone at my school. The superintendent got me in touch with a local camera manufacturer, which followed my design and made a prototype. There was an article in the paper with a photo of me on the school's roof, looking through the telescope at the night sky. The local network news covered the story. We made popcorn, and when my face came on the television screen, my mother cried. My father mussed my hair and kept repeating, "Look at that. Just look at that."

The following spring, I got accepted into Princeton and Harvard and every school I applied to. Don't get me wrong: I was a good student. Plenty of As. High SATs. But thousands of kids with As and high test scores get rejected from the top schools.

No, it was the telescope lens.

Was it a clever school project? Sure. Was it worthy of all the attention? Not really. But teachers wait years and years for a student to take the initiative in a scholarly pursuit, and when they see it, it's as if all of their years in the profession—the meager pay, the administrative headaches, all those parents to deal with—finally amount to something. My letters of recommendation must have made me out to be the next Stephen Hawking. Colleges evidently saw me as their budding cosmologist to round out their well-rounded class, when the truth was, all I'd done was invent something that'd already been invented. I wasn't even especially interested in science. But growing up in a city where the night sky is a constant dull orange, I just thought it would be nice to see some stars for a change.

. . .

At Princeton I was struck by how everyone around me seemed to get on so easily so quickly. I'd left Bayonne, driven an hour or so on Route 1, and arrived at another world, one that I didn't quite trust. My only prior visit hadn't prepared me at all. It'd been a cold, rainy day in April. I'd taken an abbreviated campus tour, returned home soaking wet, and come down the next day with a head cold. But now, under a rich blue sky, kids loafed on the quad in laughing clusters while others threw Frisbees and footballs and still others sprawled on blankets as if they'd spent their whole lives among centuries-old Gothic buildings and flagstone walkways cutting through acres and acres of sweet-smelling grass.

Some of them had. In my incoming class there was a Purdue and a Chrysler and the children of national politicians. And while not everyone was from a rich or famous family (plenty of others, like myself, worked food services to help pay for their education), it was hard to ignore the fact that the guy down the hall had the same last name as one of the new buildings on campus, and that in the dormitory adjacent to mine lived an actual Middle Eastern princess.

In those first baffling days of my freshman year, everyone seemed to be forming fast friendships. They seemed to know instinctively which organizations to join, which to avoid, which of the "eating clubs" had the best parties on tap for the weekend, and how to get passes to those parties.

Even my roommate had slid easily into Princeton life. The day he moved in, he taped inspiring quotations to the wall over his desk. "The reward of a thing well done is to have done it.—Ralph Waldo Emerson." And: "Anything in life worth having is worth working for.—Andrew Carnegie." Lying in our extralong cots late that night, we gave each other our brief histories, and then I asked him if he'd like me to set my alarm.

"I already have mine set for four thirty," he said.

I asked if he was serious. Classes were still a week away.

"If I wanted to sleep," he said, "I would have stayed in Missouri."

He had worked hard and traveled far to arrive, finally, someplace worthy of his ambitions. And he was going to make the most of it. During our weeklong orientation, he bought a new computer and began to read ahead for his classes. Once the semester began, he awoke for crew practice at dawn, and was showered and off to the library before I was out of bed. Within two weeks, he'd already decided to major in political science, joined the debating society, and begun to spend time with a pretty sophomore, the daughter of the U.S. ambassador to Chile.

Had he prepared for this life at some exclusive high school, an Exeter or Andover? No. He'd come straight off a midwestern farm, where he got up before dawn each morning for several hours of chores before school, which, from the sound of it—leaky ceiling, shared textbooks—was barely a school at all. Yet here he was, succeeding.

That seemed to be the common trait among the people here. They succeeded. They had succeeded in order to be invited here. And now that they'd arrived, they would prove themselves all over again.

Impressive? Damn right—but I didn't care for any of it. Everything about the place intimidated me, and I longed for those simple afternoons of music, marijuana, and local girls who didn't care if I was ambitious or lazy, a Rockefeller or a Buttafuoco. I would have taken solace in my coursework, but that was another problem. I'd always sailed through school without much effort. But now, my calculus class was quickly losing me. My natural ear for music took me only so far in a music theory class where half the students had studied classical piano since the age of three.

And what I'd assumed would be the gut course—the required freshman writing class—ended up being an intensive study of modern European authors: Malraux and Mann and Pirandello and Beckett and Sartre and Camus.

Two weeks into the semester and I was swamped. I hadn't even done a load of laundry yet.

Sunday afternoon, I returned to my dormitory from brunch to hear, coming from a nearby window, the whiny jangle of a badly played electric guitar. I followed the sounds of the guitar down the hallway and knocked on the door.

The guy opened the door wearing pajama bottoms and no shirt. He was pale and stick skinny with longish hair and an unsuccessful blond beard. Smoke curled in front of his face from a cigarette, which he plucked from his mouth.

"Gotcha," he said. "I'll turn it down."

"Oh, I don't care about that," I said. "Do you mind if I bum a cigarette?"

In the time it took to smoke one of his cigarettes, I learned that Jeffrey Hocks, from Los Angeles, California, was having as hard a time adjusting to Princeton as I was.

"I really wonder," I told him, "if I'm meant to be here at all." It was a relief, saying this aloud. Having somebody to say it to.

He motioned toward his desk chair and told me to grab a seat. He sat on the bed. "I *know* I'm meant to be here," he said, "but that doesn't help any." And then he went on to reveal his exceptional talent, which was even less exceptional than my own. He was a legacy. His father, two uncles, and grandfather had all gone to Princeton. He was simply keeping the tradition alive. "I had no choice," he said. "My baby clothes had tigers stitched onto them."

Both of Jeffrey's parents were microbiologists at UCLA. They hoped that their son might decide to become a groundbreaking researcher, too. But if not, they'd be satisfied if he became a surgeon, or a partner in an international law firm, or really anything at all as long as it was incredibly impressive.

He took the last drag from a cigarette and dropped it into an empty soda can. "But do you know what I think? I think I'm meant to be a world-class guitarist."

His playing had been so awful that I looked at him and said nothing. He grinned. "I'm kidding. I just started playing over the summer. How about you? Do you play an instrument?"

We smoked most of the pack and talked for the next couple of hours. I learned that the only thing keeping Jeffrey in school was that modern European authors class. He'd already read "Tonio Kröger" and "Death in Venice," which had been assigned, as well as all the other stories in Mann's collection, which hadn't. Twice a week, our professor spoke in his resonant baritone to several hundred of us with great urgency from behind the podium in the McCosh lecture hall, removing and replacing a pair of glasses every few minutes from the bridge of his distinguished, birdlike nose. Apparently Professor Rinehart was quite famous, and we freshmen were lucky to be taught by him prior to his retirement at the end of the year. He'd begin to speak the moment the bell rang and seemed to have his lectures perfectly timed so that they ended just as the bell rang again fifty minutes later. I loved the music of his voice, the rhythm of his extemporaneous phrases, but I never knew what to write in my notebook or what to think about as I read for class.

Jeffrey told me that I should be reading for the beauty of Mann's language and the depth of his sympathy for outsiders and misfits. Hearing this, I felt guilty and sophomoric for my own lack of sympathy in my earlier attempts to read the work. I vowed to give it another try when I returned to my room.

"That's Mann in a nutshell," he said. "Read for that and you'll be fine. You might even come to like it."

Jeffrey was right. I did come to like it. Or at least I convinced myself that I did.

But Jeffrey's own interest in the modern European authors class, I learned soon enough, had less to do with modern European authors and more to do with the striking young woman who sat in the front row of the lecture hall. I'd noticed her, too, since early in the semester. She was curvy and blonde. She wore heart-stopping skirts and scuffed cowboy boots. Jeffrey and I began to refer to her as Dallas, since in our eyes she could pass for a Dallas Cowboys cheerleader a whole lot easier than a Princeton University freshman. And yet she seemed almost possessed in class, writing nonstop in her notebook, as if her method was to transcribe the professor's entire lecture and then sort it out later.

One day, Dallas raised her hand during class. This simply wasn't done. Professor Rinehart would talk for fifty minutes and then the class would applaud. (This always amused me. I suppose that the professor gave good lectures, but also Princeton students liked knowing that they attended a college where the professors' lectures received applause.)

The day that Dallas raised her hand, Professor Rinehart had been talking to us about Sartre's play *No Exit*. Her hand went up with just a few minutes remaining in the class. At first he ignored her. Then he stopped speaking and asked, "Is there a problem?"

"Not a problem, Professor. Just a question."

The accent was all Texas drawl, and Jeffrey punched my leg and whispered, "*See?*"

Students sat up straighter. A few nervous titters. We were all waiting. We were five weeks into the semester, long enough to crave something unusual.

"And what question is that, Ms. . . . ?"

"Paige."

Rinehart nodded. "A literary name."

Jeffrey and I had started sitting to the side of the lecture hall so that we could steal looks at Dallas. Her face lit up. Even her teeth were pretty. "Well, I guess I never thought of it that way."

Some more laughter, lots of glancing around.

"Now, what is your question, Ms. Paige?"

"Well," she said. Two syllables. "You've been telling us about Sartre, how he believed in people's ability"—here she checked her notes—"'to choose their own essence.' But I was wondering . . ." She glanced around, aware now of the crowd watching her, the gaze of six hundred eyes in the faces of three hundred honor students and valedictorians, each with an exceptional talent that had led them to this university, this classroom. "I was wondering if you, you know, think it's a good play."

For a reason wholly unclear to me, the lecture hall erupted in laughter. The professor let this go for a moment, then began to rap his knuckles on the podium until the room quieted again.

"Would you mind if I turned the question back to you, Ms. Paige?" He removed his glasses and narrowed his gaze. "Do *you* think *No Exit* is a good play?"

"Me? Actually, I loved it." She smiled again, then cut it short. "But that's my question. I mean, when Garcin chooses to stay in that room with those awful people, rather than leave hell, his failure is in needing their judgment. That's his big flaw, isn't it?"

"One could reasonably make such an argument."

"But do you think Garcin maybe represents Sartre himself, who as a writer had no choice but to rely on others' judgment? You know, his critics and audiences?" She shrugged. "It just seems like an irony we haven't talked about, and I wondered what you thought."

No laughter this time. Right from the start, I felt there was something a little cinematic about life at Princeton—the Gothic buildings, the manicured grounds, the students and professors

57

who knew their roles and played them well. Sitting in this lecture hall, carved gargoyles eyeing me from the ceiling at all four corners, I imagined this moment as the film's turning point. Cue the soundtrack, the moment of emotional release where the class gains newfound respect for the student in the front row with brains and beauty both. And the professor—cue that smile of his, thus far concealed and so all the more surprising for its easy warmth, a smile that reveals the man's firm exterior as but the shell of an egg that, once cracked, gladly spills its sunny yolk.

His smile, however, never made it beyond my imagination's private screening.

"The last time I checked," Rinehart said, with all the kindness of an electric eel, "this class runs exactly fifty minutes. Isn't that right, Ms. Paige?"

She nodded, her own gorgeous smile suddenly nowhere in sight.

"Yes. That *is* right. And so our brief banter, yours and mine, has now deprived the class of a full minute. Multiply that by the three hundred or so of your fellow young scholars, and that's approximately five collective hours of time that we'll never see again. Now then"—he placed the glasses back on his nose—"shall I return to the lecture I've taken the time to prepare?"

Eventually, people stopped looking at her and began to set down in their notebooks our professor's immeasurable wisdom. Jeffrey, too, opened his notebook to a fresh page and began to write. Seconds later, he slid the notebook over to me.

In large letters it read, "I'm in love."

You're not alone, I thought. My classmates might have laughed at first, but they weren't heartless. Dallas would fare just fine in the stories told tonight at dinner tables across campus.

But after class, Jeffrey did what others didn't. He introduced himself. I left through a side door, giving him space. Letting the rejection—for how could it be otherwise?—happen where I wouldn't see. An hour later, the pounding on my dorm room door woke me from a perfect nap.

"Me and Dallas," he said, breathless, as if he'd been running. "We have a date later."

"Really?" I was incredibly impressed. "Where?"

"We're going to the library to study."

I laughed. "I'm not sure that counts as a date."

"No, Will—we're meeting in the *reserve* room."

The reserve room was the one place in Firestone Library where quiet talk was permitted. And they let you in with coffee.

"I stand corrected," I said.

I was only kidding, but his face lit up. "She's brilliant, you know. I can tell. And that accent . . . Oh my god. Okay, buddy, I'll see you later." He turned to leave.

"See you later," I said, still half dazed from my nap. "Say hi to Dallas for me."

He laughed and turned toward me again. "By the way, her name's Sara."

By that evening, he'd come down from his high.

"She actually wanted to study," he told us in the cafeteria. We were eating that night with Nolan, my roommate. He'd broken it off with his sophomore. Now that he was spending more time in the room, we'd gotten to be friendly.

"Imagine," I said. "Studying in the library."

"I know—it sucks. Because she's amazing. She wants to be a writer. And she isn't just talking about it, she's doing it. She writes stories all the time, and she's going to apply to take a class with Ray Campanaro next semester."

Tonight the cafeteria was serving pork loins, an unfortunate entrée too often thrust upon us. Up and down the cafeteria's long wooden tables, students were eating cold cereal, salads, heaping plates of instant mashed potatoes.

"You should offer to read her work," Nolan said. "You know, before she applies to that class."

"That's a good idea," Jeffrey said. "But I'd only be doing it as a friend. She has a boyfriend back home. By the way, we were right—she is from Texas."

"I hate it when they bring up the boyfriends back home," I said.

"The kiss of death," Jeffrey said.

"Doesn't have to be," Nolan smirked.

"Yeah, well she brought him up about nine hundred times. He's a baseball player." Jeffrey stuffed a forkful of mashed potatoes into his mouth.

"Texas is a long way from here," Nolan said.

"Maybe it won't last with this ballplayer," I said. "You never know."

"Sure," Jeffrey said. "Maybe she'll wake up one day and tell him that he's too good-looking and all-American for her, and that she prefers the nerdy, unathletic type."

We all laughed and finished dinner, having no idea that several months later this was essentially what she would do. This sexy, intelligent woman would fall for him. They would date all four years, and then after graduation they would move to California together and get married in a Pacific Heights mansion overlooking the bay and the Golden Gate Bridge, a view that they would, in time, buy for themselves. Young and in love, they would settle in the right city at the right time. And along with a million other prospectors in that modern-day Wild West, they would soon discover untold riches and ride the wave of their American Dream right into a new, shimmering millennium.

CHAPTER 6

"H OW COULD YOU LOSE all that money?" I asked Jeffrey, alone with him now in the control room. Through the window, we were watching Nolan speaking to Marie, preparing her for our desperate bribe.

"Everything was tied up in company stock when it crashed," Jeffrey said. "I held on, figured it couldn't get worse. But it did. It got a lot worse—as in, it's all gone. And now I have mortgages on my house, and houses for my parents, too, and Sara's parents."

He had always been an unlikely millionaire. He might have been a Princeton legacy, but he was no go-getter. He'd thought about going to graduate school in English, maybe becoming a professor, but then he missed all the application deadlines. Story of his life. In that modern European authors class, he pulled a C for the term. He became so interested in Thomas Mann that he decided to read his collected works instead of what was on the syllabus. The papers he wrote always came back with gushing comments about his insightful readings and the quality of his prose, but marked way down for being days or even weeks late.

When it became April of our senior year and he still had no plans, he decided to look for a job and then apply to graduate school in the fall. He applied for a few computer programming jobs in California, despite having no formal training. He figured that if he could get it, a job writing code in shorts and a T-shirt in a warm climate was a reasonable way to spend a year. In 1994 companies were desperate for programmers. When a start-up company in San Francisco made him an offer, the path of least resistance was to take it. Then the path of least resistance was to keep it. He was a quick learner and kept getting promoted. After a year he was making six figures. After two years, he stopped telling me his salary.

The nineties dot-com boom was on. Stocks were soaring and portfolios bursting. (Not mine, though. I had no portfolio. What little money I made playing the drums was tied up in things like groceries. And heat.) I remember Evan, who'd majored in economics before going to law school, explaining to us once why Internet stocks were wildly overvalued. How a market correction was only a matter of time.

"People will lose everything," he'd warned.

Jeffrey didn't want to hear it. The business he'd been working for since graduation was about to go public. He stood to make millions.

"You're telling me that you don't have any money invested in Yahoo or AOL?" he asked Evan.

"Well, of course I do," Evan had said, and shrugged. "Because, you know, what if I'm wrong?"

He wasn't wrong, though. And now the wave that Jeffrey was riding had evidently come crashing down, as all waves must.

"And you know I don't care about money," Jeffrey was saying now. "You know that, Will. But *you* try kicking your folks and your wife's folks out of the houses you bought for their retirement."

"They don't know what happened?"

"I'm not sure what Sara might have said. We're not on the best terms right now."

I told him I was sorry to hear that. "You two always stuck together no matter what."

"Yeah, well. It's pretty grim this time."

"Did she tell you who the other guy was?"

"No. I assume it's probably somebody from her work." Sara worked as an editor at a small literary press that published very good writers that nobody ever heard of.

"I guess the other guy isn't really the point," I said.

"Will, let me tell you something—when your wife sleeps with another guy, the other guy is *always* the point."

I didn't know what to say to that, so we watched Room A for a while in silence. Nolan was sitting on the floor across from Marie. They were engaged in conversation. Marie nodded slightly at something Nolan said. An encouraging sign, I hoped.

"I can't tell you how sorry I am," Jeffrey said after a while, "dragging you into this."

"I know you are," I said. "But if *this*"—I nodded toward Room A—"doesn't work, we'll need to let her go."

It wouldn't be so hard. Just say a silent prayer of apology and hope and then reunite her with the world beyond this recording studio. Tell her to walk two blocks to the gas station at the corner. She could call a cab or the police or whomever she wanted. And I would call Cynthia and begin to prepare her.

Right now my wife was probably helping to give our niece, Anne, a bath, or reading her a bedtime story. Anne was three years old and loved giraffes.

"My niece really likes giraffes," I told Jeffrey.

"Hmm?"

I shook my head. "Cynthia has no idea about any of this. It feels strange, knowing before she does that her life is about to change."

"I wish we could hear what's going on in there," Jeffrey said, nodding toward Room A.

63

"I'm sure he's doing the best he can."

"I'm sure he is, too," he said. "But best for whom?"

I looked at Jeffrey. "What do you mean by that?"

He raised his eyebrows, as if I were being intentionally obtuse. "Come on, Will. The man's a snake."

"Nolan? No, he isn't," I said. "Why would you say something like that?"

"Of course he is. Everyone knows that. I know he's your friend, but you don't actually think you can *trust* him, do you?"

I was stunned. I wanted to remind him of exactly who had done the kidnapping and who was busy right now trying to set things right. But before I could say anything, Nolan stood up in Room A and let himself out. He shut the door behind him and locked it.

Overhead, the rain on the roof sounded like the rotors of a dozen helicopters. I imagined the inevitable convergence on our windowless hideout: the SWAT teams, the police cars, the fire engines, the ambulances. The television news. But there were others out there, too, looking on, speechless in their horror and disappointment: my mother and father. My dead grandparents. Teachers who'd put their best hopes in me. The small, squinty kid in my third-grade class I'd given my windbreaker to one day because he told me he was cold. A peppermint-scented girl named Veronica, who, the summer I turned thirteen, called me a *gentleman* and kissed me on the boardwalk in Point Pleasant. I had led her through the funhouse and promised not to scare her. And I hadn't.

The ambush was inevitable. The only surprise was that it hadn't happened yet.

I looked at my watch: 8:10 already.

I tried to read Nolan's expression as he walked slowly back to the control room.

Walk faster, I thought. *Walk faster.*

CHAPTER 7

"WE'VE GOT ONE ETHICAL girl in there," Nolan said, back in the control room. "Good kid. Wish I had her campaigning for me door-to-door." He sat down. "I offer her a thousand dollars, and she says, 'Taking a bribe would be wrong.' I finally convinced her at least to think it over." He shook his head. "I even told her to let me know if a thousand isn't enough. But do you know what the real problem is here, Will? Failure of imagination."

"Whose?" I asked. "Hers or ours?"

"Hers! She can't imagine living her life with a secret like this. It's too big. All she can imagine doing is running straight to her grandmother and then both of them running straight to the police."

"You can't blame her," I said. "She's terrified right now."

"Maybe I could try talking to her," Jeffrey said.

"No," I said. "We could go around in circles forever. I'm sorry, but . . . no. Every minute she's here makes things worse for everyone. We have to let her go." Even as I said this, I was looking to Nolan for an objection. Some last-ditch plan that would save us. He said nothing, just returned my gaze, and I realized that he was looking to me for the same thing. "All right, then," I said. "It's settled."

I hoped there would be time, after letting Marie go, to phone Cynthia. I needed to let her know that our lives were going to change. That they already had.

As I was thinking about using the telephone, it rang. My ring-tone played the Popeye-the-Sailor theme song. A happy little melody. This connection to the outside world startled me completely. I removed the phone from my pants pocket and looked at the display.

"Huh."

"Who is it?" Nolan asked.

"It's Evan."

"Answer it."

I hesitated.

"*Answer it.*"

So I did.

"Save me some beer, you dickwads." The connection was full of static. "I'll be at the Newfield station in, oh, about thirty-five minutes."

"You're on the train now?"

"Yup."

"What about all your work?"

"Right, so picture this. I'm working on this memo that I'm told has to be e-mailed out tomorrow morning? Hard deadline and all that? Then I find out from the dipshit partner that the client's going to be at his daughter's wedding tomorrow. He won't even be *checking* e-mail until Monday. So I said to myself, the hell with it. I'm going to see my friends."

"Evan," I said, "you can't come tonight."

Nolan was glaring at me, whispering, "*Call him back.*"

"Look, I need to call you right back."

"What do you mean, 'I can't come.' I'm coming."

"Two minutes, I'll call you back."

"The pleasure will be all mine," Evan said.

I hung up the phone. "I know what you're thinking," I said to Nolan, "but forget it."

"You were being rash. I thought we should discuss it for a minute."

"He's our friend," I said.

"Our friend the lawyer," Nolan said.

"But this isn't his problem."

"He'll know how to help us."

"What's to know? We fucked up. The three of us. That's all there is to it. We shouldn't be drawing Evan into it."

"It's not drawing him into anything," Nolan said. "This is what he *does*. He works to get people out of bad situations."

"Jeffrey," I said, "help me out here."

Jeffrey shrugged. "Evan's an adult. The man can make his own decision."

"Not if we're making it for him."

"When he gets here," Nolan said, "he can turn right around and leave. Hell, he can call the police himself, if that's what he wants. But why not let him size up the situation?"

If I picked Evan up at the station, it would be another hour before we were back here, and that was assuming the traffic had lightened up by now. We shouldn't wait that long. Waiting had gotten us into trouble. "Or we could let her go right now," I said.

Nolan frowned. "Go ahead, Will. Do it. Let her go." When a couple of seconds passed and I hadn't moved, he said, "We need to be honest with each other. If you aren't going to set her free, then don't threaten us. If you are, then go ahead and do it already. No one's going to stop you." He crossed his arms and watched me.

I knew he was calling my bluff, but he was also giving me the chance to call his. If I went to set her free, would he let me do it, or would he try to stop me? Would he stop Marie? *How* would he stop her—to what lengths might he go? It was beginning to dawn on me that I was a little afraid of Nolan.

I handed him my phone. "You call him."

Nolan took the phone from me and dialed Evan. Waited. "No, it's Nolan," he said. "What time does your train get in to New-field? Okay. Will's going to meet you at the station. What's that? All right. Consider it done. See you soon."

He tossed me back the phone. "Evan hasn't had any dinner. He'd like a pizza."

I'd first met Evan through Nolan. The two of them had become fast friends and fierce opponents in Princeton's debating society. Debating held no appeal for me, but the society had lots of money and threw lavish receptions. I'd gone with them to one—a state supreme court justice spoke about constitutional law, though what I remember most were the crab cakes and the innumerable bottles of wine—and afterward we went to a couple of dorm parties across campus. When we left the last party, it was one of those cool autumn nights that smelled of grass and distant burning leaves. A perfect night for walking hand in hand with one's girl-friend or for cementing newly formed friendships.

We found ourselves across the street from McCarter Theatre, one of the tallest buildings on campus, and decided it would be an awfully good idea to hurl rolls of toilet paper off the roof.

We went into the nearby Wawa and bought enough toilet paper to serve a large family well into the future, and then we crossed the street to the theater. I remember looking up at the fire escape—a ladder leading straight up into the sky—and having second thoughts. I overcame them. We adventurers must push fear aside.

With one arm around a pack of toilet paper and the other locked around the ladder rungs, I started to climb. It was at least ten or twelve stories to the top and slow going. I didn't look down. Nolan and Evan stood lookout at the base of the ladder and failed miserably, because suddenly a deep voice was shouting at me to come the hell down off that ladder.

I looked down. My friends and a uniformed campus policeman and a few other passersby were all looking up at me from below. Way below. For a moment I froze. Then I dropped the package of toilet paper and began a slow descent.

The moment I was back on firm ground, the police officer shined his flashlight in my face and asked if I was a student.

I told him I was.

"Let me see your student ID," he said.

He shined his flashlight on it, then on my face again.

I grinned widely.

"This isn't funny," he said, "so shut your fucking mouth."

His manner startled me. University police, called proctors, were extremely well-trained men, gentlemen really, who knocked on dormitory room doors when parties became too loud and reminded us to please keep it down. They carried flash-lights, not guns, and weren't prone to gruffness. What we didn't know then was that the prior spring a student had fallen nearly to his death while climbing this exact fire escape, while in this same inebriated state. He was still in the hospital, and the family had filed a multimillion-dollar lawsuit against the university. Our small prank therefore loomed large in the eyes of campus police.

We were freshmen, though, and ignorant of any number of things that later would seem like common campus knowledge.

"Sorry," I said.

"I don't care about sorry. I care that you coulda been killed, or killed somebody else."

"With toilet paper?" I asked.

"You throw something off the roof, hit a car that's going by, car swerves off the road and hits a telephone pole or a student, you're damn right with toilet paper. Or you fall, hit your head, who do you think takes the blame for that? You? Some spoiled, snot-nosed freshman? No, not hardly." His voice was raised, and a few other students had started to look on. "Anyway, I've *seen* your ID, and I *know* you're underage. And I also know you were all told about academic probation during your orientation."

Princeton was swallowing up a good deal of my parents' life savings, and the possibility of jeopardizing my education sobered me right up. Suddenly I *felt* like a spoiled, snot-nosed freshman. "I wasn't . . ." But I didn't know what to say. How do you explain that you're so happy to have actually found a few friends in a place so foreign from the place you used to call home, and that to celebrate your good fortune you wanted to rocket rolls of toilet paper from the town's highest building into the starry autumn sky? "The thing is . . ."

"Please." Evan had stepped forward and put a hand on my shoulder. "Will wasn't ever planning to climb all the way up or throw toilet paper off the roof."

The officer had shut off the flashlight and put it back in its holster. Now he crossed his arms. "He wasn't, huh?"

"No. He was just seeing if it was *possible* to climb the fire escape. He wasn't going to go any higher. And that toilet paper . . . well, we'd bought some at the Wawa because they'd run out at the dorm. Which is where we're heading. Home. To bed." He lowered his head deferentially. "I promise."

The officer stared at him for a while. Without uncrossing his arms, he said, "What's your name?"

"Evan Wolff."

"You a freshman, too?"

He said that he was.

The officer watched him some more, deciding.

"I want the three of you out of my sight. And *you*"—he pointed a thick finger at Evan—"are in charge of seeing that *he*"—he pointed at me—"goes straight back to his room and goes to bed. Is that clear?"

"Yes, sir," he said.

"Now give me that," he said.

I handed over the bag of toilet paper, and we all said thank you, and then we got the hell out of there. We'd laugh about the incident the next day, but truthfully our run-in with the campus policeman left me feeling uneasy, and I vowed not to behave like some privileged jerk again.

On the walk home, I made a point to thank my lawyer.

"You really want to thank me?" Evan said. "Then treat me to a round of golf next week. I'm broke."

I knew he was into golf. I'd never even picked up a club and couldn't understand why anyone would want to.

"I've never played before," I said.

"Perfect," Evan said. "Then we'll be betting a dollar a hole."

A few days later, Evan, Nolan, Jeffrey, and I were working our way through eighteen agonizing holes at Springdale Golf Club. The experience was unspeakably frustrating, and I resolved—after handing over eighteen dollars to Evan—to give up the game forever. It was too hard, and too expensive. A complete waste of time.

CHAPTER 8

RETURNED TO ROOM A, unlocked it, and went inside. Marie sat against the wall, the blanket covering her feet.

"Feeling any warmer?" I asked.

She looked up at me and shrugged.

"Mind if I sit down?"

She shook her head.

I sat across from her, not too close. "We thought you might be hungry, so we ordered you a pizza. Everything on it. The works."

"Oh," she said.

"What?"

"It's nothing."

"Tell me. Please."

"I'm a vegetarian."

So simple a task, and I'd messed it up. "We'll get you another—"

"Forget it." She scratched her neck. "I'm not really very hungry."

"I'm happy to order another one."

"It's okay. I'll just pick off the meat. Picking off the meat isn't such a big deal, all things considered."

Sitting this close, I could tell she was a smoker, and I was glad to learn this fact about her. It made her seem a little older, a little less fragile—a little less like we had irrevocably tarnished something that'd been flawless.

"So, what did you think your day was going to be like when you got up this morning?" I asked.

She looked around the room, at the microphone stand, the monitor, the headphones lying on the floor. "I guess pretty much like this."

She didn't smile, but I felt grateful for this small joke.

Normally, when nobody is speaking, there are plenty of sounds all around us, the ongoing accompaniment to our lives. We might pay them no mind, but they're always present: a clock's ticking, a refrigerator's humming, cars passing by, leaves blowing down a sidewalk, a plane high overhead. We don't know real silence until we're exposed to it. Here in this small recording room, sheets of thick foam covered the walls. Carpet covered the floor. Even the rain, audible in the control room, couldn't penetrate the thick ceiling insulation in this part of the studio. The only thing to hear was our own breathing and our blood pulsing past our ears.

I credited this unnatural quiet with helping me to forge fast connections with the musicians who came here to record. Without that connection, you can't ever hope to see the project you're working on together with a singular vision. A lot of the recording process is talk. What are we going to do in this next take? What are we trying to achieve? And the studio itself helps us with these conversations. With the background noise gone, we hear one another with greater precision. Timbre, inflection, intensity—these are the raw elements that first the ear, and then the brain and the gut, transform into feeling and understanding.

I hoped that the studio would come to my aid now, and that Marie would hear in my words the full spectrum of regret that I was feeling.

"We've got another friend coming," I said.

She didn't react for a moment, and I got to hear my blood some more.

"He's a lawyer," I continued. "We're hoping he'll be able to help us straighten all this out."

More silence. Then: "And you're telling me this because . . ."

"It means this is going to drag on a little longer. At least another hour or two, until he gets here."

"Oh." She had been joking with me a minute ago, but now her eyes got wet and she wouldn't look at me. "I was supposed to go straight home when my shift ended at eight."

"Your grandmother is probably getting worried."

She shook her head. "No, I'll bet she's isn't. She's probably glad I'm not home."

"I see," I said, not seeing at all.

"She's been on my case to take the SATs. This morning we had a pretty bad fight about it."

"Is that such a bad idea?"

"Yeah, it is. I don't want to go to college. I want to move to New York and be an actress."

I nodded. "Acting's a really hard business." In the midst of all this, I could give advice. Sure I could.

"I've had leading roles in my high school musical the past two years."

"Are you a triple threat?"

"What's that?"

"Singing, acting, and dancing. If you can do all three, you're called a triple threat."

"I can't dance too well. I'm a good singer, though. Really good.

People tell me all the time. Even today, I'd just started my shift at noon and was sort of singing to myself, I don't even remember what it was, but I was singing and didn't know there were any customers in the store, but there was this lady who came out of the restroom and she was like, 'You know, you should be on Broadway.' And I could tell she meant it. It wasn't just some dumb compliment. So, yeah, I can sing." Her eyes weren't watery anymore.

"Is this where you work?"

"Yeah."

"It's a recording studio, isn't it?"

I told her it was. "And a record company." I said it to see whether I still believed it.

"Has anybody famous ever recorded here?"

I told her I had no idea.

She looked outside the glass door into the main recording room. "Why did your friend kidnap me?"

"He doesn't know."

"That's not a good answer."

"Maybe. I don't think it's such a bad answer, either. Haven't you ever done anything and not known why you did it?"

"I guess. But even then I think I usually know."

"Then you're smarter than the rest of us."

She chewed on that for a minute. "When you're out getting the pizza, would you buy me a pack of cigarettes?"

"Sure," I said.

"You aren't going to tell me I shouldn't smoke?"

"No," I said. "All things considered, I'm happy to buy you cigarettes."

"You know, you don't seem like the kidnapping type."

"I'm not the kidnapping type."

"Don't take this the wrong way, but you are." A hard point to argue. "I wouldn't tell anyone, by the way. I know that's why

75

you're all freaking out and offering me money and stuff. All the things I said in the car, I only said them because I was so scared. But I can keep a secret. My friends, they don't ever worry about telling me their secrets, because I view a secret as a sacred trust. One of my girlfriends, I'm not going to tell you her name, but anyway, she told me about an abortion she had when her boyfriend knocked her up. She didn't even tell the guy, but she told me. And I promised to keep it secret, and I have. So I know you probably don't believe me, but I'd keep this whole thing a secret and nobody would get in any trouble."

"I know you believe that," I said.

"I believe it because it's the truth."

"Marie," I said, "this would be a very, very hard secret to keep. *I* couldn't do it. Neither could my friends. And that's what matters, isn't it? Not what *you'd* do, but what they can imagine themselves doing if they were in your shoes."

"Your friends should have a little more faith in other people."

I smiled.

"Will," she said, "can you do something for me?"

"What's that?"

"Give me your hand."

I didn't want to touch her. I wanted to cling to whatever propriety I could. But suddenly she leaned toward me and her two hands were surrounding my own. My wife's hands were slim and soft. She took great care of them, and they always smelled faintly of moisturizing cream. Marie had the hard, sweaty paws of a high school kid.

"I want you to pledge to me," she said, looking me in the eye, "that you won't let your friends cause me bodily harm."

Bodily harm? Exactly like a teenager, I thought. She'd found a way, even under these circumstances, to be overly dramatic. I was completely charmed.

"I've already told you, nobody's going to hurt you."

She yanked her hands away. "When you said it before, you were just being nice. You hadn't really thought it through. Now . . ." She took my hand again and sat up a little straighter. ". . . I want you to pledge it and mean it."

"Marie, I promise. You're safe."

"Then *pledge* it."

"All right. I pledge that you're safe. I pledge that you will not come to any bodily harm."

She kept holding my hand until she had reached some sort of decision about me. Or maybe it was simply more teenage theatrics.

"I believe you, Will," she said. "You'll protect me."

I was nearly out the door when she called my name again. I turned to face her. "She's not all bad," she said.

"Who isn't?"

"My nana." For the first time, she smiled a little. "She wears pink all the time—sweaters, hats, gloves. And even though she's over eighty, her hair is still black. And she doesn't dye it or anything. It's kind of cool. Anyway, I just thought I should say that. Because I don't hate her or anything. I mean, she raised me. I don't take that for granted, you know. I actually think about it a lot. She probably thought she'd have a normal person's old age, and then suddenly she's got *me* to raise." She shook her head, as if thinking what it must have been like raising a girl like her. "So I don't hate her. She's just old. Her mind is sort of going. But I actually really love her."

"I'm glad," I said. I turned to leave again, and again she stopped me.

"Hey, Will?"

"Yes?"

"Marlboro Lights," she said.

77

CHAPTER 9

T HE SUN HAD SET. Streetlights were lit. Up and down Lincoln Avenue, shops and restaurants and apartment buildings still stood. Drivers took no notice of me. Neither did the pedestrians who walked under umbrellas or darted from awning to awning in the light rain. Away from the studio, Friday evening was unfolding with impossible ordinariness.

When I tuned the car's radio to the news, instead of reports of a kidnapping, there was talk of power outages in Hudson and Essex Counties. Delays easing up at the Lincoln and Holland tunnels.

But it looks like we're on tap for a pleasant weekend! said the woman's voice.

I listened and waited. Business news. The Dow closed down fifty points for the week. The Federal Reserve was rumored to be cutting interest rates again.

And after the break, have you ever suspected that your dog might be a genius? Ernesto Sanchez interviews the headmaster of a new school for gifted pooches—

I shut off the radio and noticed, in the space between the seats, my Albright-for-Congress hat. I'd removed it before going into

Antonello's for dinner. Remarkable, I thought, how one minute you were optimistic enough to print your dream on a hat, and the next moment . . . this.

What if I were to keep driving? Just disappear? I played with the idea of starting over, new home, new identity. Maybe grow a beard. Become the captain of a Caribbean fishing boat. I understood right away how absurd this was, but I allowed myself a brief mental getaway to Fantasyland as I drove the very real streets of downtown Newfield toward the railroad station and into the parking lot. Only when, several minutes later, the train came into view and groaned to a stop did I reluctantly shake off images of palm trees and white sand.

I believed it was rotten of us, fooling Evan into coming. But he was a lawyer, a good one, and nothing seemed more valuable at that moment than his sage advice. I arrived just as the train did. Evan stepped onto the platform along with the dozens of other passengers returning from their long workday. He had on khakis, an orange golf shirt, and a Mets cap and was carrying his suitcase and golf bag. Unlike the rest of us, Evan was a serious golfer. His father had played varsity in college and made sure that Evan had grown up playing, too.

We shook hands, and I took his golf bag from him. As we walked to the car, he told me that Meghan, his new girlfriend, had just landed a gig as lighting designer for the revival of *Fiddler on the Roof*. I'd only met Meghan once, at a dinner party Evan had thrown around the holidays, and had liked her immediately. She had an honest, toothy smile and a habit of swearing like a sailor when telling stories. A vast improvement over his last girlfriend, the actuary.

He was launching into a story about a party he and Meghan had gone to last weekend when I said, "Evan, hang on a second."

"What is it?"

79

"Let's sit in the car," I said. "We need to talk."

We put the suitcase and golf bag in the backseat and got in my car. With the engine running, I explained that Jeffrey, Nolan, and I had gotten ourselves into serious trouble. And that we had no clue what to do about it.

"Tell me what happened," he said.

I really wanted to. It was good to see Evan, extremely comforting, and I felt a strong desire to unburden myself and tell him everything. But I knew I shouldn't, for his sake. Luckily for him, he'd gotten tied up at work just long enough to be uninvolved. And I knew that the right thing was to keep it that way. "I can't," I told him. "It's bad, though."

"How bad?"

"Really bad."

The train chugged to a start and left the station. We watched it go. When the station was quiet again, Evan asked, "Did one of you kill someone?"

Three hours earlier, the question would've seemed absurd. "No."

"Look, whatever's going on, Will, you need to tell me. You'll need a lawyer."

"Maybe so." I tried to word this delicately. "If you learned that a crime was being committed . . . you know, in progress . . . you'd need to report it, wouldn't you?"

"That's right," he said.

"Then I can't tell you anything else."

A quarter mile down the track, the train rounded a curve and blew its whistle. Then it was out of sight.

"Then what the hell am I doing here?" he asked. "I mean, if you can't even tell me . . . Look, maybe I can offer you some *hypothetical* advice?"

Hypothetical advice, it suddenly occurred to me, was exactly what he was doing here. "A hypothetical situation would be okay for me to talk about?" I asked.

"Just be careful what you say."

"All right." I paused, considering my words. "Let's say that, hypothetically, three men had gotten themselves involved in a situation."

I was looking out the front windshield. Stragglers were getting into their cars and leaving the parking lot for a well-earned weekend. Early Monday morning, they'd be standing at this same train platform, carrying the same briefcases.

"Are the three men equally responsible for their . . . situation?"

"Say that one man is most responsible, but the other two didn't do anything to make it better or to stop him."

"Go on," he said.

"And say that what happened was inadvertent."

Evan looked at me. "What does *that* mean?"

"It was an accident."

He was shaking his head. "I'm already skeptical. You'd be surprised how many so-called 'accidental crimes' aren't so accidental. You bring a loaded gun where it doesn't belong, the gun goes off by accident—that isn't really an accidental crime, is it?"

"Then I guess I mean it wasn't planned." I wasn't going to get into details. "So now these three men want nothing more than to set things right. But they aren't sure how, without . . ."

"Without facing the consequences."

"That's right."

The small ticket office by the platform was shutting down for the evening. Out front, a gray-haired woman in a large yellow sweater briskly swept a broom across the pavement. A man of about the same age was on his knees by the door, tying twine

81

around stacks of unsold newspapers. I couldn't help wondering about tomorrow's front page.

"Maybe there are mitigating circumstances," Evan said, more to himself than to me. His eyebrows raised. "Was there a car involved?"

He must have seen the surprise register in my face.

"That's what I thought," he said. "And I'll bet there was drinking."

"A little," I said. "Nobody was drunk, if that's what you mean."

But he'd evidently come to a conclusion. "Time is critical." And just when I thought that, impossibly, he'd figured out about the kidnapping—that maybe he'd already heard about it on the radio—he said, "In New York, a hit-and-run is a third-degree felony. That's three to five years in prison. Doesn't even matter if anybody's injured. I'm sure the law is similar in New Jersey." He watched me closely. "The driver of the car is probably terrified, but he needs to understand that the longer he waits to turn himself in, the worse off he's going to be. And that by waiting, he's making things a lot worse for his friends."

We watched the man from the ticket office stack more newspapers.

"If he wants to help his friends," Evan said, "he'll confess. He'll take the blame. Maybe even suggest that his friends tried to get him to stop the car, but he refused. Do you understand this hypothetical advice I'm giving you?"

I was thinking about Jeffrey, how when earlier he'd offered to take the full blame, Nolan and I had called him naive. We were wrong, though. *We'd* been naive. And how much time had passed now? I glanced at the clock on my dash. Almost two hours since she'd first gotten into my car. Sitting there with Evan, feeling the weight of each passing minute, I wished that I were back in the studio urging Jeffrey on. Write that confession! Take the blame! It seemed so obvious, now. He had gotten us into this trouble. Only he could get us out.

"I need to get going," I said.

"Are you sure you don't want to tell me any more?"

I wanted to, but I wasn't going to. "Thanks," I said.

"Suit yourself." He said he'd wait here at the station for the next train. We got his things out of the backseat.

"I was looking forward to golfing this weekend," he said, and put a hand on my shoulder. "I was going to play well. I just dropped four hundred bucks on a new Callaway driver."

"Some other time, I hope." We shook hands.

"You've got to remember," he said, looking me in the eyes, "that these are lifelong decisions you're making now. Decisions that you can't unmake. So please, Will, if you think there's any way I can help—"

"I'll let you know. I promise."

I got into the car, still wishing I could have told him more, yet relieved to have spared one friend. But before I'd driven even ten feet, he was waving his arms at me. I stopped the car and rolled down the passenger-side window. He jogged over.

"Get rid of your cell phones! They can be tracked, even if they're turned off."

I thought about the phone in my pocket. Nolan and Jeffrey must have had cell phones, too. I thanked him again, rolled up the window, and left him standing there in the empty parking lot with his confusion and his golf clubs.

CHAPTER 10

A BRIEF STOP FOR PIZZA and cigarettes—pack of Marlboro Lights for Marie, pack of Camels for myself, plus two lighters—and then back to the recording studio. Would Marie eat with freedom imminent? It seemed important to come through with the meal I'd promised. Especially after convincing the restaurant to change the order from "the works" to something called "crazy veggie."

I had a cigarette lit before the key was even in the ignition. As I drove, I smoked and listened to the radio. The whole way to the studio I kept switching stations but heard nothing of our transgressions. When I parked my car behind the studio it was 9:40. It'd been more than two hours now, so why no word? It seemed very strange.

"Where's Evan?" Jeffrey asked, seeing me enter the studio alone.

"I told you, I didn't want him involved."

"But we need him! He could've—"

I held up a hand. "Save your breath. He's already on his way back to New York, so there's nothing to discuss. One of you, help me carry this stuff over to Marie."

Nolan watched me a moment, then took the bag of soda over to Room A. He opened the door and we slipped inside.

"What's this?" I asked. Two buckets were on the floor, one empty and the other partially filled with water.

"I had to pee," Marie said.

"The other's so she can wash her hands." A roll of toilet paper was on the floor, too.

"You couldn't walk her to the bathroom?" I asked.

"Marie," Nolan said, "have as much pizza as you like. Will, let's talk outside a minute." We left her the box of vegetarian pizza and a liter of soda, as well as the cigarettes and lighter. I followed Nolan out to the main recording room. "No, I couldn't walk her to the fucking bathroom," he said. "This isn't summer camp."

I knew he was right. "Sorry."

He nodded. "So you didn't tell him anything?"

"Not much. We kept things hypothetical. He said we should get rid of our cell phones. They can be traced."

Nolan's eyes widened. "Shit, he's right." He looked around the studio. "Is there a hammer around here?"

There wasn't. But just off the main recording room was a storage closet containing heavy gear. "I have something that'll work."

In the closet was a large canvas bag filled with drum hardware. I opened the bag and removed a metal cymbal stand. A minute later, our cell phones, batteries removed, were in the plastic bag that our soda had come in. The bag lay on the studio's wood floor. The three of us stood over it.

"Who wants the honors?" I asked.

Nolan took the cymbal stand from me. "Stand back," he said. And then he began to smash the bag. Each time the metal slammed into the bag of phones, the loud crack made me wince.

After seven or eight smashes, he said, "I really needed that," and then he gave the bag one final smash. Other than hitting a bucket of golf balls sometimes, I wasn't the sort of person who relieved his anxiety with violence. Still, I regretted having been so quick to pass up the job.

We looked in the bag to survey the damage. Satisfied, Nolan handed me the cymbal stand, which I returned to the canvas bag in the closet.

Back in the control room, I relayed what else Evan had told me. "He said that you were right, Jeffrey. You ought to write out a confession, take the blame. And that way, maybe Nolan and I can negotiate some lesser crime. He said it's worth a shot, anyway."

"Jesus." Nolan massaged his forehead with his fingertips as if touching a crystal ball. He must have been seeing his own bleak future. "This is just . . . Jesus Christ."

"Sorry, Jeffrey," I said. "I don't like that the whole burden's going to fall on you. But I hope you understand that's the way it's got to be. You need to write a confession and take the blame."

In Room A, Marie had finished a cigarette and was now eating a slice of pizza. I watched her take another bite, then bent down to get a notebook and pen from beneath the sound console so that Jeffrey could begin writing.

"Yeah, I can't do that."

I sat up. "Come again?"

"I can't. Not anymore." Jeffrey chewed on his lower lip and looked up at the ceiling as if measuring his words carefully. Then he looked back at us. "I've had a little time now to think things over, and . . . well, you guys should've stopped this. Stepped in when it mattered. I lost my mind there for a minute or two—hell, I'll admit that—but you should've stepped in. You're supposed to be my friends, aren't you? Will, you should've stopped the car, but you didn't. And where were you, Nolan? You should've been concerned about the girl instead of your political campaign." He shook his head. "No, it's like you said earlier—we're all to blame."

Nolan, who until now had been silent, was out of his chair in a flash. Before I could react, Jeffrey's chair rolled backward and banged against a rack of sound gear. His hands flew up to his mouth, where he'd just been punched.

Nolan swiped the notebook and pen from me and stood over Jeffrey's chair, staring him down. "Write the fucking confession, you son of a bitch!"

"I'm bleeding!" Jeffrey said through his hands.

"Write it!" He threw the notebook into Jeffrey's lap.

For the second time in five minutes I felt jealous of Nolan. Even more than wanting to throw a few good punches Jeffrey's way, though, I wanted a signed confession. "Nolan," I said, "get Jeffrey a roll of toilet paper from the bathroom." When he didn't move, I yelled, "Do it!" He left the control room without a word.

"He fucking hit me," Jeffrey said, and slowly lowered his hands. The blood covered his fingers, his teeth, and his lower lip, which was swelling purple.

"Are your teeth okay?" I asked.

He felt around them with his tongue. "I think so." He wiped his mouth with the bottom of his shirt. The shirt came away with enough blood to make my stomach twist. He looked at the blood and shook his head. "I didn't deserve that."

I had no response.

"All I was doing," he said, "was explaining how simpleminded it is to think this was all my fault."

"How about we don't talk right now. Let's just be quiet, both of us, until Nolan comes back."

"Fine with me." He tested his teeth again with his tongue. Marie caught my eye and looked away. Had she seen the punch? If so, it would only confirm her fear that sooner or later, something brutal was coming her way.

87

"Anyway," Jeffrey said, "I didn't see either of you guys rushing to set her free."

"We were trying to *protect* you."

"Yeah, well if you really wanted to protect me you would've ended this as soon as it started. You could've stopped the car or driven—"

"Just shut up," I said. "I don't want to hear it."

Jeffrey winced, then reached into his mouth with his thumb and forefinger, and tugged. "This one's loose. I can wiggle it a little. Man, he's going to pay for that."

I couldn't sit there any longer. "I'm going to see what's keeping him." Jeffrey seemed more interested in his face than my immediate plans. From the doorway, my voice under control again, I said, "I'm sorry about your tooth. But Jeffrey?" I waited until he was looking at me, his fingers still in his mouth. "Write the fucking confession. And make it good."

The bathroom looked like it was straight out of a 1950s high school. Blue tile, two stalls etched and inked with graffiti, stained urinal. Part of my job was to keep the bathroom clean. Now and then we'd hire an intern for minimum, some college dropout with fantasies of recording platinum records at the Hit Factory, and the first thing I'd delegate was bathroom duty. The interns never complained, because their fantasy always began with paying their dues in exactly this manner.

Nolan was leaning over the sink, splashing water on his face. "Hand me some paper towels, will you?"

I did. He stood up and wiped his face. Balled up the towels and pitched them into the trash. "I don't blame you for sending Evan home, by the way. It was a decent thing to do."

"Thanks," I said, "but maybe it was decent *and* stupid."

"This is really something, huh?"

I agreed. It was something.

"Think he'll write the confession?"

"After the punch you threw?"

"Oh, come on. He'd made up his mind already."

"You knocked one of his teeth loose."

"Good." He was studying himself in the mirror now. Even after a full day—this day—his hair was perfectly in place. His shirt looked freshly ironed. He could've walked up to a podium and given a speech, and nobody would know he had concerns beyond his constituency. Still, he must have seen some nuance I'd missed, because he frowned at his reflection and turned away. "Why now?" he asked. "That's what I don't understand. I was going to be a United States senator, Will. I was going to win that election. I had him beat."

It seemed likely. His rival was an aging baby boomer with unnaturally white teeth and the angry tan of a pro golfer. Before becoming a congressman, Stan Byers had run an insurance company into the ground. He called his state *Missoura*, winked a lot, and warned his God-fearing constituents that without his stewardship, they could kiss the Second Amendment good-bye. Which was nonsense—Nolan was hardly some urban liberal. He was born and raised in Missouri farm country and had won marksmanship trophies in high school. At Princeton he'd been head of the debating society, where he'd learned skills he'd put to good use in his current position as state senator for the Twelfth District.

In a sense he'd been working toward this election for as long as I'd known him—paying his dues, working to perfect the strange art of becoming a national figure. The election was still half a year away, but his lead in the latest polls was more than the margin of error. Surely he'd begun letting himself imagine the confetti falling and the marching band playing in his victory parade.

My own dreams lacked that sort of spectacle. But they were mine, and I'd been working toward them with quiet diligence.

For a moment I entertained the idea of recording Jeffrey without his knowledge. Maybe I could coax him into a confession that exonerated Nolan and me. It wouldn't be hard. The band this afternoon had left in a hurry, so the main recording room was already miked. If I could get Jeffrey into the recording room, and if I were in the control room alone and could load up the reel-to-reel . . .

It would never work. For one, Jeffrey now seemed convinced that we all shared responsibility for what'd happened. He was being very egalitarian that way. But also, I knew I couldn't scam my friend—even Jeffrey, even now, even if it meant saving myself. I had neither the talent nor the constitution for subterfuge.

Nolan looked at his watch. "Fuck, it's getting late. I should've called Ronnie before we busted the goddamn phones." Ronnie was his campaign manager. "I know it's bad timing, but if I don't check in with him and he can't reach me on my cell, he's going to panic. And trust me—we don't want Ronnie panicking."

"You're probably better off calling from a pay phone anyway." I told him there was a phone at the gas station two blocks away. "But can I call Cynthia first? She goes to bed early when she's at her sister's."

This was completely illogical of me. Time was precious. But I had a sense it might be the last time I spoke to her as a free man.

He nodded. "Try to make it quick, though."

I told him I would. Then I hesitated. "Do you think it's at all strange that the robbery hasn't been on the radio? When I was in the car, I kept listening for it."

He thought for a moment. "I think every single thing about this fucking situation is strange."

I went into one of the stalls and came out with a roll of toilet paper. "Do me a favor." I tossed him the roll. "Take this in to Jeffrey. And try not to kill anyone while I'm gone."

90

CHAPTER 11

I HAD CHANGE ON ME, but not enough. The gas station attendant changed a five-dollar bill for me. (*Sure, I remember the guy,* I pictured him saying to the police. *Gave him twenty quarters.*) The phone was attached to the station that only partially blocked the wind that'd kicked up. I called Cynthia's cell, and when the electronic voice told me how much money to deposit, I began to feed the telephone with quarters.

Since our niece regularly woke up at dawn, spending the next fourteen hours wearing everybody out, Cynthia went to bed early when she stayed there. She could already be asleep. And even if she were awake, she might let my call go through to her voicemail, not recognizing the number.

Then I heard that single word—"Hello?"—and my chest tightened. A giant chasm opened up between what I knew and what she didn't, and I had to force myself not to confess everything.

"It's me," I said. Deep breath, I told myself. Take a deep breath, and lie to your wife. "My cell isn't working for some reason. How're you doing?"

"I'm good," she said. "Tired."

"Me too. We went to Antonello's for dinner."

91

"Did you have a good time?"

Just a few hours earlier I was ready to announce, *You and I are officially in the record business.*

"Sure," I said. "It was okay."

"Did you have a lot to drink?"

"Not too much. Why?"

"You sound funny."

"I *am* funny."

She didn't laugh, but I knew she was smiling. "Oh, so get this," she said. "Anne was riding her tricycle around the driveway, and I was drawing a road for her with colored chalk . . ."

I listened, but less to the story itself than to her voice. The lightness of it.

She didn't talk for long. Didn't want to keep me on the phone. "Thanks for checking in," she said, "but you should get back to your friends."

I told her good night.

"Have a good time," she said. "Enjoy golf tomorrow."

I said I would.

"Good night, Will," she said.

"Wait."

"What is it?"

I needed to get off the phone. Return to the studio. Nolan was waiting.

"Tell me something first," I said. "Before you hang up."

"Tell you what?"

Anything, I wanted to say. *Tell me anything.* Instead, I asked her about the traffic on the Jersey Turnpike. If it was heavy.

I returned to the control room and told Nolan where to find the telephone. I handed him the rest of my quarters and my building key so he could let himself back in.

"Where's Jeffrey?" I asked.

"Bathroom. Trying to fix his face."

After Nolan left, I sat down and waited. Marie was turned away from me, facing the rear of Room A. I felt a strong curiosity about her, and a desire for her to like me, and I wondered if this was true of all kidnappers.

At least a full minute passed before it dawned on me. There she sat, not thirty feet away. It would be easy. I could have her out and into the cool night air in half a minute. Nothing was stopping me. Except for me.

Once, I saw a hypnotist perform at a bachelor party. When he told his subjects that they couldn't get out of their chairs, they really couldn't. They struggled with all their might—teeth gritting, muscles tightening—but not one of them got out of the chair. I was commanding myself to get up. And I was also commanding myself not to.

There were a hundred reasons to let her go, yet I felt locked to my chair. It wasn't only the fear that she'd tell. I still believed in Nolan, and in myself. Believed that we'd find a way out of this with our lives more or less whole. I didn't believe this completely. Just enough to cause me to hesitate, until Jeffrey appeared in the control room's doorway, a big wad of paper towel pressed to his face. As he stepped into the room, the big box of untapped courage inside of me snapped shut.

"How's the tooth?" I asked.

I felt chilled, looking at him. His fat lip curved upward like a grotesque grin.

"It's still in my mouth." He sat down on the sofa. "You smell like smoke."

I removed the cigarette pack and lighter from my pants pocket and handed them to him. Then I watched him try to hold a cigarette in his busted lips.

"Why did you say earlier that Nolan was a snake?" I asked. We obviously weren't going to make a move until Nolan returned, and I wanted to get to the bottom of something.

He lit the cigarette and took a long draw, like he'd been waiting all his life for that jolt of tar and nicotine. He exhaled and handed me back the pack and lighter. "Oh, pick your reason."

"No, I'm serious. Tell me why you said it."

"You're telling me that you disagree with the assessment?"

"Yes, frankly, I do."

Another draw of the cigarette. He shut his eyes in bliss, or maybe pain, and exhaled a stream of smoke. "After all these years, Will, your naïveté continues to astound me."

CHAPTER 12

I T ALL WENT BACK to Nolan's first political campaign.

Before then, I'd never traveled west of the Mississippi River. A year earlier, with my band stagnating and love life nonexistent, I'd have gladly traded the callous streets of New York for twenty million acres of corn and soybean, for wide autumn skies unspoiled by smog. For four weeks, that would've been a real treat.

By the summer of 1996, though, High Noon was performing in better venues and beginning to generate a little attention. Low men on various music-industry totem poles were starting to make vague promises. When Nolan called and asked for my help, I knew that the rest of the band wouldn't take well to my leaving.

But it'd always been my conviction that nothing trumped loyalty to a friend. So I begged the band for their understanding—and if not that, their forgiveness—and I agreed to fly to Missouri in early October and stay there through the election.

Then Cynthia came into the picture.

When I met her, she was a senior editor at *Center Magazine*, a Manhattan arts and culture weekly. One night she happened to catch the band's set, and afterward she came up to us and asked for an interview. Even the low-wattage room didn't dim her intelligent blue gaze. I liked looking at her. A red beret capped her head like a cherry on a sundae, and a small stud pierced her nose. Her smile was friendly and unguarded. She looked like the girl next door if the girl next door had spent a year in Europe.

She plucked a golf pencil from behind her ear, and in the little notebook she was carrying she scribbled down the date and time when we would meet. She thanked us repeatedly, as if we were the ones doing the favor.

We all met up later that week at an Irish pub near the NYU campus. Cynthia set a tape recorder on the table, and for the next two hours she ordered pitchers of McSorley's and asked us questions. I liked that she talked about music as if it mattered, but not as if it mattered more than it actually did. And I liked her vocabulary, such as when she asked the band if we thought that grunge was here for good or "evanescent." This turned me on.

When the interview was over, she stopped the tape and my bandmates all made polite excuses and left. Only much later, when our relationship was secure, would I reveal to Cynthia the secret behind those quick exits. It'd all been prearranged. *I don't ask for much*, I'd said to my bandmates before the interview, hand on heart. *Please—give me this chance alone with her.* The guys, romantic fools the lot of them, agreed.

Alone with Cynthia, over the next two hours I fell in love little by little.

There was beauty, of course, but this was New York City, where beautiful women seemed to outnumber the pigeons that flocked every park and street corner. No, what got me was that in a city of manufactured looks, manufactured personalities, everything calculated and posed, she seemed genuine. Everyone I met those days claimed to earn a living as a musician or writer or actor or painter. Hearing people talk, one could only conclude that the city must have been suffering from an alarming shortfall of waiters and receptionists.

Yet Cynthia didn't hesitate to tell me that *Center Magazine* was new and underfunded. Also, that despite having the title of senior editor, she made most of her money working as an administrative assistant for a public relations firm. I revealed my own secret: to help with bills, twenty hours a week I worked for minimum wage at a recording studio.

"Occasionally they let me near the sound console," I explained. "But mostly I answer the phones, clean the bathroom, and go on sandwich runs."

"You and I live glamorous lives." She smiled and patted the back of my hand.

When we left the pub, I walked her to the subway and asked for her number. She had that notebook with her, but she wrote her number on the palm of my hand. We saw each other twice more that week. And for the first time I understood why so many sentimental movies took place in Manhattan. The city's grit and trash suddenly seemed coated with a romantic veneer. I found myself smiling to pretzel venders and subway-token salesmen, buying candles and artwork to spruce up my crumbling, roach-riddled apartment. And hoping.

The article came out two weeks later. In my view, she'd made the band out to be far more interesting than we actually were.

"You should be our publicist," I joked.

"Actually, I'll probably move into PR eventually," she told me. "It pays a lot better than arts journalism."

More significant than the substance of this exchange, however, was its location: my apartment. Specifically, my heretofore unremarkable bed, new candles burning on the nightstand, music from a nearby street fair wafting in through the open window.

I leaned over and kissed her. She kissed me back. Then we just lay there awhile, enjoying the music. We were lazing away a perfect, autumn Sunday afternoon, after spending our first night together. Exactly two days before I had to leave for fucking Missouri.

I packed my suitcase, endured a terrifying flight through black thunderstorms, and landed in Kansas City. Rented a Chevy Blazer. *Be sure it's an American car,* Nolan had warned. *People notice these things.* Then drove ninety miles into Missouri's heartland, to the Albright family farm in Nodaway County.

When I'd met Nolan that first day of our freshman year in college, I'd asked him what town he was from.

"Town?" He'd shaken his head. "No town." If you needed to send him a letter, he'd said, you used the zip code for Stokesville, five miles to the south.

In the last several years, however, the city limits of Stokesville had expanded those few miles to include the farm and the land around it. Farmers saw the city's expansion as an opportunity to sell their land for development. Not Nolan's parents, though, despite their property's appealing location at an intersection of two county roads. They still worked their hundred-acre farm as the town steadily encroached on them. Driving to the farm, I passed a lot of new construction—a residential neighborhood, a row of stores—and I could see into the future to a time when there would be car dealerships and chain restaurants and gas stations, eventually a shopping mall, and then it would look exactly like the America I'd grown up knowing.

Although Nolan rented an apartment in town, he still referred to the farm as home. From there he ran his campaign. As I pulled up the driveway, a small black terrier ran in front of my car. I stopped the car and got out, and the dog barked comically and spun around in a few circles. A moment later, Nolan came outside.

"When'd you get Cujo?" I asked.

"My mother got him from the pound a couple of months ago. She said she'd always wanted a little dog."

Nolan's mother was responsible for his interest in politics. She'd studied political science in college and, for a couple years, had an administrative job at the statehouse in Jefferson City. That was before meeting Mr. Albright and moving to Stokesville, where she became a more than capable farmer.

But in the spring she'd been diagnosed with breast cancer. Radical mastectomy, chemo, the whole mess. Nolan hadn't told me much—it obviously upset him to talk about it—but he did say it'd come as a real shock. His mother had gone to her doctor several months before and been assured that the lump she thought she felt was nothing to worry about.

"How's your mom doing?" I asked.

"I don't like the wig," he replied. "Makes her look old. Otherwise, she's doing all right." He sighed. "I mean, no she isn't. But we're trying to be hopeful, you know? Anyway, she likes me running the campaign from home. That way she can still feel part of it." He bent down to pet the dog, which had flopped over and was wriggling on its back. I noticed its collar had rhinestones on it. "Molly's a good dog. We had a couple of hunting dogs growing up, coon hounds. They were good dogs, too, but this one's different. This one's my mother's dog."

Nolan took one of my bags, and we went inside, led by Molly. The house was two stories and decorated with simplicity, even elegance. I hadn't ever been to his family's farm before, and certain touches—a retro-looking leather sofa, a framed Rothko print—struck me more as SoHo than Missouri. (My urban bias would dissipate in the weeks that followed to the point where, upon returning to New York, I'd find myself bristling at rude waiters and jerking awake at night with every passing wail of a patrol car or ambulance.) The house's single nod to its rustic location was a cow skull hanging over the mantel.

A dozen or so people of all ages were standing around the living room and looking grave. Nolan explained to me that they'd convened in order to assemble the one thousand yard signs that were due to be delivered that morning—they were already weeks overdue—but he'd just gotten word, moments before I arrived, that the delivery was being delayed again.

"I needed for them to be made locally," Nolan explained, "but I'm starting to think the manufacturer doesn't support our campaign."

"You mean they're intentionally—"

"Welcome to Missouri politics." He clapped his hands. "All right, people," he said to the room, "we have work to do, signs or no signs."

They divided into canvassing groups and spent a few minutes looking over maps and lists of registered voters. Then they went out to their cars to convince the citizens of District Twelve that it was "all right to vote Albright." Nolan's father went with them—after giving me a bone-crunching handshake—wearing a T-shirt that said, "Vote for my son."

Only after they were gone did Mrs. Albright come downstairs. She had on blue jeans and a loose-fitting sweater. I hadn't seen her since graduation. I didn't remember her being a small woman, but she looked small now—shrunken, and tired. The wig wasn't so bad, though.

She smiled and took both my hands in hers. "It means so much to Nolan to have you here," she said.

I told her I was glad to come.

"You're a good friend," she said. "You always have been. Now fix yourself a snack—I'll bet they didn't give you anything on that plane."

She was right—I was starving. Nolan and I went into the kitchen and Mrs. Albright headed back upstairs. When she was out of earshot I quietly asked, "Do you want to talk about . . ."

He shook his head. "I'd rather talk about *anything* else."

So I asked him about all the canvassing his volunteers were doing. I wanted to know if it actually worked.

"You don't win elections around here with radio or TV ads," he said. "Not that we've got the money for that anyway. Here, the personal touch is everything. Meeting voters, shaking their hand, hearing what they have to say, telling them what you're all about. Reminding them that you're from these parts, and your family is from these parts." His voice seemed to slow down a notch. I detected the drawl that seeped in sometimes during a college debate. "And it doesn't hurt to have a secret weapon."

"What's that?" I asked.

He laughed. "*You*, that's what. The volunteers are dedicated and some of them are even smart, but not one of them can really think, let alone write a good sentence." My job, he explained, besides helping to keep the volunteers organized, was to crank up the campaign's publicity effort—writing press releases to all the local papers, letters to the editor, and updates to the campaign's newsletter. Plus, I'd overhaul any campaign literature that I felt needed it.

He showed me the magazine rack with all the press coverage so far: newspapers, mostly, but a few glossy magazines—*Missouri Monthly* and the *Princeton Alumni Weekly*.

On a table in the living room was a computer and laser printer. Nolan opened a file on the word processor. "Here's my position on every issue that affects our district," he said. "Take the afternoon and read it all. Tonight, you can ask me anything you don't understand. But now," he said, heading for the door, "I have the important job of getting a haircut." He grinned. "In Missouri, hippies don't win elections."

When he left, I opened the *Princeton Alumni Weekly* to the half-page article about Nolan and sat down at the table with it.

Since college graduation, the *Alumni Weekly* appeared in my mailbox with surprising regularity given the number of times I moved from apartment to apartment. Sometimes I'd flip through the magazine and read about a famous alumnus or a winning sports team. And I'd always look at the "Class Notes" section for my year. When I first graduated, I'd read about students enrolled in law school, medical school. I'd read about weddings. So many weddings. Sometimes there'd be a photograph of the happy couple surrounded by fifteen or twenty other alumni in their suits and dresses.

Soon after came the babies, and with them the clichés—"bundles of joy," "prayers answered," "little miracles"—along with interchangeable, fat-cheeked photos.

And then, life's housekeeping apparently over with, my classmates got down to the serious business of achieving. They became partners at law firms, consulting firms, investment firms. They became venture capitalists. They traveled to countries I'd never heard of to stamp out diseases. They climbed unclimbable summits, swam unswimmable rivers. They produced Hollywood movies and published novels and, like Nolan, created important organizations.

The article about Nolan focused on the nonprofit organization he'd founded. It summed up what I already knew. The year after graduation, he interned for a Missouri congressman in Washington, DC. While there, he started up Students for Peace.

The organization pays for children aged ten to eighteen to attend weekend-long events centered on the idea of peace—among individuals and among nations. Students attend workshops, debate ethical issues, and interact with politicians, ethicists, and other leaders, culminating in a hands-on project promoting peace. In its first year, guests included author Kurt Vonnegut, former president Jimmy Carter, and the director of Princeton University's Center for Human Values, Janet Vogel.

When asked about his organization, Albright stated, "We tend to think of children as insular and self-centered. But I'm always amazed, talking with them, how concerned they are with their community, their world. Our organization is designed to empower these kids, to let them know that they have every right to care about peace even though they aren't of voting age."

Albright founded Students for Peace in 1995 while working as a congressional intern in Washington, DC. The organization is currently based in Albright's hometown of Stokesville, Missouri. Tax-deductible donations can be sent to . . .

I set down the magazine and scrolled the document titled *Albright on the Issues*. It ran sixty-four single-spaced pages. World peace wasn't on the agenda. This was a state election, and the concerns were domestic: economic development, education, infrastructure, health care.

I was willing to help sell the product of Nolan Albright to whoever wanted to buy it, but I'd never written a press release in my life. I began to fantasize about Cynthia, the real PR pro, trading in her pumps for cowboy boots and coming out here to work with me on the campaign. Our romance blooming under the wide Missouri sky.

And then I began to read.

Those yard signs were becoming the bane of the campaign, and their continued absence made them seem all the more critical. None of us knew for certain whether or not Nolan was going to win. The incumbent was retiring at the end of the term, and our opponent, like Nolan, had never run for office before. Ed Cassidy was twice Nolan's age. He owned several mammoth car dealerships across the state, and back in September he was running a couple of percentage points ahead of Nolan in the polls. But polling wasn't especially precise in a district-wide election. Our real barometers were our guts and our ears.

We believed we had a shot, but Cassidy's smiling face seemed to be everywhere—his signs were in storefronts and at major intersections, and of course large banners stood in the parking lots of his dealerships. Driving around the district, it would've been easy to conclude that Nolan simply didn't exist.

And so when one cool morning a dusty diesel truck bearing the name "Show-Me Sign Company" finally clanked into the Albrights' driveway, Molly's approving bark spoke for all of us. Over the next couple of days, I learned the roads of northwest Missouri. For me these were the best days of the campaign, driving alone under deep blue skies into small towns, along rivers, and through field after field of spent corn. Sometimes I'd drive into a neighborhood to deliver a half-dozen signs. Other times I'd travel fifteen or twenty miles on remote roads to drop off a single sign that hardly anyone would ever see.

If nobody was home, I'd leave the sign on the front stoop. But as often as not, somebody would be there to thank me, maybe offer a glass of water or cup of coffee. We might chat for a minute. And talking with them in their front yards and their kitchens, catching a glimpse of their landlocked lives, for the first time I found myself believing that there were other places to live out one's life besides a city.

I wouldn't act on that belief for several more years—not until the shooting that drove me out of New York. But rural Missouri gave me the first inkling that there were ways to be content without having to become the white hot center of everything.

. . .

A few days before the election, campaign headquarters started receiving calls that yard signs were vanishing in the night. To retaliate, I showed up at the house that night carrying two "Vote Cassidy" signs that I'd daringly swiped from the lot of one of Cassidy's own car dealerships. I'd done it as a prank—to lighten the mood, I guess—but Nolan wasn't amused.

He took me aside. "Elections can be brutal, but there are rules."

"Okay," I said. "Fair enough."

"I want us running a clean campaign, is all."

"Understood."

He sighed. "You've been a tremendous help to me, Will. I can't thank you enough."

Later, after everyone else had left for the night and Nolan's parents had gone to bed, Nolan and I poured tumblers of Scotch and sat down on the living room sofa. Molly immediately jumped up between us and rested her snout on Nolan's leg.

"As a kid," Nolan said, "I remember sitting right here, in this room, watching Ronald Reagan bait the Soviet Union on TV. I'm sure you remember all that 'Evil Empire,' 'Star Wars' end-of-the-world bullshit."

I did, vaguely. At the time, I was more interested in *Star Wars* the movie.

He sipped his drink in thought. "I was ten years old, but I knew trash talking when I heard it. And Reagan was the most reckless trash talker I'd ever heard, because thousands of nuclear warheads were pointed at him. And at me—and my friends and my parents. Though my parents didn't seem to think much about it one way or the other. I could see it for what it was, though—reckless and stupid. As far as I was concerned, he was going to cause the end of the world." The dog's stomach gurgled. "So that's when I decided to write him a letter."

105

"Who? Reagan?"

"Of course. And not some childish, emotional plea, either, but a reasoned argument for using the office of the president to end the risk of nuclear war."

He was looking at the dog, not me. The story seemed to embarrass him, and I wondered why, until I remembered the fan letter I'd written at about the same age to the actress Carrie Fisher. I'd slid the letter into an envelope I'd made out of aluminum foil so it would stand out. *I'm not asking you to marry me,* I'd written. *But I know we'd be friends.*

"So what'd you say in the letter?"

"I said that name-calling only increased the likelihood of a brawl. Basic school-yard diplomacy." He looked up at me. "People were people, I figured. How different could it possibly be between leaders of nations?" He shook his head.

"I take it you never heard back."

"Two weeks," he said. "It came quickly, I'll give him that. I remember coming home from school and seeing it on the kitchen table. Nobody else was home. It was a thin envelope. But it didn't need to be thick. All it needed to say—and I was sure that it would—was that Reagan had seen the error of his ways." He finished his drink in one long swallow, set the tumbler on the coffee table, and looked at me again. "Two sentences. I'll never forget them." His eyes widened. "Hold that thought—I still have it."

He was off the sofa and down the hallway toward his bedroom. While waiting, I gave the dog a good scratching behind the ear, earning a thankful groan.

Nolan returned from his bedroom with the envelope, now faded from time. He opened it and removed the single page, folded in thirds, and handed it to me. I unfolded it. The letter was typed on stationery with the presidential seal.

October 12, 1982

To my friend Nolan Albright,

Your thought-provoking letter leaves me heartened. It is because of young Americans like yourself, concerned with the important issues of the day, that I feel optimistic about our nation's future.

Sincerely,
Ronald Reagan

I handed it back to Nolan.

"At least it's personalized," I said. "And nice enough."

"*Heartened?*" He glared at the letter as if he'd received it only minutes before instead of fourteen years ago. "He was *heartened* by my letter? Hell, he missed the whole fucking point."

"It probably wasn't Reagan who wrote it, anyway."

"Yeah. Tell that to the kid who's lying in bed every night, scared shitless, sure the world's going to explode before he's even kissed a girl. This letter only made things worse." He refolded the letter. "That's when I made a deal with myself. Two promises, for when I became an adult. Number one, I'd make sure that no kid went through what I went through. And number two, I'd help kids make a difference, so they wouldn't have to lie in bed at night feeling powerless. In return for those promises, I'd stop worrying about the state of the world until I turned eighteen, when I'd be old enough to be taken seriously. That was the deal I struck, the promise to myself that saved my life. And it's the promise I'm keeping today."

He looked at his watch, then down at the carpet, then back at me and grimaced. I didn't want him feeling uncomfortable—his story had moved me deeply, and I nearly confessed my short-lived Carrie Fisher crush.

107

"When you write your presidential memoirs," I told him finally, "be sure to include this chapter."

Nolan slid the letter back into its envelope. He looked at me and smiled politely. "Let's just win this one first."

The evening before the election, Evan and Jeffrey flew into town to show their support. When they arrived at Nolan's house, we said quick hellos and put them to work on the phones. But work got interrupted when Luke, a senior at Northwest Missouri State and one of Nolan's most dedicated volunteers, came into the house in tears.

"He ran right in front of my truck . . . ," he was saying to anyone who'd listen. ". . . It was so dark . . . I didn't see . . ."

Molly.

Mercifully, it'd been quick. By the time we made it outside and down the long driveway to the road, the dog was already lifeless. I hadn't ever seen a dead dog before. Its tongue really did hang out. We stood over it—Nolan, Luke, myself, and a few of the morbidly curious among the volunteers—not knowing what to do. A minute later, Nolan's parents followed us outside with a flashlight.

"Maybe I should go home," Luke said.

Nolan's mother nodded, her eyes wet. She was shivering. "Maybe you should."

"Mom . . . ," Nolan began.

His father shut off the flashlight. "Come with me, son," he said to Luke, and led him away from the street, toward the shed. They returned with a wheelbarrow.

Late that night, after the volunteers had all gone home and Evan and Jeffrey had left for their motel, Nolan and I took care of some sad business at the edge of the backyard and the corn crop.

The weather had been mild lately, and the ground gave easily. I'd thought we might put the dog into a box first, some makeshift coffin. Instead, without ceremony Nolan lifted the dog out of the wheelbarrow and set it down in the hole. He must have noticed my expression, because he said, "It'll decompose faster this way." He scooped up some dirt and let it fall onto the dog in the hole, then offered me the shovel in exchange for the flashlight.

"I'd rather not," I said. "I know it's just a dog, but . . . I'd just rather not."

"I understand. It's morbid. I don't like doing it, either. Though I guess it's better to be the one with the shovel than the one in the hole." He added more dirt to the grave until there was a small mound, which he patted down with the back of the shovel.

"Please tell me," he said, as we walked back toward the shed with the shovel and wheelbarrow, "that this is not an omen."

I stopped walking. "Nolan, this is *not* an omen. This was an accident."

"I just really want to win this, you know? It's probably a couple of years too early for me to be running. I know I don't quite have the experience yet, or the name recognition. Or the money." He glanced back toward the house. "But I really want to win this one. For her, you know what I mean?"

"Of course I do." I felt as if I needed to say more. "Look, you've worked your ass off and run a good, honest campaign. You're going to be a great politician. The best kind, because you actually give a shit."

He nodded. "All right. I'm convinced." We returned to the house.

Twenty hours later, we crowded into the lounge at the Regency Hotel in Stokesville. Under a ceiling of helium balloons, about fifty of us—volunteers, family, friends, and media—watched the

TV over the bar, waiting for the returns to come in. Nolan's mother buzzed around the room in a purple dress, thanking everyone and expressing confidence that the state of Missouri had chosen wisely. She looked better than I'd seen her since my arrival. Nolan's father was being quieter, sipping his whiskey and studying the television.

Nolan had written his acceptance speech, and in my shirt pocket was a list of people he wanted to be sure to thank. Beer and wine flowed freely. On the bar were trays of food—deli sandwiches, a cheese platter, plenty of desserts—and coffee. We were hunkering down for a long night.

We needn't have been. The polls closed at seven. At seven thirty, the stunningly pretty newscaster said: *And in the Twelfth District, Ed Cassidy successfully jumps into state politics with an easy victory over his young rival, Nolan Albright.*

She flashed her perfect white teeth.

CHAPTER 13

"SO DO YOU REMEMBER how the night ended?" Jeffrey asked me now.

I remembered Mrs. Albright kissing her son on the cheek and, thoroughly deflated, going off to bed. Mr. Albright walking over to his son, shaking his hand, and frowning.

"You lost," he said, "but I suppose you did the best you could."

"I don't know," Nolan replied. "I thought I did."

His father went in the direction his mother had gone, and then others left, too, and then a handful of us headed up to our defeated candidate's suite to watch the TV news and finish off whatever wine hadn't already been consumed. Our numbers dwindled. Nolan clicked off the TV.

I have nothing, he said, the melodrama of the inebriated. *It's all over for me.*

"Sure, I remember," I said to Jeffrey now. "Nolan got drunk and kicked us out of his hotel suite."

I didn't see him until the following morning. Jeffrey, Evan, and I were having breakfast at the hotel restaurant around eight o'clock when the elevator doors opened and out he came, looking uncharacteristically disheveled. No morning run. He came over and took the fourth seat. He picked up the menu and looked at it, though there was no need. Nolan always ate a bowl of oatmeal with a banana for breakfast.

The waitress came over. "Pancakes," he said. "And a cheese omelet. And a Coke."

"How're you holding up?" I asked, when the waitress had gone away.

"My head is killing me."

When the food came, he didn't touch any of it. Just stirred the eggs around in his plate, sipped the Coke, then stood up and shook each of our hands. "I'm sorry, but I really need to get the hell out of here." He dropped some bills on the table and left, and I didn't see him again until the following spring, when we all met up for golf in the Great Smoky Mountains of Tennessee. By then he was back to his old self, and thoroughly optimistic about the next election two years hence—an election he'd go on to win decisively, and without my help.

"You're leaving out something important," Jeffrey said, "after he locked himself in his hotel suite."

"What's that?"

"He called my house."

This didn't make sense. "In California?"

"Of course."

"But you were with us in Missouri."

The look he gave me said, *No shit.*

"He told her he loved her, Will. Three in the morning, and he wakes her out of a dead sleep and says he loves her."

"No."

"He told her he's *always* loved her."

"Jesus—when did she tell you about it?"

"When I came home. I'm about to go to bed after a full day of travel, and Sara mentions it like it's no big deal. *Did you know that*

Nolan Albright called me late last night? As if I could possibly know. I almost threw up, hearing about it."

"What did she say to him?"

"She told him to go to bed. I told her she should've told him to fuck off, but apparently she felt sorry for him because of how badly he'd gotten whipped in the election." He looked out into the hallway, as if Nolan might've been standing there, listening this whole time. He lowered his voice. "You don't *do* that, Will. You don't phone your friend's wife like that. Not after—"

"He was drunk. I'm not excusing it. But people say things when they're drunk."

"They tell the truth! *That's* what people do when they're drunk."

"So what?" I said. "So he made a mistake. What do you care? You're the one she married."

His body seemed to be tensing up just thinking about it. His hands curled into fists. "Who did he think he was, huh? The Great Gatsby? Did he think he was some self-made big shot who could waltz in and steal my wife away?"

"Gatsby ended up dead in a swimming pool."

"Yeah, that's true. Served him right."

"Come on, he was depressed. You were there. You saw it."

"Still, that's no excuse."

"Isn't it? Are you really going to sit here and claim you can't understand how a depressed person might do something he'd later come to regret?"

We both looked over at Marie.

"Sara's my *wife*," Jeffrey said.

"Yes, that's what makes it wrong. I see that."

"It revealed a lot, is all I'm saying. I know you don't like to think badly of anyone. That's why I never told you any of this before. You like to have your little golf weekends and make insipid toasts and pretend we're all still best friends. You pretend that history doesn't exist. But it does. And the truth is that Nolan tried to betray me that night, just like he betrayed me before."

Ah. So that's what this was all about. Not some election-night impropriety. No, this went back further, to matters I'd assumed were long settled.

"You don't know for sure that Nolan ever betrayed you," I said. When he shook his head, dismissing the notion, I said, "Come on, Jeffrey, you were the English major. You know that life and literature aren't the same thing."

I was about to say that we'd been through all this before, when Nolan returned to the studio carrying a large cardboard box.

"That electronics store down the street has excellent bargains," he said, set the box down in the control room, and tossed me my keys.

The box said Magnavox.

"You bought a TV?" I asked.

"Had to. So we can watch the news."

"Did anybody see you?" Jeffrey asked.

"Of course. But nobody's looking for me. I'm invisible. Unlike you—jeez, sorry about your face. Is it broken?" The fresh air seemed to have done him good. Our predicament hadn't changed any, but I was glad to see Nolan fresh again and no longer angry.

"You knocked a tooth loose," Jeffrey said.

"Damn. Really sorry about that. It was wrong of me. I shouldn't've done it." He held out his hand for Jeffrey to shake. Jeffrey hesitated.

"Oh, don't be a baby," I said. "Shake his goddamn hand and send him the dental bill later."

Jeffrey shrugged. They shook hands, and then we went into the main recording room, where there was more space to set up the TV. As I expected, the reception was terrible. The TV had come with rabbit ears, though, and after carrying it around the

114

room from spot to spot, two New York stations finally began to reveal themselves—NBC and ABC—both distorted, but good enough.

Crime dramas on both stations. All that seemed to play on TV anymore, besides reality shows, were crime dramas. For a few minutes we sat on the floor and flipped between stations. We watched the badge-flashing, the interrogations, the rough arrests. At no point, however, were any of these programs interrupted for the real crime in progress. No words at the bottom of the screen informing crime-addicted viewers that an actual girl had gone missing.

"Jeffrey," I said after a few minutes, "why doesn't anybody seem to be looking for us? Do *you* have an explanation?"

"No," he said. "None."

"Why don't you tell us exactly what went down at the Milk-n-Bread," Nolan said.

Jeffrey watched the screen for another minute, then reached for the TV and muted it. "First of all," he said, "you guys need to understand how fast it all happened. I'd planned to buy a thing of Tums. I was feeling really ill. And, no, it wasn't the clams. Listen—Sara only told me about the affair two days ago. She said she had to tell me because . . . she's *nearly* certain the baby's mine, but . . . well, you get the idea. So, yeah, I've been feeling pretty fucked up. Anyway, there was an old lady in the store, and when she left I looked over at the register and noticed that the cashier and I were the only two people left. And maybe she looked a little like Sara—okay, I can see that now—but it wasn't anything I thought too hard about. Believe me, I never in my life thought about robbing a store or kidnapping somebody, but it was like this moment opened up and it became doable. If that old lady had stayed it never could've happened. I just stood there at the register a moment, because I was sure somebody else

115

would walk into the store, or another employee would come in from some back room or the bathroom or wherever. But no. And right then I knew I could do it. You know how we've talked about how a good quarterback can see the whole field and know exactly how it'll look a few seconds later? That's how it felt. I saw the play come together, and I knew exactly what to do."

I didn't like the quarterback comparison. It meant that alongside whatever remorse he might now claim to be feeling, he was still feeling the rush, the residual amazement at what he'd done.

"All right, Joe Montana," Nolan said, "describe the play."

"She rang up the Tums, and I handed her some money, but the instant the register opened, I looked out the glass door and said, 'Oh my God, she fell,' or something like that. Marie must have known the woman, because she gasped and said, 'Mrs. Tyler?' And I said, 'Yeah,' and then she ran for the door."

"Without shutting the register?" I asked.

"I made it all sound really urgent," he said. "So yeah. I leaned over the counter and grabbed a handful of bills from the register and stuffed them in my pocket. Marie didn't even notice—she was already opening the door to go outside, so I hurried up and went with her, and then when we were out there I took her arm and said, 'Hurry, follow me,' and that's exactly what she did. She must've thought your car was the old lady's car right up until the last second. It was dark and rainy, and it all happened so fast, I don't think she knew what was going on until she was already in the car. I know I didn't." He looked at us, as if trying to gauge our reaction. "It sounds really calculated, but that's not how it felt. It felt as if I hadn't even decided to do it until it was already done."

I thought I understood better now why the authorities might not have been notified. Marie had been alone in the store. She'd come outside willingly. There was nothing to see and no one to see it.

"But here's what I still don't get," I said. "Her shift runs noon to eight. I looked at my watch. "It's now after ten. So what happened when the new employee showed up at eight and didn't see Marie? And what about her grandmother? Wouldn't she be worried by now?"

"Two hours late coming home?" Jeffrey said. "That isn't so long. Think about when you were a teenager and—"

"Stop." Nolan was staring at me.

"What is it?" I asked.

His gaze stayed on me. "How do you know when her shift started?"

"Because she told me," I said, feeling a little proud that I was the one she'd confided in. "She was scheduled from noon to eight, and at eight she was supposed to punch out and go home to her grandmother."

Nolan was shaking his head. "No, something's not right. We need to have a chat with Little Red Riding Hood. Right now."

I glanced in her direction. Like me, she'd been devouring one cigarette after another. "Am I missing something?" I asked.

"Yeah, Will, you are. She's been bullshitting us."

CHAPTER 14

I CRACKED OPEN THE DOOR to Room A, leaned my head in, and told Marie that we'd like to talk with her. "There's more room out here," I said. "Can we trust you not to make a break for it?"

Trust and precaution, however, need not be mutually exclusive. We had already moved some equipment—a couple of amplifiers, that big canvas bag of drum gear—in front of the exit leading to the hallway. It would be impossible for her to make a fast escape even if she wanted to.

Marie nodded. I opened the door farther and stood aside as she slowly got up, stretched, ran a hand through her hair, and then emerged. The moment she left Room A she glanced over to the blocked doorway. Then her gaze moved to Jeffrey and Nolan, who were seated on folding chairs. I took a seat behind the drums and noticed that The Fixtures had stuck one of their bumper stickers onto the snare drumhead. I began to work the sticker off with my thumbnail. I was always peeling bands' bumper stickers off things.

"Please," Nolan said, pointing to the empty chair beside him. Marie took a seat. "Look, we'll get right to the point. There's something we don't understand, and we'd like to hear what you

118

have to say about it." Her eyes widened a little. She waited for him to continue. "Will, why don't you explain it."

Marie looked like a model student—hands folded in her lap, head lowered in deference, or perhaps in an imitation of deference. "You told me earlier," I said, "that you were working the noon-to-eight shift."

She nodded. "That's right."

"Okay, that's what confuses us."

I didn't enjoy having this conversation. It felt as if we were antagonizing somebody we had no right to antagonize. For this reason, I suppose, I'd sat at the drums. This was where I felt most comfortable, partially obscured behind cymbals and tom-toms. "You told me you're a junior in high school."

"A junior," she said. "That's right."

"But today's Friday." I shrugged. "So we were wondering how it is that you could be working the afternoon shift."

She looked up at the ceiling. If we'd been in a house, we would've heard the ticking of a wall clock. A refrigerator might have clicked on. Instead, we heard only our own breathing.

"We didn't have school today." Her foot began to tap on the wooden floor. "It got canceled."

I glanced at the other guys, then back at her. "Can you tell us why?"

This was a job for a lawyer, or for someone like Nolan who enjoyed trapping people with his words.

"It was a teacher convention," she said. "In Atlantic City. They have those conventions all the time."

They don't have them all the time. They have them once a year, and in the fall. Years of public school education had permanently etched in my brain this two-day vacation, occurring each year just before the weather turned too cold for outdoor play. I couldn't recall, now, whether the convention was in September or

119

October, but it wasn't in April. I remembered always being surprised that we would be granted a reprieve from classes so close
to the beginning of the school year.

"I'm sorry, Marie," I said, "but that doesn't sound right."

"There's no need to lie to us," Nolan added. "We're on your
side here."

"But I'm *not* lying." More foot tapping. "I mean . . . maybe it
wasn't the convention. Okay, I might have that wrong. The thing
is, I had to take the day off from school anyway, because the store
needed someone to cover. Okay? That's the whole story."

Nolan's response was instantaneous: "That may be the story,
but we'd prefer the truth."

"What?" She glared at him but then looked away. Her voice
raised in pitch, and her breathing quickened. "I'm *telling* you the
truth."

Jeffrey, who'd been listening quietly until now, put up a hand,
silencing her. "You aren't in school anymore, are you?"

"What?" she repeated, and I was reminded of myself as a teenager, choosing deafness rather than defiance as a means of dodging the probing questions of a teacher or parent.

"Did you drop out of school or have you already graduated?"
Jeffrey asked.

"I don't like this," she said. "It isn't fair."

"No, it isn't." Nolan's voice softened. "It's completely unfair
what we've done to you. But the one thing we're going to need
from you in order to get through this together is honesty. We've
done a terrible thing, the three of us. We know that. But we've
also been straight with you from the beginning. This was an accident. We never planned for it to happen. I really hope you believe that, because it's the truth. And it's also the truth that we
want nothing more than to get you home, and the sooner the better. Do you believe me?"

She sighed. "Whatever."

"I really hope you do, Marie." I wondered if she cared whether or not we were truthful. None of it changed the fact that she was here, and we were here, and several hundred pounds of musical equipment blocked her exit.

"But this truth," Nolan was saying, "this honesty, has to cut both ways. Because the more we find we can trust you, the more we're inclined to keep on trusting you. But if we find that we *can't* trust you, then that's a problem. So please, tell us the truth. Are you or are you not still in high school?"

First, nothing. Then a barely detectable shake of the head.

"Is that a no?" Nolan asked.

She said, "I graduated last year."

"So that makes you, what? Nineteen?"

"Yeah," she said.

I was confused. "Why did you tell me before that you were still in—"

"Because you're all a bunch of kidnappers! I'm sorry. I know you think you aren't, but you really, really are. And I thought that if you believed I was just some high school kid, maybe you'd feel bad and let me go."

"Thank you for being honest," Nolan said.

Easy for you to say, I thought. I was the one she'd confided in. Now, hearing the truth, I couldn't help feeling a little betrayed. "What about your grandmother?" I asked. The pink sweaters. The jet black hair. I felt as if I'd be able to recognize the old lady shuffling down the streets of Newfield. I'd even begun to think that maybe I had. "Is she just someone you made up?"

"No!" She sounded offended but then caught herself. "I wouldn't lie about her. She raised me, just like I said. Only, I don't live with her anymore."

"So who do you live with?" I asked.

121

"I don't live with anybody."

I hadn't considered that Marie might have been fabricating parts of her story. But why shouldn't she? From the moment Jeffrey had forced her into my car, her one concern would have been her own survival. If she'd had money, surely she'd have given it to us in exchange for her freedom. But the only currency she had was our perception of her. And so why shouldn't she bend her life story a little, mold herself into someone she thought we might feel protective toward and unwilling to harm?

"Look," she said, "I'd show you my ID except, like I told you, my purse is in a locker back at the Milk-n-Bread. But I swear I'm not lying." She must have felt the need, now, to prove her candor beyond any doubt, because she began to describe for us her lonely life. A life unlike the one I'd pieced together from the few details she'd already told me. I'd envisioned a difficult but comfortable life with her grandmother, energized by school and friends, punctuated with her after-school job at the Milk-n-Bread to help pay for clothes and movie tickets. I had it wrong. There were no movie nights in Marie's life. The Milk-n-Bread job was full-time. She lived in her grandmother's house and paid whatever bills she could. Her grandmother's dementia, meanwhile, had become bad enough that last year Marie had to put her in a nursing home. "Some depressing place in Elizabeth called Timber Cove."

I knew the place, and it *was* depressing—from the outside anyway. The old structure stood ominously on Route 1, its bricks yellowed and tarnished. I assumed it used to be a psychiatric institution or maybe a veterans hospital. You could tell it wasn't where people of means took their aged and infirm to live their final years in serene dignity. When you drove to the airport, you passed it just before miles and miles of power plants, or, as I'd called them as a kid, "fog factories."

"Is it Alzheimer's?" I asked.

She shook her head. "Parkinson's. But she's eighty-three, you know? And Parkinson's can make you senile. Or it was the medications she's on. But it was getting bad. I couldn't leave her alone in the house. I came home once from work and she'd burned her arm really bad from the iron. I had to rush her to the ER, and in the car she kept screaming the whole way, and I had to roll down the windows because I could smell her burned skin."

So there it was. She lived alone at the house, worked at the Milk-n-Bread, and visited the nursing home when she could, even though her grandmother was becoming more confused and less likely to call Marie by the right name.

"But no," she concluded, "I'm not a student or even a kid. I'm nobody. And there isn't a single person who knows or even cares that I'm here right now. So there's your honesty. And if it makes you want to kill me"—she held out her arms to us, naked wrists facing the ceiling—"then go right ahead and get it over with."

Her attestation of adulthood was undercut somewhat by her continuing flair for the dramatic. The gesture wiped away any hurt feelings I had at having been lied to, and I found myself feeling a great deal of compassion for this young woman with a dead-end job and problems beyond those for which we were directly responsible.

"For God's sake, put your arms down," Nolan said. She lowered her arms to her sides. "You're here because the three of us made some bad decisions, no more and no less. Personally, I don't care whether you're sixteen or nineteen or ninety. What matters is that we all keep on telling the truth."

She glanced toward the blocked door, then back at Nolan. "Okay. So what else do you want to know?"

We wanted to know why there hadn't been a single mention of the robbery on the radio or television. We wanted to know how it could be that nobody knew of her disappearance.

As she answered our questions, it was the closest we all ever came to talking like regular people. We began to understand why the police hadn't yet pounded down the door. No other customers or employees had been in the store when she'd left. The store's surveillance camera hadn't worked since she'd taken the job.

And what about her replacement, we wondered, arriving at eight o'clock to find Marie nowhere on the premises?

"I'm not really known as the most reliable employee," she explained. "It wouldn't be the first time I ducked out before my shift ended."

"But someone must be expecting you at home," I said. "A boyfriend?"

She shook her head. "I meant it earlier when I told you I could keep this secret. I know you thought I was just a kid then, but now you know I'm not a kid. And I don't have anyone to tell. So I hope you can believe me."

I wanted badly to do just that. Probably if at that moment Nolan or Jeffrey had said, "Sure, Marie, we believe you," I'd have helped to move away all the stuff blocking the door and, despite any feelings of trepidation, bade our hostage farewell. I'd have hoped for the best.

But as I'd told Marie earlier, it didn't matter whether she could keep our secret. All that mattered was if we could imagine keeping it ourselves if we were in her shoes. How much, in other words, did we trust ourselves?

Nolan's answer came when he stood up, walked over to the drum set, lifted up a cymbal in its stand, and hurled it across the room. It was a large cymbal, an eighteen-inch crash, and crash it did—violently so, before skidding toward the wall. I jolted in my seat. Marie gasped.

"I DON'T KNOW WHAT THE FUCK TO DO!" he shouted.

These were words I thought I'd never hear come out of Nolan's mouth. Like the cymbal crash, they echoed crisply off the wooden floor and then were sucked out of the air and into the panels of soundproofing foam mounted on the walls.

Nobody moved or spoke for a few seconds, and in this silence the plan came to me fully formed. I became, for an instant, the quarterback able to visualize the entire field and all the players on it.

"Nolan," I said, "please sit down for a minute." He seemed not to mind taking instruction for a change. "Good. Now—Jeffrey, Nolan—I have an important question for you both. A simple question." They were looking at me intently. "Do you believe her?"

She'd lied to us once; there was no reason why she wouldn't do it again. And yet I found myself believing her. I did. And I wondered if the others did, too.

Jeffrey studied her a moment. "Yeah," he said.

"I don't know," Nolan said. "Sure, why not."

Hearing this, I went over to the door leading to the hallway and, trusting that I was doing the right thing, began to remove the equipment we'd stacked there.

"What are you doing?" Jeffrey asked. "Hey, wait a minute."

"Will?" Nolan said, but that was all. He didn't get up to stop me. Good. I didn't want to stop. Didn't want to second-guess myself or have Nolan or Jeffrey try to talk me out of what I was doing—because they probably could have.

When there was nothing blocking the door any longer, I returned to my chair.

"Please, Marie," I said, "would it be all right if I asked you just a couple more questions?"

She stayed where she was, though she was clearly eyeing the door.

"How much money do you make, working at the Milk-n-Bread?" I asked.

125

"Six-fifty an hour," she said.

I did some quick calculations. "So that's, what, about fifteen thousand a year?"

"Before taxes. Yeah, that's about right."

"And you say we can trust you."

Another glance toward the door. "Yes. Absolutely."

One last deep breath, as I tried to come to terms with the inevitable fact of Marie's existence in our lives. Nolan and Jeffrey were watching me closely. "Okay, then there's our answer." I gestured toward the door. "You can go." But before a single one of them could do or say anything, before they could catch a breath or even blink, I added: "*However*, Nolan would like to give you twenty thousand dollars first."

Marie's eyes widened, then narrowed. "What for?"

"And Jeffrey—he'd like to give you twenty thousand dollars, as well."

"What the hell are you talking about?" Jeffrey asked.

I explained that Jeffrey and Nolan would each give Marie a check for twenty thousand dollars. Marie would deposit the money into her bank account. "You have a bank account, don't you?" I asked.

Still looking suspicious, she nodded.

"Good," I said. "You'll endorse the checks and deposit them into your account."

"News flash, Will," Jeffrey said. "I don't have twenty thousand at my immediate disposal."

"Then sell a car." This was *my* plan, and I didn't have any time for bullshit. "Do what you need to do. In the meantime, Nolan will loan you what you need."

"I don't get it," Marie said. "What am I supposed to do with all that money?"

Nolan's icy expression was beginning to melt. "Whatever you want," he said.

"That's right," I said. "Quit your job, and go back to school. Move out of your grandmother's house. Take a vacation. It'll be your money. Yours to use however you want."

As we explained the offer to Marie, her continued presence in that chair filled me with gratitude and hope. It seemed nearly impossible that we weren't hearing echoes of her footfalls, the door shutting behind her. Yet here she remained.

"Forty thousand dollars." She said the words slowly, as if trying to imagine the sum. And even though this was my idea, I couldn't help thinking about where those forty thousand dollars had been allocated only hours before and silently mourning the brief financial solvency of Long-Shot Records.

"You told us you can keep a secret," I said. "Well, this will give you some incentive to be true to your word. If you ever tell the police about us, it'll be hard to explain away all this money you've willingly accepted from us. There will be a money trail, and any story you might tell about a kidnapping will be complicated by that fact."

"It's not an ideal plan," Nolan added, "but everyone will make out okay this way. It's a lot of money, Marie, and it sounds like you could really use it."

She closed her eyes a minute. She must have been imagining all the ways that money would make her life easier. "Just say for a minute," she said at last, "that I agreed to this. How will I know for sure you'll keep your word?"

Nolan removed his wallet from his pants pocket and handed her a business card.

"Because the three of us want nothing more than to forget any of this ever happened. Because I'm a state senator running for national office, and I know you hold all the cards in this relationship, and I believe that you know it, too. This money isn't a gift, it's insurance. And for that insurance, you'll be earning more than two years' salary. Not a bad day's work." Marie looked at Nolan's card and put it into her back pocket. "So what do you say?" he asked.

She said, "This is crazy."

"You're considering it, though, aren't you?" When she didn't answer, Nolan said to Jeffrey, "Checks won't work, though. My checkbook's in Missouri. I assume yours is in California. But we can wire money directly to her bank account."

"There won't be any endorsed checks that way," I said.

"Still, the money will be in her account," Nolan said. "There will be an electronic record of the transaction. That's the best we can do. I think it's good enough."

"And if I *don't* agree to this," Marie said, "I can just get up and leave?"

"That's right," I said. "It's completely up to you."

She nodded. "But if I do agree—then what happens?"

"We'll drive you to your house," Nolan said, "so that you can get your account information, and then we'll go to a Western Union office and wire the money to your bank."

"Or," I said, "in the spirit of trust you can leave on your own, go home, and then call us here with your account information." I looked at my friends for any objections.

"Forty thousand dollars," she said.

"Forty thousand," I said. It was a sleazy deal we were making, and I would have to find a way to live with that. Incredibly, though, it seemed like we were all going to agree. Marie would sleep in her own bed tonight, and so would I, and then tomorrow we could all begin to pretend that none of this had ever happened.

"And there's no catch?" she asked.

"No catch," I said.

"That's right," Nolan said.

There was a beautiful silence, the silence of a decision nearly made. Jeffrey seemed to find no joy in breaking it.

"Actually," he said, "if we're going to do this right, then there *is* one catch. And it's a big one, and nobody's going to like it."

PART TWO

CHAPTER 15

I AWOKE BECAUSE OF THE pain in my shoulder. I rolled onto my back, but that also ached. In fact, I seemed to hurt just about everywhere. The hard floor underneath me reminded me of yet another reason why, in my experience, camping was better imagined than experienced. And this floor lacked even the earth's slight give; nor was there a soft sleeping bag anywhere in sight.

It was dark—I had dimmed the overhead hours earlier—and very quiet. I lifted my head (there was one comfort, at least—an old sweatshirt I'd been using for a pillow) and saw the lack of activity around me. Earlier, we had carried the sofa from the control room into the main recording room. The sofa was only a loveseat, but Marie was small and seemed comfortable on it, curled on her side underneath the blanket that, if everything went according to plan, would soon return to its designated place inside the bass drum. Closer to me on the floor, Jeffrey was lying on his back, eyes closed, using his jacket for a pillow. His breathing was deep and even and, it appeared, peaceful.

I tilted my watch to catch the room's dim light: 4:10 AM. I'd been asleep for nearly an hour. I'd thought I would only rest my eyes for a while, as I'd done the nights before Cynthia and I fled

133

New York, when I used to sit by the window and worry one hour into the next.

And yet when I'd lain down tonight, I'd felt as tired as I'd ever been in my life. In a recording studio it is difficult to tell day from night, but apparently not impossible—eventually the body takes over. Evidently my exhausted body knew that night had come. Then again, for millennia human beings have fallen asleep in more perilous circumstances than ours—with tigers on the prowl, in frigid temperatures. Right now, how many people were sleeping exposed to the elements in Bayonne or New York or Detroit? And how many others, across the globe, were right now in dreams while around them war threatened to gut them or blow them to pieces? We call ourselves human, think we're rational beings, but we're animals first with animal needs. We can't help risking the big sleep for the little one. It seemed absurd, lying there in the studio, that I'd ever stayed awake all night long for something as monumentally trivial as a term paper.

Nolan was awake. He lay propped up on an elbow, looking at the television, which flickered silently and gave the room a slight strobe effect.

Earlier, I had wanted to run out briefly for essentials. Now that everyone's stay here was more or less voluntary, I began to feel a little like their host. I thought we ought to have toothbrushes, for instance, and contact lens solution. There was a twenty-four-hour supermarket a couple miles down the road, and I didn't believe that it would be a risk for me to go there. But I was persuaded otherwise. Better to stay here. Stay unnoticed. For one night we could do without the comforts of home.

The plan—the catch—was to give Marie's story twelve hours. First she tells us that her grandmother will practically notify the White House if she isn't home promptly at eight o'clock, then she tells us that her grandmother actually lives in a nursing home.

First our arrest seems imminent, then she tells us that not a single person knows she's missing. We believed the second story because it filled the holes in the first one. It explained why we were not yet in custody. But there could be other reasons, other explanations that we simply hadn't thought of.

So before going through with my plan, a plan that would irrevocably tie us all together, Jeffrey had proposed—insisted, really— that we wait. That we stay right here in the studio, where we'd be insulated from the outside world, and continue to watch TV and see if the kidnapping story broke. If after twelve hours—by ten thirty tomorrow morning—there was no word of any robbery/ kidnapping at the Milk-n-Bread or anybody reporting Marie missing, then we could assume that she was telling us the truth: that there was no surveillance tape at the store, and nobody to report her missing at home. In that case, the deal was on. In the meantime, the door leading from the recording room to the hallway remained unlocked and unobstructed. If at any time she wanted to abort our agreement, she was free to walk out the door. Of course, if she was telling the truth, then there'd be no need to.

Jeffrey was right. We didn't like this. It seemed foolish to maintain our proximity to Marie a minute longer than necessary, let alone for twelve more hours. But Jeffrey had insisted, and Nolan soon came around to his way of thinking.

"It's better for all of us in the long run," he said to me. "We need to know for sure that we can trust Marie, and she needs to know for sure that she can trust us."

"We're only talking twelve hours," Jeffrey added, "and for most of them we'll be asleep."

Fat chance of that, I thought. And yet, amazingly, I had dozed. And beside me Jeffrey was dreaming of flying, maybe, or dunking a basketball, or perhaps he was reliving his first date with Sara in the reserve room of Firestone Library, sipping their coffees and

135

whispering back and forth, their whole future still tantalizingly ahead of them.

As I lay on my back, trying to ignore the hard floor beneath me, I thought about what Jeffrey had said earlier. I knew that Nolan once had a thing for Sara, but I assumed it was short-lived. I remembered the cold, rainy afternoon of our sophomore year when Nolan stopped by my dorm room and asked if we could go for a walk. Never mind the freezing rain—he needed to talk through a problem he was having, and he preferred to do it on the move. He was always on the move.

I needed to return my car to the parking lot at the edge of campus, so we drove there together and then walked back toward the dorms. But he wasn't talking. He was kicking a rock in front of him, until it rolled into the gutter. Then he said, "So I'm sort of in love with Sara."

I nearly laughed. "Oh, is that all? Come on, we all are." Jeffrey had a habit of telling Sara that she was the prettiest girl in the room. This wasn't mere flattery. We had all become friendly with her by then, and despite the various imperfections that had come to light— like how, despite her high grades, she seemed to require constant reassurance from her professors; like how one of her front teeth wasn't real, having been knocked out by a field hockey stick in high school gym class—I nonetheless continued to view her as someone on whom the Great Sculptor had worked overtime.

Unlike many women her age, Sara seemed to recognize the power of her body, of her beauty. She hadn't yet learned this lesson that day of freshman year in our modern European authors class. She hadn't imagined just how threatening her sexuality might seem, even to an internationally renowned academic like Professor Rinehart. But this was a lesson she came to learn, and in the three years I'd known her she had changed in subtle ways, toning down the makeup, dressing a little more like it was 1994 in

136

Jersey and the trend in fashion was to obscure rather than reveal. She had changed just enough to make her time at Princeton easier.

Except at parties. Then the hair came down and the cowboy boots came out, and, in her words, her "inner Texas" got unleashed onto an unsuspecting campus.

Yet even then she was no flirt. Guys would seek her out, laserlike, standing too close, shouting over some band playing Pearl Jam or Nirvana and toasting her plastic cup of beer with their own. She would slip away gracefully and go over to Jeffrey and put her arm around his waist—or, in his absence, she'd come over to one of us and say, "Save me." So you'd engage in the easy banter particular to a guy and his buddy's girlfriend. And you couldn't help feeling proud, knowing that you were the one that the prettiest girl in the room had chosen as her knight in flannel armor.

At one of these parties, when intoxication had sufficiently lowered my inhibitions, I asked her what exactly she saw in Jeffrey. Simple curiosity. He was my friend, but she seemed out of his league.

"I know he won't beat the shit out of me," she said with little hesitation. Then, as if basing her next words on my reaction, she grinned. "I'm kidding. I mean, books." Before Princeton, she went on to explain, she'd never met a guy who read books outside of class. Then, as if unsatisfied with literature as an answer, she went on to mention his smile, his sense of humor, his intellect. Then her face lit up again, as if just remembering something. "And he loves me."

But now Nolan was telling me that he, too, loved her. "I'm being serious," he said. "I've thought about this for a while. I think I'm in actual love with her. I'm talking about we-can-be-together-forever kind of love."

Nolan's romantic exploits rarely included the same woman for very long. He wasn't looking for love, and—the way he told it, anyway—he seemed remarkably candid about this fact with the women he dated. He believed that his liaisons were in fact far more honest and respectful than most long-term, monogamous relationships, which, as he described them, were typically nothing but cauldrons of manipulation and hurt feelings. My own theory was that his philosophy came second to his actions. He was a good-looking guy with a magnetic personality. He found romantic partners easily.

He'd never given me any indication that he gave the matter of love any thought at all, let alone "forever," and I could only assume that he had surprised himself, as well.

"It's too bad she's with Jeffrey," I said.

"Yeah. Too bad."

"But she *is* with Jeffrey. So . . ."

In January, the Gothic buildings, leafless maples, and brown athletic fields looked dreary and ominous. I sloshed through a puddle.

"It kills me, you know," he said, "seeing them together."

"I understand," I said, "but that's how it is."

"God, Will, what does she see in him?"

"Oh, don't start blaming Jeffrey. That isn't cool."

"Maybe. It's just that I've never felt this way about anyone."

"You never kept any of them around long enough." His record, I believed, was a month. "You've known Sara now for two years. Which of your girlfriends have you known that long?"

It was a question I could've asked myself. I'd dated a few women, and none of them had aroused feelings in me that remotely suggested forever.

"Good point," he said.

We passed a cluster of dormitories built during World War II, squat ugly structures with names like "1942 Hall" that resembled army barracks and were consistently bypassed, I'd noticed, on campus tours in favor of the older, ornate buildings for which the university was known.

"Look," I said, "if they were to break up sometime down the road . . . maybe that'd be a different story. But otherwise, you can't make a move. You just can't. It's that simple."

"It is?"

"Of course. So you'll just have to put her out of your mind. Anyway, it's not like you have any trouble, how do I say this . . ."

"If you're going to tell me that there are plenty of fish in the sea, I'm going to beat you senseless."

But then he thanked me for listening to him, and soon we reached our dormitory, where we lived in adjacent singles. After I went into my room and he into his, we never spoke of the matter again. Within the week, Nolan had begun a brand-new liaison, and I could clearly hear the honesty and respect coming from the other side of our shared wall.

So it surprised me to learn about Nolan's election-night confession all those years later. However ill-advised, it did reveal a level of longing and romantic depth that I hadn't known he was capable of feeling.

But also, if Nolan really had confessed his love to Sara while in some drunken, postelection despair, why would the incident, now six years in the past, continue to bother Jeffrey? Except, I knew why. Jeffrey had linked that transgression to another, earlier one. And the combined effect was evidently to tarnish Nolan irrevocably in Jeffrey's eyes.

Before today, I hadn't the faintest clue that one of my closest friends was deemed a serpent in the eyes of my other friend. And wasn't that the strangest thing of all? Jeffrey had been able to conceal those feelings from the rest of us all these years. The Jeffrey I'd met twelve years ago would've been incapable of that sort of deception. It was why I'd liked him immediately—his transparent, somewhat bewildered expression was a refreshing change from the guarded gleam I saw in the eyes of so many future lawyers and CEOs and bankers on campus.

Jeffrey's parents must have protected him well, because except for the cigarettes, he'd seemed a young eighteen when I first met him. He seemed a bit immature, or—to take his age out of the equation—prone to emotional swings, and I used to imagine that somewhere in the world there was an artist searching fruitlessly for his temperament.

As I was thinking about Jeffrey, he let out a heavy sigh in his sleep and rolled over onto his side.

I wondered what, exactly, had changed him. What about his personality had led to today's blatant unhinging? Was it personality at all, or was it circumstance, or some amalgam of the two? And if so, were any of us immune?

Once this evening's agreement had been reached, and the twelve hours lay long before us, we had little to say to one another. We were talked out, and so we watched TV. At eleven o'clock we watched the local news, anxiously waiting, but then the hard news was over and we were looking at sports highlights, then a map of the United States—plenty of sun over much of the country—and then eleven thirty arrived and with it the brassy riffs signaling the beginning of late-night television.

Nolan, Jeffrey, and I came up with shifts to watch TV. Jeffrey until 1 AM, Nolan from 1 to 4, and me from 4 to 7. None of us believed that we'd actually get any sleep, but all the same it felt productive to make a plan.

The moment of truth came just after midnight, when Marie asked where the restroom was, and I told her, and then she walked out of the recording room and into the hallway, shutting the door behind her. We all looked off in our separate directions, waiting, until after what undoubtedly seemed longer than it was, there came the unmistakable sound of water rushing through pipes, the studio's one important acoustical deficiency. (During recording sessions, nobody was allowed in the john while the tape was rolling.) Another minute passed, and then the door, improbable as it seemed, was opening again, and in the doorway stood our lovely, trustworthy hostage, hands and face washed, makeup removed, ready to settle in for a night on the sofa and earn her forty thousand dollars. Our slumber party had begun.

I went over to Nolan now and sat down on the floor beside him.

"You should've woken me up," I said quietly. "It's my turn."

"That's all right," he said. "I'm not tired."

"You've been awake a long time."

"I don't mind." On TV a man with enormous biceps was stuffing broccoli into a juicer. He stood on one side of a kitchen island, and his four friends stood on the other side. The muscled man handed one of his friends the glass of bright green liquid, and the friend took a sip and said, "Mmmm," and high-fived the man who'd made the juice because it tasted so good and healthful, and then their other friends applauded.

"So I guess it was all a matter of settling on the right price," I said.

Nolan looked at me. "How so?"

"We raised our price from one thousand to forty thousand inside of three hours."

He shrugged. "She's smart. She's one of us." He looked back at the TV. "That's why it'll be good to never see her again."

141

We both watched TV awhile. "Why don't you try to get some sleep," I said after a few minutes had passed. "I'll take over."

"It doesn't matter," he said. "None of this matters. None of it makes any sense."

"What doesn't?"

"Any of it. Giving her forty thousand dollars. Staying here overnight."

It did make sense, though. However strange this day had been, now we had a plan where before we didn't.

"Everything's going to work out," I said.

"Oh, come on, Will. Wheeling and dealing with some nineteen-year-old? This isn't getting any better." He looked at me. "There's a simpler solution. You know that."

"Don't."

"I'm not saying we *do* it, so relax. I'm just saying that when no one knows you're missing, then it means you won't be missed." He shook his head. "Look, forget it. It's late, and I'm exhausted, and I'm only acknowledging what we've all been thinking."

"No one's been thinking that."

"Of course you have."

"No," I said. "I haven't." I watched him closely for a moment, but he was looking at the TV impassively, impossible to read. "Things are going to look different in the morning." I hoped that would be the case. I needed Nolan's usual hopefulness. I needed to believe in his belief. "And you need to rest your eyes awhile."

"Maybe later."

"Then do you mind if I watch with you?"

The strongman transformed sweet potatoes and beets and spinach into tall glassfuls of juice. The audience oohed and aahed. It was beautiful to watch how happy they all looked, even if they were only actors.

CHAPTER 16

W E DECIDED TO END our vigil early. There was no reason not to. At eight thirty in the morning, Nolan was still sitting in front of the TV. The rest of us had slept a little, but Nolan's eyes were bloodshot, his shirt untucked, his hair no longer perfect. It had taken eighteen hours, but he finally looked as rumpled and spent as the rest of us.

It appeared that Marie was telling the truth. There was nothing about her on TV overnight and nothing this morning. As far as the media were concerned, yesterday was nothing but a day with some bad storms that'd since moved off the coast. I was anxious to leave yesterday behind and get on with today. Yesterday we'd kidnapped a girl. Today we would set her free.

At a little after nine, Nolan shut off the TV and rubbed his eyes. Blinked a few times and stood up. "How about let's get this show on the road already," he said, massaging his neck. "Any objections?"

There were none.

I put the blanket, which Marie had neatly folded and then draped over the arm of the sofa, back into the bass drum. I asked Jeffrey to help me carry the sofa back into the control room.

Without my asking, Marie held the doors open for us. When we went back into the recording room, she sat at the drum set and tapped a couple of the drums with her fingertips.

A pair of drumsticks was lying on the floor tom. "Here," I said, handing them to her. "You can try playing if you want."

She looked at me a moment, then took the sticks. A couple of light taps on a tom-tom. On a cymbal. Abruptly she stopped, got up from the seat, and handed the sticks to me.

"You do it," she said.

The drum set was mine. Or it used to be, anyway, charged on my Visa card the year I graduated college and paid off slowly over the next several years. Before that, all I had were the secondhand drums my parents had bought me when I was twelve years old.

The newer set was the best purchase I'd ever made, and well worth going into debt for. The shells were made of birch, with a beautiful red lacquer finish. All the best hardware. I'd taken excellent care of them, too, somehow keeping the drums free of nicks and scratches even as I hauled them in and out of a hundred clubs crammed with drunk, careless patrons.

The best part of the drum set, however, wasn't even the drums at all, but the cymbals. There were a ride cymbal, two crashes, a splash, and of course a hi-hat. Most people don't think about the importance of cymbals, but drummers do. The cymbals are like the drummer's signature. Choosing them had taken hours at one of the giant music stories on Forty-eighth Street in Manhattan. Finally, as one employee began to dust the equipment, and another began to vacuum the carpet in some other part of the store, I decided on a series of Zildjian "K" cymbals for their dark, mournful tones.

After Cynthia and I moved to Newfield, the drums and cymbals remained in their cases for months, stacked in a corner of our bedroom. Eventually I gave them to Joey as a gift for the studio. I only ever sat at the drums anymore to tune them up for a band. I couldn't remember the last time I'd actually played them, but I wanted to now. They were sharp and shimmering—a wonderful instrument—and I wanted Marie to see me play, to know about this other side of me, the musician. It's hard to imagine, now, what I'd hoped to achieve, but it seemed important then to prove to her, in the last few minutes of our ordeal, that I wasn't just some twisted man who locked people in closets.

I sat down at the set, and with everyone watching I began to play a simple funk beat, nothing fancy. I'd replaced the drum heads before The Fixtures had begun their sessions, and the drums had a nice *thwap* to them. They sounded pure and full of tone even when you hit them softly, though they always sounded best when you hit them hard. So I hit them hard.

What a release, banging on a set of drums! I had forgotten. I'd forgotten, too, what it felt like to have a group of people watching me play and thinking, *This guy's good.* Even Marie. Ever since jamming with Burn in Ronnie Martinez's musty basement I'd come to know the look on someone's face of being transported, however briefly, to a place they hadn't expected to go. I threw in a couple of fills, complicating the beat a little, some syncopation, off-beats on the ride cymbal, ghosting on the snare drum. And as I played, it felt as if I were controlling our collective pulse. Everyone's trust was in me, and it was well-placed trust because I knew exactly what I was doing, and even now—especially now, after everything that happened after—I wish that I could've found a way to keep that one beat going without ever stopping. Because for the briefest of moments there was only this rhythm I was playing, only this rhythm and nothing else—no kidnapping, no desperate plans, no deception. For thirty seconds, maybe a minute, all of that was forgotten.

But every song ends. I ended mine with a couple of cymbal crashes that echoed and then died away, and then the room fell silent.

145

Everyone let the silence linger a moment, until Marie looked at me and said, "Sweet."

I smiled, set the drumsticks on the floor, and left the recording room for the bottle of Jack Daniel's I kept in a drawer in the control room. When my bands finished their final session with me, I liked to have a toast with them, unless they were underage. And sometimes even then. No matter how difficult the recording might have been—even in the best of circumstances there are usually some disagreements and hurt feelings—the whiskey toast always made for an uplifting coda to the project and left the band feeling like they were wrapping up something important.

This morning our toast would go beyond music. It would be a toast to freedom. To the possibility of keeping a lifelong secret. And, of course, to luck. I wasn't sure whether we'd already been granted luck or whether we'd need it sometime in the future, but I felt that the role of luck ought not be dismissed, though others might call it fate.

I returned to the recording room with the whiskey and four plastic cups. Poured a small amount in each cup and handed them out.

Only then, cups in hands, did I realize my mistake. I'd meant to cement something between us, to express goodwill. But our parting was nothing to celebrate. No doubt we all wanted to forget as quickly as possible that we'd ever been together at all. So nobody said anything—there was nothing to say—and we all just looked into the bottom of our cups, saw what we saw, and swallowed.

It was time then for logistics. Time for Marie to walk out alone, go home, and call us at the studio with her bank information. Nolan and Jeffrey would then wire a lot of money, and we'd all try to live our lives.

Marie was rubbing her thumbs over the top of her plastic cup, still looking into it. She bit her lip and looked up at us.

"So I've been thinking," she said, and hesitated. The words dangled in front of us.

My body must have sensed something before my brain did, because my gut seized in pain as if the whiskey were tainted. I needed to sit down, but I stayed standing and gently rubbed my stomach outside my shirt, trying to massage away the pain.

"What have you been thinking?" Nolan asked.

"Well, a lot of things."

I couldn't help it—the pain was too much. I sat down on the floor and leaned against the wall.

"I had all night on that couch," she was saying, "and I thought about a lot of things. And what I've decided is, well . . ." She sighed. "Forty thousand isn't enough."

I squeezed my eyes shut. "Don't do this, Marie," I said.

"I'm not doing anything," she said. Her tone was tinged with sarcasm, even a bit of confidence. I opened my eyes again. Something important had happened overnight while I had been sleeping. She looked different—her eyes more severe, a darker, more calculating blue—and I couldn't imagine ever thinking she was sixteen. "It's just that, the way I figure, I'm standing between all of you and a lot of trouble," she said. "A *lot* of trouble. And I just wonder if maybe forty thousand dollars . . . you know, all things considered . . . might be a little stingy."

"It isn't," Nolan said. "It's generous, and you know it."

"Maybe," she said. "You could be right. But my nana, she used to pay a neighbor's kid forty dollars to cut the grass. He was a nice little kid in the sixth grade, but sort of dumb. I think he might have been retarded. But as I was lying on that couch last night, I kept thinking about him, and about how you're all important men. Family men, too. I think you'd do pretty much anything to avoid . . . well, you know. And all night I kept asking myself, am I only a thousand times more important to these men than some

147

retarded kid who cuts my nana's grass? And my guess is no. I'll bet I'm way more important than that."

Her voice exuded confidence, but her hands squeezed the empty cup and shook slightly.

"Cut to the chase." Nolan's gaze bored into her. "How much do you want?"

Her brilliance, if it could be called that, was in recognizing the power she had over us and having the nerve to act on it. Had she named her price at that moment, she almost certainly would've gotten it. Her mistake was to equivocate.

"Well," she said, looked up at the ceiling as if considering the question—blatant theatrics—then back at Nolan again. She shrugged. "That depends."

"It depends?" He laughed dismissively, then narrowed his eyes. "All right, fifty thousand." Silence. "Sixty." He shook his head. "Fuck, I knew this was all a waste of time. Now get the hell out of here before I throw you out."

"No, wait a second!" Too late, Marie caught her error. She had vacillated when decisiveness was called for, and now her moment was slipping away. She could see her two years' salary vanishing before her eyes, and suddenly I understood what Nolan had meant last night, how everything depended on trust. Without trust, a deal like this meant nothing. "I want more money, that's all." Her voice was desperate and shrieky. "That's all I want. Come on, I don't have *anything*, and . . . you just have to give me more."

Nolan stepped closer to Marie. "I'm going to ask you one last time. How *much* more?" She was still avoiding his eyes, so he put a hand on her arm and said: "Give me a number, Marie."

The physical contact. That was *his* error.

"Hey!" She yanked her arm free from his grip and backed up like a wild animal that had inadvertently crossed paths with another, larger one. "Don't touch me." She looked over at Jeffrey.

148

"Get him away from me!" The irony of that glance over to her abductor for assistance wouldn't hit me until later.

It worked, though. "Leave her alone, goddamn it," Jeffrey said.

Jeffrey's admonishment proved too much. That, I still believe, was what sent Nolan into action. He pointed a stiff finger at Jeffrey and held it there a second—not a word got said, but I'd never seen a more threatening gesture—and then he reached out and grabbed Marie by the wrist and tugged her toward him. For a second I thought, *Here it is, he's going to kill her*—strangle her, or beat her to death—but when he had both hands around her, he pulled her toward Room A. She was fighting to get away, kicking her legs out and twisting her arms, but Nolan was strong, and in no time he had the door held open with his foot and was shoving her inside. I sat against the wall, my gut screaming, watching as she jammed a foot in the doorway, but her foot slowly slid backward as Nolan forced the door shut until it clicked, and then he locked it.

He turned around to face us, and that was the instant when Jeffrey—I had forgotten he even existed these past few seconds—rushed forward and swung the cymbal stand down on Nolan's head.

Long ago, Jeffrey and I had bonded over stories of the brief, traumatic year we'd each spent in Little League, him in California, me in New Jersey—the dropped fly balls, the thinly veiled frustration of our coaches, the sad look on our teammates' faces when it was our turn to bat. I was no slugger, but Jeffrey's batting average had been a perfect zero.

This time he connected.

It was the same cymbal Nolan had thrown yesterday, the same one I'd set up again last night and had ended my drum solo with this morning. When it hit Nolan, it made a dull crack. It was a glancing blow, the equivalent of a foul ball, but enough to drop

149

Nolan to his knees. At first Nolan looked down at the ground and did nothing. His hands covered his ears, and he shook his head a few times, the way that cartoon characters shake off an injury and become whole again. Then he looked up at us and lowered his left hand. He looked stunned but not visibly injured, though his other hand still covered his right ear.

"Nolan," I said, "take your other hand away."

Slowly he lowered his hand. His right ear was practically torn off.

"Oh, shit," I said, my stomach giving one last mad lurch. "Oh, Jesus."

Every little kid who's ever skinned a knee knows that it takes a few seconds for the blood to start. But you know it's coming.

This was a hundred times worse. Blood hadn't yet started to flow, but I could see the deep gouge where the top of Nolan's ear met his head. His eyes widened. Not because of the pain, not yet, but because of the horror he must have seen in my face.

"Is it bad?" he asked.

"I know where the nearest hospital is," I said. "Don't worry. I'll get you there fast."

"How bad is it?"

I shuddered. "It's deep. Shit, it's really deep. We need to get you—"

"Show me," he said. "Show me in the bathroom."

"All right, but hurry." I helped him off the ground and told Jeffrey to stay right where he was. I opened the door for Nolan, then led him to the bathroom. On the way, the blood started to flow. In the bathroom I wetted a stack of paper towers and handed them to him. "You need to apply pressure."

He was turning his head in the mirror. "I can't see it! Fuck, Will, I can't see it. Tell me what's going on."

Blood was oozing from him, turning the floor beneath us crimson. I forced myself to look at the wound. Nothing but blood. "I can't tell. You need to stop the bleeding."

"I can't without seeing. You need to do it."

I didn't want to touch him. What if the ear came off in my hand? But I did anyway. I gently pressed his ear to his head with one hand, and held the wad of paper towels to the wound with my other hand. In seconds the blood had soaked the towels.

"This isn't going to work," I said. "We have to get you to the hospital."

"Try!" he said. "Please." So I got more paper towels and tried again. He shivered. "It really hurts. Oh, man."

"I know why you don't want to go to a hospital," I said, "but you don't have a choice."

He was breathing deeply, slowly, trying to regain control. He reached up and took my place holding the paper towel against his ear. "There's always a choice."

"You know what I mean," I said. "This is a serious injury."

"I fucking know that!" he cried.

I washed my hands under hot water, scrubbed them with soap. We stood there, Nolan pressing the paper towels to his head, me looking on to see if the blood flow was slowing. And gradually—after fifteen or twenty minutes—the paper towels I handed him weren't immediately turning red.

"Why would he do this to me? Huh, Will? Why would he hit me like that?"

"He must've thought you were going to hurt her," I said.

"Well, I wasn't." He sounded out of breath.

"Or maybe he'd reached his limit of being a kidnapper." But what I really believed, though didn't say, was, *It's because he thinks you slept with his wife.*

151

We stood there another minute, watching the paper towel fill with blood again. And then, as if reading my mind, he said, "I'll bet it was revenge."

I'd been tearing more paper towels out of the dispenser. I froze. "How do you figure?"

He looked at me strangely. "What do you mean? It's simple: I hit him in the mouth yesterday, he hits me in the head today."

"Oh. Yeah, I guess it could be that." I handed him the paper towels.

After another fifteen minutes, during which time I tried to clean blood off the bathroom floor, Nolan pulled the ball of paper towels away from his head and I made myself take another look. He was still bleeding, though less so, and I could see now that the wound wasn't as dire as I'd first thought. The ear wasn't going to come off. Still, the cymbal had sliced deeply into the cartilage, and the angle between his ear and his head seemed to have shifted by a few degrees.

"You've got to get stitched up," I said. "Otherwise it's never going to stop bleeding."

He nodded, and I thought I'd finally gotten through to him when he said, "How's your sewing?"

The implication made me queasy. "No. Forget it. Not a chance."

"Yes," he said.

"No." There was absolutely no way. My hands were already shaking just thinking about it. "Anyway, you'll want a plastic surgeon. This is your face we're talking about."

"It sure is. So you're going to have to be careful." When I tried to protest again, he cut me off. "Listen. This is nonnegotiable. Forget the hospital. Got it? When I'm back in Missouri—if I'm *ever* back in Missouri—I'll have my doctor tend to it. He's a good man who won't ask questions. Until then, I'm in your hands."

CHAPTER 17

L AST NIGHT THIS STRETCH of town would've been deserted. The only people who came out at night here were either looking for trouble or already in it. But now it was a bright Saturday morning, and plenty of people were on the sidewalk feeding meters and pushing strollers and holding kids' hands. My window was cracked open, and I smelled fresh bread. The sign hanging over the bank said it was fifty-two degrees. It would have been a perfect morning on the golf course.

I headed back into the outside world to get Nolan the supplies he needed. I was driving too fast, but for the first time since Friday night the kidnapping had been relegated to some less critical place in my mind. Right now I had an urgent task to do. Doing it was almost a relief. Almost. At the pharmacy, just a mile or so from the studio, I rushed from aisle to aisle, not knowing exactly what was required. Everything I knew about first aid centered around what to do until the professionals took over. What, though, if the patient refused the professionals?

I found gauze and Band-Aids and first-aid tape. Several kinds of pain reliever. I grabbed a bottle of Pepto-Bismol for my own stomach. Could you buy surgical thread at a pharmacy? Maybe not. But then, in the next aisle, I came across a small sewing kit. A needle was a needle, I figured. Thread was thread. I looked at it and looked at it, then walked away, then returned. Could I actually sew thread through someone's flesh? I'd never even sewn on a button before. I imagined Nolan, liquored up from my whiskey, gritting his teeth as I pushed the needle through his ear with all the skill of an ape.

Disinfectant cream. I'd almost forgotten. My decision postponed, I returned to the first-aid aisle, and that was when I saw, on the bottom shelf, the First Aid & Survival Kit. Professional Series, it said. Eighty-nine dollars. I bent down, set everything I was carrying on the rack, and read the list of contents: dressings, tapes, ointments, medications, antiseptics . . . the list went on and on. There seemed to be an entire hospital inside.

And then from behind me: "Good morning, dickless!"

I turned around. Bobby Hazen was standing in the aisle wearing a Night Ranger concert T-shirt and black parachute pants. His hair was sticking up and he was holding a Dunkin' Donuts coffee, with which he saluted me.

I gave him a noncommittal "What's up?" and continued evaluating the first-aid kit.

I knew Bobby from back when we both lived in the Village. He was one of those guys who'd spent his teenage years cocooned in his bedroom with his acne and his Fender Telecaster and emerged like some soft-spoken guitar god that everyone wanted in their band.

The coincidence of running into Bobby wasn't so great. Despite his frequent New York gigs, he'd moved to Jersey a couple of years ago, to his brother's place not far from here, to save on rent.

"Lycanthrope," he said. "Tell me that's not the shit." I hadn't seen him in probably a month or more, but our conversation about naming his new band continued as if there'd been no interruption. "Seriously," he said, "what do you think?"

This was no time to engage him in conversation, but I didn't want him to think I was acting strangely. So I told Bobby that Lycanthrope was about the worst name I'd ever heard, which was saying a lot considering what I'd heard.

He gave me the finger, yawned, scratched his stomach underneath his T-shirt, and told me about his gig at Blackbirds this coming Thursday. Blackbirds was a small club in the East Village whose dubious claim to fame was that the Spin Doctors had gotten their start there fifteen years earlier.

"We've been working a cellist into a few tunes," he said. "She went to Juilliard for a year."

"Why only a year?"

"You're missing the point. The point is, she's killer. And really hot." He sipped his coffee. *"Really* hot."

Bobby was my last remaining link to a life I once led, and seeing him always aroused my pity and envy.

"I'll try to be there," I said, and looked at my watch. "Look, I gotta run."

He grinned. "You'll be there, huh? You're such a fucking liar." He slapped my back and went in search of whatever it was he'd come in for.

"I'm not lying!" I called after him. I meant it, too, or at least I wanted to mean it. But seconds later I was carrying the First Aid & Survival Kit up to the checkout counter, and my thoughts returned to injured ears and stolen people.

The clerk ran the kit through the scanner. "I'll bet you're a speedboater," he said, "am I right?"

"No," I said.

"Rock climber?"

I shook my head. "Sorry." I ran my credit card through the machine.

He handed me my receipt and I signed it.

"Well, whatever it is," he said, "you be careful."

I didn't know Evan's cell phone number from memory. It had been stored in my own cell, now smashed to bits. If his home number wasn't listed, then I would have to drive back to the house to get it out of my address book. With Nolan's injury there wasn't time for that. I parked my car at the gas station, exchanged some singles for quarters, and dialed directory assistance. The operator asked me to repeat the last name three times, and then to spell it. Finally I was given the number.

I got his answering machine. There was no choice but to leave a message, simple and unambiguous: *Call me at the studio. It's urgent. We need you here.* I left the studio's phone number on the machine.

And then, as an afterthought: *Be sure you erase this message.*

Not until I'd parked behind the studio again, and my stomach cramped up so hard that I saw floating flecks before my eyes, did it occur to me that I'd forgotten to take the Pepto-Bismol up to the register.

CHAPTER 18

I SAT THERE WITH THE engine running, hugging my gut and waiting for the pain to pass.

How was it, I wondered, that I'd crossed over to a world that
gave weight to the rules of revenge? We were merely four friends
who met up each year for golf. For some good meals and beer and
cards. For joking around and reminiscing.

What could be simpler?

In all the years we'd spent together, I hadn't once considered
whether Jeffrey might still harbor some deep grudge. And why
would he? He'd married Sara. He'd gotten the girl. He'd won.

So why, then, the violence? Why the attack? Did he really believe he'd been protecting Marie from Nolan? Or was it something else? And did he himself even know? This was, after all, the
same man who'd kidnapped Marie fewer than twenty-four hours
earlier. All I could come up with was that his recent problems
with Sara must have dug up emotions that'd been buried ever
since that one fraught night nine years earlier.

It almost hadn't been a problem, either. We'd just about graduated. Only a couple more days. We'd already stripped our dorm
room walls of posters and prints and bulletin boards, stuffed dirty

clothes into suitcases, stacked textbooks and notebooks and a year of assignments into cardboard boxes. Sara had even begun to tape shut some of the boxes in her room. She just hadn't gotten around to taping all of them.

That close.

The weekend before graduation, Princeton University transformed itself into a many-ringed circus. Everyone other than seniors had already left for the summer, their now-vacant dorm rooms rented out to thousands of alumni who returned to campus for the school's annual reunion. In all the major courtyards across campus, enormous tents had been erected, under which, for three days, alumni and their families would be treated to gluttonous meals, live music, dancing, and unlimited alcohol, all in the service of maintaining strong ties between the university and its alumni—and, some would readily admit, encouraging alumni donations.

It really was some party, though. The rumor was that it was second only to the Indianapolis 500 in terms of kegs of beer consumed. Three days of parties, of games for the kids, guest lecturers for the scholarly minded, service projects for the service project–minded, three days of reuniting with lost friends, lost loves, three days of social (and, it would be fair to say, sexual) intercourse, and all of it culminating in a parade—called, naturally, P-rade—where Princetonians wore their orange-and-black garb (each reunion class having come up with its own themed clothing, strangely a source of little embarrassment to accompanying spouses) and marched through campus just as previous generations had marched before them. Leading the P-rade was the oldest living alumnus, riding beside the university president in an orange and black golf cart. Bringing up the rear an hour or so later were eleven hundred inebriated, raucous graduating seniors staggering their way toward the end of college and the beginning of the rest of their lives.

Alumni and their families traveled far and wide to be here. Watching them, we couldn't help imagining ourselves in five or ten or twenty years, returning with our own spouses, many of whom we hadn't yet met, with our children whose births were still years away. We wondered what our future selves might be like, and what we'd think of them. And we wondered what that older self might have in the way of advice or wisdom for a twenty-one-year-old just now on the threshold of leaving the security of this privileged place.

Quickly, though, we stopped wondering and started partying. Final exams were done, senior theses turned in, and so we drank. And then we drank some more. Thursday, Friday, then the P-rade on Saturday. By Sunday we were wiped out. The alumni were leaving. By dinner they were gone, all twenty thousand of them. The circus had left town, and now only the tents remained. Late Sunday night, against official university policy and at the risk of getting injured or, worse, busted by campus police so close to graduation, several of us planned to adhere to another Princeton tradition.

We would go tent sliding.

The idea was to boost one another up onto one of the tents, crawl up to its apex, and slide down again on the steep mountain of thick canvas, ideally stopping before reaching the edge and the ensuing eight-foot drop to the grass below.

I'd never done this before. But a group had planned to meet up at midnight and head over to the fifth-reunion tent, the largest on campus. It had started to drizzle earlier, the first time in days, and we hoped the water would add an element of speed to the descent.

At nine thirty, Sara phoned my room and asked if I'd seen Jeffrey. I told her not since dinner.

"That's weird," she said. "He was hanging out in my room, but when I came back from taking a shower he was gone."

She didn't sound overly concerned, though. They were the rare couple, I'd noticed, that hadn't become strained as gradua-tion neared. It seemed that graduation was rarely a time of unity. More often it caused outright breakups or, for the warmer of heart, vague promises of long-distance relationships. We were an ambitious bunch, eleven hundred Jack-in-the-boxes full of poten-tial energy, just waiting to be sprung upon the world. This was no time for diversions, no time for compromise. All we had to do was to follow the path that our education had cleared for us. Even a good campus romance, even love, had little force to deflect the pull of an acceptance to a top medical school or a plum job at a New York consulting firm.

Jeffrey and Sara were an exception. On Tuesday they would be shipping all their belongings, except for a suitcase or two, to their respective parents' homes, and then casting off together in Jef-frey's boat of a car, his 1982 Ford Taurus station wagon with 150,000+ miles, bound for San Francisco. There he would pro-gram computers—though he really didn't know very much about programming computers—for a company so new and under-funded that the CEO, a twenty-six-year-old UCLA dropout, car-ried his coffeemaker from home to work every day so the company wouldn't have to spend twenty dollars on another one. (Jeffrey had told me this detail, one of many that he found charming rather than alarming, upon his return from interviewing there. He interviewed at several other companies, too, but had liked this one best. *They think big*, he'd explained.) Sara wanted to spend the next year or two working on a novel. Once she and Jeffrey settled somewhere, she'd take part-time work—as a barista or maybe a bartender—for extra money.

That was their plan. Compared to the plans of many of our peers, it seemed like a recipe for starvation. But they'd be starving together.

160

I had started seeing a political science major named Wendy just a few weeks earlier, and unlike Jeffrey and Sara, we would be starving separately. Or rather, I would be starving alone. She'd made it clear on our first date that she wasn't going to get involved in anything complicated right now, not with Michigan law only three months away. When I told her that I was heading for New York after graduation to play the drums, and that a long-distance relationship probably wasn't in the cards, she seemed pleased, and our springtime romance was on.

I'd spent much of the day with Wendy, and now she was having some sort of last-hurrah dinner with her suite mates and would catch up with us at midnight by the fifth-reunion tent. At eleven o'clock I was in my room, just sitting with the bay window open, looking out into the dark courtyard and killing time before we all met up in an hour. There was a pounding on my door. I got up and opened it.

Jeffrey stood in the doorway looking wet from the rain, blood-shot eyes, hair a mess. Definitely drunk. He came in and sat down on the floor. The night was warm and humid, but he was shivering.

I asked him what was wrong.

"Can I borrow a T-shirt?" he asked. "This one got wet."

All my things were in boxes. I dug around until I found a T-shirt and tossed it to him. He pulled off the wet one and put on mine.

"Thanks."

He was breathing heavily, and when he looked up at me, it wasn't the rain making his eyes wet.

"Jeffrey, what is it?"

Outside, the most determined of us were still in full party mode, despite the hangovers and the rain. A drunk student was announcing to the whole courtyard how fucking drunk he was, and in response a second guy yelled at him from inside one of the dorms to shut the fuck up, and in response to *that* the first guy reminded the second guy that it was a free country, and then his belch echoed across the quad.

"It's Sara," Jeffrey said.

"What? What about her?" The way he looked, my first thought was that she'd just broken up with him.

"I can't believe it."

"Tell me," I said.

"She cheated on me."

At that precise moment, another partier outside began singing a loud, off-key version of the "Love Boat" theme. *Love, exciting and new . . .*

"What are you talking about?" I said. "How do you know?"

Come aboard, we're expecting you . . .

"I . . . that guy really needs to shut up." Jeffrey got up and slammed my window closed. He sat down again. "I need a cigarette," he said. "I really need one and I'm completely out."

"All right," I said, except that I didn't have any. I left him in my room and banged on a couple of doors, returning a minute later with the last of a pack, borrowed from a guy at the end of the hallway I'd been trying to avoid all semester, an aerospace engineer named Gilbert who apparently played the bass and was always asking me to "rock out" with him.

Jeffrey struggled to breathe normally—he was still crying a little—and lit his cigarette. Took a long drag. Then he told me what'd happened. How the information had come out in the worst possible way. In one of Sara's short stories.

She'd been taking the advanced fiction writing class that semester with Tanya Mahoney. Since freshman year she'd been trying to get into that class.

"She said she didn't want me reading her work this semester, that she was 'getting close.' To a breakthrough or whatever. I wasn't suspicious," he said, "only curious. I mean, for four years I'd read every word she ever wrote."

They were the ideal couple that way. Sara loved to write, and Jeffrey loved to read. She wouldn't show her work to anybody besides him, but he was always bragging about her talent, saying it was only a matter of time before she began to publish her stories.

After dinner that night, he'd been alone in her dorm room while she went to take a shower. While she was out of the room, he'd noticed in one of the open boxes a pile of her stories.

"What do you mean, you 'noticed' a pile of stories?"

"Okay, I dug a little. I was curious. I hadn't read anything of hers for months." He pulled a bundle from the back pocket of his jeans. "Maybe I was a little suspicious. It's possible. I don't know. Anyway, here. Read it."

"You stole her story?"

"Yeah, I took it and left. I couldn't stand to be there when she came back. Go on—read it."

I unfolded the pages he'd given me. Sara was always telling us that her stories went long—twenty, thirty pages. This one was short, though, just eight pages. It was dated from the middle of the semester and titled "The Three-Day Affair."

In the late afternoon of the third day, they lie in bed, the food between them in white cardboard cartons. The chow mein, perfect. The Szechuan shrimp, too spicy. Insanely spicy. She asks if he is perhaps trying to kill her. Just the opposite, he says. He is trying to save her. Save her from going to California.

He's my boyfriend, she says. He needs me.

If there is a hell, she thinks, I'm surely going there. And then she adds "overly dramatic" to her list of faults.

I'm not talking about your boyfriend, he says. I'm talking about earthquakes. I'd hate to see you caught in one.

You can't expect me to change my whole entire life based on three days, she says. It isn't fair.

She blames her yellow curtains, through which the soft afternoon light is making this young man who is not her boyfriend look beautiful. She searches his face for a scar, a pimple. Some blemish to find distasteful so that she can focus on it when she remembers him. She hunts for a mole.

I hear there are wildfires, he says. You could get trapped. Your house could burn to the ground.

Please, don't joke, she says. I don't want any jokes right now. She sets the box of shrimp on the bedside table. I don't want to think about anything, she says, and kisses him below his eye. His eyes are pale blue, like the Midwestern sky of her imagination, nothing at all like the cold dark waters off California's rocky coast.

Then I'll tell you something that isn't a joke, he says, and kisses her, beginning at her mouth and working his way to her throat, the hollow of her collar bone, down her body lower and lower. Soon, she is clenching her teeth. She begins to moan softly as their third afternoon together slides slowly toward . . .

I turned the page and kept reading. The boyfriend has taken a trip to California to interview for jobs as a computer programmer. He is made out to be a decent person but a bore and an unsatisfying lover. The man with whom she has the affair is handsome and ambitious and bound for success in Washington, DC. He has always pined for her, and she for him, but neither one ever acted on their desires until now. He wants the story's narrator to break up with her boyfriend and come with him to DC.

The story ends ambiguously, as if the character, or perhaps the author, hasn't decided. Her boyfriend calls on the phone from

Newark Airport, having returned from his trip. He says the interviews went well, and he can't wait to see her.

I love you, he says.
She grips the receiver and squeezes her eyes shut, imagining.
I love you, she says.

He was looking at me, waiting for my verdict.

I shrugged. "It's a short story. It's fiction."

"Bullshit," he said. "It happened. I went to California to look for a job. She stayed here and had an affair. My God, Will, it's so . . . *detailed*."

He was right about that. The story, despite its lyricism, was overtly sexual. Its climax was not solely literary.

"You shouldn't have gone through her things," I said.

"That's not the point."

"It sort of is. I don't see how you can confront her about this now without coming across—"

"She cheated on me, Will! And the way she describes me . . . my God, she thinks I'm a total loser. And bad in bed. She should just tell me, if that's what she thinks. I can take it. But she shouldn't cheat on me." He was up now, pacing my small room. "And all the stuff about the other guy, the things he did with her . . . I'll never get that out of my head. Not ever." He went over to the bay window and cracked it open. He crushed his cigarette on the stone wall outside and dropped the butt out the window.

"She's still planning to move with you to California, though," I said.

"Yeah. That's the plan."

"And is that what you want, too?"

He was looking out the window. It was still drizzling. A few guys had come outside and were throwing a football around in the dimly lit courtyard.

"More than anything," he said.

"Then you need to get rid of that story and hope she doesn't notice it missing. Forget any of it ever happened. Leave it alone."

"How can I? I mean, you read it."

I shrugged. "Tell yourself she made the whole thing up. I mean, that's a possibility, isn't it?"

"Yeah, right. And I'm sure you figured out who the guy is. The guy in the story." When I didn't answer right away he said, "Come on, Will. Nolan's moving to DC. And the physical descriptions . . . It's him. You can't pretend it isn't."

"Maybe," I said. "Maybe not."

Three woman had joined the football group. They seemed to be taking on the guys in a game. One of the girls kicked the ball, and the guy ran it back for a touchdown. Whooping and high-fives ensued.

"You can't accuse him," I said. "There's no way."

"How can you defend him?"

"I'm not defending anybody. I'm saying you're getting your facts from a piece of fiction."

"So you don't think it happened?"

"I'm saying you can't know for sure." I handed him back the story. "Not without asking her, and you can't ask her. Look, maybe it's just her imagination, completely made up, but she knew you'd get upset if you ever read it. Isn't that a possibility?"

"So being with Nolan is her fantasy—is that what you're saying?"

"I'm saying it's a short story. It's a class assignment. It's fiction."

He sighed and said nothing.

"All I know is," I said, "she told you she wants to move to California. With *you*. So accept that. Move to California, get married, have twenty kids, and live happily ever after."

"And that's it? Never mention any of this to Nolan."

I nodded. "Exactly. Never mention it."

"You know he's talking about us all getting together next winter someplace for a weekend of golf. I couldn't do that, Will. I couldn't play golf with the guy."

"Then don't," I said. "You never have to see him again if you don't want to. But can I make a prediction? I'll bet that by next winter, this will all be behind you. All of this will seem like it never happened."

"Keep your friends close and your enemies closer. Is that what you're saying?"

"No," I said, "that isn't at all what I'm saying."

He shook his head. "I don't know if I can just forgive and forget."

He could, though. Or if he couldn't, then he must have come to terms with the part of himself that resented ambiguity and learned to live with not knowing. Some would call this growing up.

The next winter, we all met up in Sedona for a weekend of golf, just like Nolan had talked about. Every year after, we'd pick a different spot. And not once did Jeffrey bring up the three-day affair that he had read about.

"You know," he said, "I'm no writer. But if I were to describe Sara in a story, even if it were fiction, I'd never demean her. Never."

"I know you wouldn't," I said.

The rain lightened up suddenly, like someone turning off a faucet. Moments later, the phone rang. It was Evan. "It's time," he said. He and Nolan had finished the bottle of tequila in his room and were ready to slide down some tents.

"We'll meet you downstairs," I told him, and hung up the phone. "You still up for this?" I asked Jeffrey.

"I don't know." He shrugged. "Sure, why not."

I saw this as the first sign of his willingness to let the mystery die. I was glad. I didn't want high drama. These were our last days together for a long time. They were hard on us all.

A few minutes later, Evan, Nolan, Jeffrey, and I were participating in one of our last-ever Princeton rites. When Sara caught up with us, she said, "Jeff, where've you *been*?" and he shrugged and said, "Just shooting the shit with Will," and she punched me on the arm and said thanks a lot for letting her know, and that was that. To Jeffrey's credit, he didn't brood or ruin anyone else's fun. It helped that Sara was acting affectionately toward him. They held hands and slid down the tent together.

Wendy showed up at midnight with several of her suite mates, and she kissed me with sweet alcohol breath, and everything about the night made me sad. The moon shone through a light layer of clouds, which then drifted away, and a light breeze rustled the leaves of the elm trees that bordered the courtyard. At first I was afraid the tent wouldn't hold us, but I was wrong. It was a sturdy structure. I sat at the very top of it, underneath the stars, and looked out across campus: Blair Arch in the distance, the bookstore, the smaller library where I used to study during my perplexing freshman year. Graduation wasn't for another two days, but I was already feeling nostalgic for the place.

We climbed and slid and got muddy and behaved exactly like alumni desperate to relive their youth.

CHAPTER 19

I TOOK A BREATH, AND when I couldn't hold it any longer I got out of the car and went inside the studio with my first-aid kit. Nolan was seated at my chair in the control room, a wad of paper towels pressed to his ear but otherwise looking fully alive.

"I thought you'd fled to Mexico," he said.

"Don't think I didn't consider it." I set the kit on the couch and began to peel the tape off the box. Through the window I could see Jeffrey sitting in the recording room, leaning against one of the walls and looking down at his shoes. "How is he?" I asked.

"How's *he*? What the fuck do I care how he is?"

I had the kit open and was dumping its contents onto the sofa. "I don't see a needle or thread in here. But there are some good strong bandages. I think that's our best bet until a professional can sew you up. I'll tape it up real well. That should keep the wound closed."

Nolan shrugged. "I'm in your hands."

"Does it hurt?"

"Like a bitch."

I handed him a packet of Advil. He tore it open and ate the pills without water. Miracle of miracles, there was also a bottle of

169

antacids in the kit, and I quickly ate a handful. My stomach gurgled in thanks.

"Not feeling so hot yourself?" Nolan asked.

"You could say that," I said, and asked him if he wanted more whiskey.

"Desperately," he said, "but I'm going to pass. I need a clear head right now."

I pushed his hair out of the way and stuck a big bandage to his head, pinning the ear in place. I began to wrap a big white length of gauze around his head at an angle so that his good ear would remain uncovered.

"That feel any better?" I asked.

"Doesn't feel any worse." With the gauze around his head he looked like a soldier whose brains and good sense had been blasted out across some rice paddy.

"I called Evan," I said. "Just so you know."

He turned to look at me. "What'd you tell him?"

"He wasn't home. I left a message for him to call here." He looked at me with disapproval. "It was stupid of me to send him away yesterday. We need him, especially now." His expression didn't change. "It's over, Nolan. The bribes didn't work. It was wrong of us to try. This is as far as we can take it."

He stared at me a moment as if he might argue my point but then looked away and nodded at the glass partition. "What about crazy man over there? You'd better tell him."

I nodded. "My guess is he'll be relieved."

Nolan moved the contents of the first-aid kit onto the floor and gently laid himself down on the couch. "If you don't mind, I'll wait here. For some reason I've got a slight headache."

When Jeffrey had taken Marie from the Milk-n-Bread, at first every minute had seemed precious. But now an entire night had passed, and the currency of time had inflated. Seconds no longer mattered, and minutes went by almost unnoticed. When I told Jeffrey that I'd called Evan, that I wanted him here when we let Marie go, he merely shrugged. "It'll be nice to see him," he said. "It's been a while."

It was noon. I spent most of the next hour trying to clean the blood off the hallway carpet. I wasn't too successful, but fortunately the hallway was always dim and the gray carpet was already terribly stained from years of grime and beer and cigarette ash.

When an hour had passed, I called Evan again from the studio's phone. The hell with not leaving a phone trail. I got his machine again and left another message—same content, more urgency. Then I called information for the number to his law firm. The operator directed me to the company directory, and after pressing the digits for his last name, I reached his work voice mail and left another message. Evan never went long without checking for messages. A client or partner might be calling. After another hour had passed, I nearly called a third time. Instead I went out to the sub shop on the corner and bought Italian subs for the guys and a veggie special for Marie. None of us had eaten all day, and my stomach was feeling somewhat better.

I handed Marie her sandwich, and as she unwrapped it I told her that Evan was coming. That we were waiting for him and then we'd let her go. She didn't deign to look at me, and started picking onions off the sandwich.

"Just remember," she said, "you made a pledge to me."

"I remember," I said.

"Good. Because I don't feel safe around those guys," she said. "I don't trust them—especially the good-looking one. Though I'll bet he isn't so good-looking now."

Standing there in the doorway I wanted to say more, but through the glass, in the control room, Nolan was waving the phone receiver at me.

While at the University of Virginia, Evan had made law review and was recruited heavily by the big firms, wined and dined and offered signing bonuses as if he were going to be throwing touchdown passes instead of writing memos and taking deposi- tions. My uncle had been a lawyer in Jersey City, estates and wills and real estate closings, but Evan's job was nothing at all like that. In the deals he worked on, billions of dollars were on the line. He wasn't allowed to name his clients, but he implied that they were the corporations that advertised during the Super Bowl.

He was calling from halfway across the country. The moment his boss learned that he wasn't taking the weekend off in Jersey, Evan was whisked away to Minneapolis. A client needed his help on a deal that was close to being finalized.

"Come home on the next flight," I told him.

"Can't do that, Will. I just got here."

"Doesn't matter," I said. "Drop what you're doing. Whatever it is. Get to the airport as fast as you can and take the next flight to Newark. Rent a car. I'll give you the address—"

"Wait a second, now. Just slow down. The client's in the next room. We're in a meeting. You're not being reasonable. So just slow down a minute and tell me—"

"Listen to me, *please*," I said. "Ditch. The. Client."

"*Will* . . ."

"Tell him someone's been in an accident. Or that your moth- er's sick. Do whatever you need to do."

"Look, the weather's awful out here. Even if I did try to leave . . ."

"Just get here as fast as you can." I glanced over at Marie. "Man, I promise you I'm not crying wolf over here."

He didn't say anything, and for a moment I thought the call might have gotten disconnected, severing my only tie to somebody beyond this recording studio. But then his voice returned.

"Give me the address," he said.

CHAPTER 20

M ARIE WAS MOTIONING FOR my attention. Lunch was done. We were waiting to hear from Evan when his flight would leave. Jeffrey and Nolan refused to be in the same room together, so Jeffrey had eaten lunch in the recording room, and Nolan and I had eaten in the control room.

I opened the door to Room A and Marie handed me the trash. Then she told me what she wanted. I had a feeling this was coming eventually.

"I know the bucket isn't ideal," I began, "but . . ."

"No way," she said. "I'm not shitting in a bucket in front of you guys, not when there's a bathroom fifty feet away."

I sighed. The bathrooms were out in the hallway, and the hallway led to the front door. "Wait a minute," I said, and shut the door. Jeffrey, who'd overheard the conversation, shrugged. "It's fine with me."

I went into the control room to relay the problem to Nolan. "Your call," he said. "Just don't let Jeffrey accompany her."

"I thought maybe you both could—"

"Forget it. I'll do it alone. I owe her an apology anyway."

"You know she's scared to death of you now."

"Then this will be a chance to show her my soft side." He got up from the sofa, groaned slightly, and went to get her. After a couple minutes of them chatting together in Room A, he had his hand on Marie's arm and was guiding her out of the studio and down the hallway.

When they were gone, Jeffrey followed me into the control room. "It's probably too late to apologize to you for everything, but I am sorry, you know."

"Duly noted," I said.

He looked around the control room. "So other than kidnapping, what do you use this place for?"

I'd almost forgotten that it was a place for music. I answered his question by cuing up a reel of tape. It was The Fixtures, the band I'd been recording all week. "They're just teenagers," I said, "but they're pretty good."

And I liked them. We got along well. I had a certain way of dealing with young bands. I'd ask them, "Are you motherfuckers ready to play some rock and roll?" And they'd answer, "Fuck, yeah! You'd better fucking believe it!" They loved that I didn't treat them like kids. That I was nothing like their parents or teachers.

When I started engineering the band's five-song demo a couple weeks ago, they said they wanted a "major-label sound." They had big plans to sell the CD at shows and mail it off to record companies. The checks that they paid me with had *Dr. Edmond Castle* printed on them. These were the well-adjusted, bright-eyed kids of doctors and lawyers, kids with just enough talent, motivation, and family backing to approach the mountain that they'd spend the next five or ten years of their lives probably failing to summit. Someday, cynicism would likely creep in as it did with most musicians, but that was still long into the future. I was glad they'd come to me. A lot of studios would've treated them like free money, putting some intern on the console who'd only ever swept the floors, and given the band a quick lesson in rock and roll being a lousy business. At least I could prolong their innocence, give them a CD worthy of Dr. Edmond Castle's generous checkbook.

"They sound good," Jeffrey said. "They're good, this band."

They were, and it felt good to be listening to music, any music. Jeffrey and I had finished the last of my cigarettes late the night before, and I had been in such a hurry at the pharmacy this morning that I'd forgotten to buy more. But my craving subsided as we were transported, for a few minutes, away from this place. Neither of us said anything when the song ended. We wanted more. We wanted the next song, and the song after that. As long as the music kept playing, time would stand still and our problems wouldn't exist.

I leaned back in my chair. I'd slept last night, true, but it'd been a wakeful kind of sleep, and now I began to dream the moment I closed my eyes. My dream was a shapeless thing, more sound than image—bass drum becoming some universal heart beating, pumping blood into exhausted arteries. It seemed to go on a long time. Then gradually my vision returned. The shape of a man in the doorway. Not Nolan. Not Jeffrey.

"Working hard, or hardly working?"

I jerked awake, and the dream zippered itself shut.

Seton Hall sweatshirt over baggy jeans. White stubble. Yankees cap.

Joey.

I sat up in my chair, then clumsily shut off the tape. "What're you doing here?" He knew that nobody was booked in the studio this weekend.

"What am I doing here? This is my goddamn studio." He glanced over at Jeffrey. "Who're you?"

Jeffrey watched me with pleading eyes. My terror matched his own.

"This is Jeffrey Hocks," I managed to say. "A friend from college. I was showing off your studio. Jeffrey, this is Joey Pitts. He owns the place."

Never a man of nuance, Joey seemed ignorant of our anxiety and shook Jeffrey's hand heartily. "Glad to meet you, Jeff," he said. "Sorry about your taste in friends." He laughed at his own joke.

When I asked Joey again what he was doing here, he whistled as if recalling a grisly traffic accident. "I had to escape my own house. The wife's meeting there with her book club. She's always reading about nuns in Bangladesh or kids in Iran who put on Shakespeare plays. Hell, I don't know. Bunch of old broads get together once a month. Way I figure, it's a chance for them to gossip and eat cake. I had to clear out for a few hours. Sometimes you gotta do that. You married, Jeff?"

"What?" He was already backing out the door.

"You'd understand if you were married. Will here understands, don't you, Will?"

Before I could answer, there came the sound of water rushing through pipes. Joey's eyes narrowed a little.

"Joey," I said, "Jeffrey and I were talking about something kind of *important*." Several weeks earlier I'd alluded to a wealthy friend who might want to invest in the record company. I hoped that Joey would get my hint and leave us alone.

"Is someone else here?" Joey asked. No suspicion in his voice, just curiosity.

Jeffrey and I glanced at each other. There was no ignoring the sound of the toilet being flushed. Then I heard a scream, blasting my heart to the top of my throat, but it was only the bathroom sink.

"Like I said, Joey, I've got friends in town for the weekend."

"Nolan's in the bathroom," Jeffrey said. "I'll go get him."

But Joey put up his hand. "Give him time," he said. "Nobody likes to be rushed in there. I'll wait."

"It's okay," Jeffrey said, "I've got to go anyway."

"Maybe I'll use the crapper, too," Joey said, and my heart lurched. "Join the crowd? Nah, I'm kidding. I don't crap more than once every couple of days. Waste of time. Bet you didn't know that Albert Einstein only crapped once a week. Da Vinci, no more than twice a month."

Go away! I thought. *Go away go away go away!*

"Nah, I'm kidding again. I'm just a constipated old man. Like you'll all be some day. Ah, youth." He grinned at us. Jeffrey slipped past Joey, out of the control room, and went down the hall toward the restroom.

Joey lowered his voice, asking if I thought Jeffrey was going to invest money in the record company. I told him I wasn't sure yet, but I was hopeful.

"I hate to kick you out of your own studio," I said, "but our chances are better if it's just a couple of old friends talking. I'm sure you understand."

Joey studied me a moment. "I'm impressed, Will. I've got to admit it. When you first mentioned starting a record company, I told the wife you were full of it. But maybe I was wrong. Maybe you can pull this off. So my point is, I'm sorry. I'm apologizing to you right now."

"Don't sweat it," I said.

"Everyone makes mistakes, though. You gotta agree with that."

I agreed. I'd have agreed to clipping his toenails if it would get him out of the studio.

"All right," he said, "I'm going. I'm thinking of bowling a few frames. You heard me! I haven't been bowling in years. But what the hell, am I right?"

He turned to leave, prompting a silent prayer of gratitude to every deity I could think of, and then he nearly ran into Nolan coming into the control room.

"Holy crap, son, what happened to you?"

"Car flipped over twice," Nolan said, "back in Missouri. I'm lucky to be alive."

I made quick introductions: "Joey, Nolan. Nolan, Joey."

"Well, it obviously hasn't knocked any sense into you," Joey said to Nolan, "because you're still friends with this guy." He winked. "Okay, fuck it, I'm leaving. Enjoy the afternoon, boys."

Before he could change his mind, I shot out of my chair and took him by the arm. I escorted my boss out of the control room. After a couple of steps Joey turned around again, and I had to stop myself from murdering him on the spot.

"Enjoy the weekend, Nolan," he said. "Jersey's a good place. Don't let anybody tell you otherwise. Or do. What the fuck do I care?"

Finally he left. After the door had closed behind him, I exhaled for what seemed like the first time in several minutes and returned to the control room.

"Holy shit," I said, trying to catch my breath. Nolan went to get Jeffrey and Marie. They led her back to isolation Room A. She went obediently inside and sat down on the floor. Nolan locked the door behind her. They both came into the control room.

"Now *that*," Nolan said, "is what you call dodging a bullet."

I nodded, glad at least to see that Nolan and Jeffrey were willing to be in the same room again.

"I'll tell you this," Jeffrey said. "That girl deserves a medal. I agree with her—forty thousand dollars isn't enough for what she's put up with."

Nolan was sitting on the sofa, eyes closed. He didn't even bother to open them as he gave Jeffrey the finger. I couldn't help laughing.

179

He opened his eyes. "Don't fucking laugh. There's nothing funny about this."

But I was giddy from the close call. The release of tension felt entirely welcome. We laugh at funerals. Why not now?

"He's right," Jeffrey said. "Seriously, Will. Cut it out."

I balled up a sheet of paper, faked a throw at Nolan, and whipped it at Jeffrey. It hit him in the head. "You fucking crazy fuckmunch," I said to him with as much feeling as those words can carry.

"What did you just call me?"

"You heard me, fuckmunch."

He smiled a little—not the crazed grin from before. A human smile. "You're right. I really, really am."

I've heard that in mountain climbing, most injuries occur on the descent. This makes perfect sense to me. One's attention can remain in a heightened state for only so long. When we head downward, we relax a little; we let ourselves appreciate the view. And that's when we find ourselves tumbling into a crevasse.

I should have followed Joey to the door and locked it behind him. Everyone makes mistakes. Joey's were trivial. He talked too much and he sometimes forgot to slam the damn door so it locked. I knew this about him. I should've followed him to the door.

I rewound The Fixtures' tape and was putting it back into its case with the easy arrogance of somebody who believed he'd be finishing that recording in a few days. That simple action, boxing up the tape for another day, revealed to me, in immediate hindsight, that at some deep level I still believed that when the weekend was over, I'd go back to my ordinary life and nothing would have changed.

To my credit, the moment I set the box back on its shelf I realized what I'd just done, and what it said about me. But by then it was too late. When I looked up again, a man was standing in the center of the main recording room, looking straight at Marie and waving.

180

CHAPTER 21

H E SOMETIMES WANDERED IN from the street when Joey left the
door unlocked, which was why I never left it unlocked.

"Get out of here!" I yelled, not that he could hear me through
the thick glass. After a quick explanation—"Homeless guy"—I
left the control room and went into the recording room. "Out of
here, right now!"

"Cute girl," he said. "Who is she?"

By now Nolan and Jeffrey were on my heels.

"She's nobody," Nolan said.

Marie was looking at us with an expression of mild curiosity.
He didn't look like the kind of guy who'd save anybody. She probably assumed he was another one of my friends.

"She's recording an album," I said. "I mean it—out, or I'm calling the police." I had him by the arm, and before Marie could
change her mind and begin pounding on the locked door, I'd led
him out of the studio and into the hallway.

As soon as I let go of him, he stopped walking. He had a moldy,
boozy smell. "My friend," he said, "those submarine sandwiches
you were out buying today were probably delicious. I could use
one of them subs myself, if you could spare a dollar . . ."

181

I didn't like the idea of him watching me without my noticing. What else had he seen? Nolan got out his wallet, removed a twenty, and held it out. The man's eyes got huge. "You're going to leave right now and not come back. Isn't that right?"

"My friend, everything you say is right." He wasn't taking his eyes off the bill.

When Nolan handed it to him, he held it up by its ends like a prize fish, then tucked it into the pocket of his flannel shirt.

"Now find some other street," I told him. "Somewhere across town." But why would he cross town, knowing he could get twenty dollars from us?

"As good as done," he said. "God bless. You're good men."

"Sure we are," I said. "Now go."

He took his time walking down the hallway and out the door. I slammed the door behind him, and like a fool hanging a smoke detector on the charred embers of his burned-out house, I made certain it was locked.

Evan called from the airport, where he'd bought a ticket for Newark. The flight was scheduled to leave at 4 PM Central Time. But weather in the Twin Cities had worsened. No spring blizzard, as some had predicted, but freezing rain and lots of it.

"So far no flights have been canceled," he said, "but it's coming down hard." He promised to call again when he had an update.

More waiting. And now the minutes seemed to matter again as they began to pile up. I paced the control room. Four o'clock came and went, and the phone continued not to ring. Then came four thirty and five, and still no word.

We had to let Marie go. That fact had always quietly filled the studio like ambient noise. You could put it out of your mind, but only for a while. There would be no money paid in exchange for her silence. Not anymore. Undoubtedly, she would go to the police, and it wouldn't be long—hours? a day?—before we were arrested. And then we would confess. We had no alibi. Also, we were guilty.

We'd been arrogant, believing that any problem could be solved as long as you had intelligence and determination and a little time. We had all those things but couldn't solve this one, and now time was up. I was beginning to feel ready. Whatever disgraces—prison? Divorce? A hungry media?—I was about to face were, for the first time, being overshadowed by a basic need to do the right thing.

And yet I strongly believed that the way we handled our surrender now would have far-reaching consequences down the road, the way that traveling a few degrees off course could mean, upon crossing an ocean, the difference between landing on your continent and missing it entirely. Although the beginning of this weekend had been out of control, the end of it was still unfolding and, I believed, still subject to our influence. Should we write up a confession? Go to the police ourselves? Have them come here? Evan would know. That was why it was so important for him to get here.

At 6:15 I called his cell again. "We're waiting for the plane to get here from L.A.," he said. "The good news is, flights are still coming in and out."

"How's it look outside?" I asked.

"Like hell. But I think they're used to that here."

By 7:00 we were all hungry. And I really wanted cigarettes. I remained spooked, however, from my run-in earlier and was afraid to go outside. So we all sat around waiting, looking at our watches and at one another and at the telephone that kept not ringing—until, finally, it rang.

There was a problem.

Evan was scheduled to change planes in Chicago, but because of his delay, by the time he'd get there he'd have missed the last plane leaving for any of the New York airports. The only other option was a direct flight to Philadelphia, scheduled to leave Minneapolis at 11:30.

If everything went perfectly, he'd land at 3 AM. We were located about two hours from Philadelphia. That would get him here shortly after 5 AM. It would mean another night in the studio.

Another goddamn night. Another ludicrous phone call to Cynthia—*Everything's great!*—followed by a thousand more years of waiting.

"Book it," I said, and then asked Jeffrey to help me again with the sofa.

Marie retreated obediently to a corner of Room A so we could cram the sofa in for her. We went through the routine again:

"Swear on your grandmother's life that you won't try to escape when we open the door."

"Aren't we past all that by now?"

"No. Swear it."

Hesitation. Then a shrug. "I swear on my nana's life."

We told her there would be no dinner tonight for any of us. Jeffrey removed the blanket from the bass drum again, spread it out on the floor, and lay down on top of it. Nolan took his spot by the television. I went to the control room and dimmed all the lights in the studio. I sat in my chair for a while and presided over my wrecked kingdom. In this artificial twilight, Marie's resemblance to Sara increased. It was more than physical likeness—it was the posture, the way she carried herself. And this, I thought, was because of the violence, or the threat of it. It produced a sort of grace, whose purpose was to mask fear. We could tell Marie a thousand times she was in no danger, but she'd never fully believe it. And why should she? To her, violence was always imminent.

184

I hadn't been witness to Sara's violence—that'd all happened long before college—but we all felt the wake of it. Every now and then—not often, maybe once or twice a year—she'd say something horrible to Jeffrey. She'd find ways to dig at his insecurities by praising her ex-boyfriend's athletic body. Telling him that some nights she craved a real man's shoulders, and chest, and cock. When this happened, he would become severely depressed until, a day or two later, they would talk and cry together and, to outward appearances, become better again. She was testing him, evidently, waiting for him to do something brutal, because in her experience that was what men did. She crossed the line to see if he would, too.

I used to wonder about her past but hadn't felt comfortable asking. And Jeffrey wasn't the type to share somebody else's secrets. Yet college, more than any other time in one's life, puts a person in situations where the questions that can't get asked get asked anyway. Sara and I were doing laundry one Sunday evening in the basement of our dormitory. This was early in our senior year. We'd both scored large single rooms, luck of the room lottery, and this night found us sitting at a rickety wooden table, sick of studying, and waiting for our things to dry. I mentioned that my mother had called me earlier in the evening and given me hell for forgetting my father's birthday ("What? Not even a card?"), and Sara asked if my parents were happily married. "Sure, I guess so," I said, and then felt funny because I knew that her family life had its problems. All she'd ever mentioned outright, though, was her hometown's unforgettable name: Slaughter, Texas.

She must've felt like talking that night, though, because suddenly she was telling me about being raised by her single mother, how she'd never even known her father.

"And I'm not one of those people who'll track him down thinking we have some magical connection," she said. "Though I imagine he was exactly like every guy my mother ever dated."

185

I asked her what she meant.

"This one guy she was with, back when I was fourteen . . ." She shook her head as if remembering, or maybe trying not to. "Leo. He owned a garage and always seemed greasy. I think my mom broke up his marriage. Anyway, he rented an apartment in town but stayed at our place a lot. Whenever he took a shower, his towel was always 'accidentally' slipping down. I used to lock my bedroom door, and I'd wake up in the middle of the night sometimes and swear I heard the doorknob rattling."

"That's incredibly creepy," I said.

"Damn right it was." A few other students were in the laundry room with us, at other tables, heads down in their books, but the sound of the machines kept our conversation private. "Then one night I came home from being out with friends, and my mom was walking around the kitchen in obvious pain, but she wouldn't talk about it. She said Leo had been there, but that was all."

"Pain where?" I asked.

"So that's the thing. I noticed she wouldn't sit down. *Then* I noticed Leo's long leather belt draped over a kitchen chair. I remember the buckle had a Cowboys logo on it. Mom didn't sit down all evening or the next day. When she was awake, she just stood around grimacing. She managed a bookstore at the time but couldn't even go to work. She refused to talk to me about it, except to say that if Leo called, I was supposed to tell him she wasn't home. And to this day I still don't know if his beating her ass was something kinky or a straight-ahead whipping. But she stayed with him. That killed me. You know, my mom's got three siblings. I don't see them much—they're scattered all over the country—but when we do I'm always amazed by how ordinary they are. Ordinary marriages, ordinary jobs . . ."

"Managing a bookstore sounds pretty ordinary," I said.

"It was an adult bookstore." She watched my face turn red and smiled. "All I know is, within the week Leo was back, showering in our bathroom, watching football on our TV."

My own life had always lacked drama. My parents had gotten along. They'd protected me and sacrificed again and again for me. I wasn't sure if this made them ordinary or extraordinary, though I knew it should've made me grateful. And it did, usually, though at the moment I felt sorry that I had nothing to share, nothing of my own to balance out her story with. All I had were questions.

"Is your mom still with him?"

"No. She finally dumped him. One night at dinner—this was during a pretty good spell, actually—he wiped his face with his napkin, like a real gentleman, and told Mom and me that he had this terrific idea. Something that the three of us could do together. He said it so matter-of-factly, he could've been talking about us all going to a Cowboys game. But he wasn't." One of the washing machines behind Sara began to shake violently as it entered the spin cycle. "Anyway, that's what it took for my mother to get rid of Leo."

I was twenty-one years old that year, old enough to know that even among friends full disclosures were rare. They always came when you least expected it—in line for burgers, or at the movies just as the lights dimmed, or waiting for your clothes to dry. And often you had just that one brief window, and you knew it wouldn't stay open for long. So you'd better find out all you could.

"Did things change after that?" I asked. "With your mother?"

"No, she just took up with another troublemaker. Some ex-army guy, retired but still built like a truck." Then she laughed. "My mom calls herself a passionate woman, and she claims her men are passionate, too. But she just uses that word to excuse people for their bad behavior. Her so-called passion leads her from one loser to the next. She was a beautiful woman, though. Still is. Very alluring. One day she'll be alone, that's for sure. I feel bad for her. And I won't let it happen to me. It almost did, you know."

"The baseball player."

She smiled. "He played backup second base for the county high school. He was always throwing the ball over the first baseman's head. Beautiful eyes, though. The boy was beautiful, I'll give him that. And not violent or mean. But a local guy. Small-minded. The sort of guy who thinks that the ultimate thing a woman would want is her name spelled correctly when it's tattooed on his bicep. You've got to be crazy to build a future with a guy like that. When I told him I wanted to go to college and become a novelist, he literally laughed, and then when he saw I was pissed he said all he meant was that there was a perfectly good newspaper right in Slaughter that I could write for." She shook her head. "Which was *extra* stupid because it wasn't a 'perfectly good newspaper.' It was a shoddily written weekly devoted mainly to church activities."

"You really need to stop bringing that guy up in front of Jeffrey," I said. "It makes him crazy."

She nodded. "I know. I hate when I do it, even when I'm doing it."

"Well, maybe just don't do it."

In that regard, our conversation wasn't just informative, it was practical. Because as far as I know, she never mentioned him to Jeffrey again.

"You know, I've never told anyone about Leo," she said, several minutes later, once our shirts were dry and folded.

"Except for Jeffrey, you mean."

"Nope."

"Just me?"

She must have seen the confusion in my face, because she smiled. "It's no big deal. I just sort of felt like talking, that's all." She shrugged. "Anyway, you're a good listener."

Her compliment filled me with satisfaction, though I didn't believe I'd done anything to earn it. "You know I'd never—"

"I know you won't. There's no need to say anything."

My fear, now, was that we were creating just those sorts of "Leo" moments in Marie, instilling the presumption of violence and betrayal in a person who hadn't asked for it and didn't deserve it. She'd been foolish, trying to get more money out of us. And greedy. But in the scheme of things her faults were small-time and forgivable.

At some point during my musings, she had lain down on the sofa. She turned onto her side and curled up her legs, making herself smaller, and then was still.

Sleep, Marie. From the control room I further dimmed Room A until it went black. *Sleep.*

CHAPTER 22

T HE PHILLY-BOUND PLANE HAD sat on the runway so long it needed to be de-iced all over again, and by the time Evan called us saying he'd touched down in Philadelphia, it was nearly five in the morning.

"Sorry if I woke you," he said.

"You didn't," I said.

He hadn't woken any of us. Jeffrey, Nolan, and I had spent these hours apart. Even after Evan's call I spent two more hours staring at my hands, wishing for my friend to get here already while simultaneously hoping he'd never arrive. At seven thirty he called again from the parking lot behind the studio, asking to be let in.

Only two days earlier I'd tried to keep Evan away. Now, despite my stiff limbs, I couldn't get to the door fast enough.

The bright morning sun nearly took my breath away. It must be how gamblers feel stumbling penniless out of a casino and being shocked that the colorful world is carrying on without them. Evan stood in the doorway, framed by the morning light. He wore a gray business suit and carried his computer bag. He looked tired, but if his expression reflected what he saw, I must have looked worse. We shook hands. "Thanks for coming," I said, and led him into the studio. "It's good to see a friendly face."

We kept walking down the hallway, past the bathrooms.

"Look, Will," Evan said, "are you going to make me guess what's going on? Or are you going to tell me . . ." We had rounded the corner into the main recording room. Evan stopped walking and looked around.

There was a drum set and guitar amplifiers and cables and microphone stands, but what he saw, I'm sure, were the pizza boxes and full trash bags, and a television, and when Nolan and Jeffrey came around the corner from the control room he saw one friend with a bandaged head and another with a busted lip. And of course he saw the girl—looking tired and miserable, but curious, too—on the floor of Room A, sitting on the sofa and looking at him quite calmly, almost as if he were the one imprisoned and on display, like at a zoo. She sat with her head in her hands, with only her gaze trained on us. She looked incapable of becoming excited anymore, of getting her hopes up, though she must have been wondering if this new man who'd entered the room was indeed the savior I'd promised or merely the beginning of some new indignity.

"What the hell have I just walked into?" he asked.

We had planned to tell him everything. Nolan, Jeffrey, and I would sit in the control room with Evan and begin back at the Milk-n-Bread, telling him what we'd done, and, as best we could, why we'd done it. We would try to convey how basic concepts like *time*, like *morality*, had become distorted and unpredictable when mixed with the impurity of panic.

Nobody would raise his voice. Nobody would interrupt. We wouldn't even rush. Evan had flown halfway across the country. Marie had been our hostage for three days. What did it matter if we explained ourselves in thirty minutes or an hour? We would confess everything and calmly ask for his counsel. We would follow his advice wherever it led us.

That was our plan, but it didn't happen. Because the moment Evan saw Marie, the rest of us were forgotten. He rushed over to Room A, opened the door, and went inside.

Their conversation looked strangely animated. Almost heated. It went on a long time, nearly an hour, and when they emerged, Evan looked distinctly perturbed. Not sad, exactly. Annoyed, and frustrated. Like a student who'd failed an exam because of trick questions. Marie was with him. Not running for the door. Just standing beside him.

We caught up with them in the main studio. "So," I said, "what's the verdict?"

Evan said nothing, just continued on with his annoyed look, lips pursed, head shaking slightly. Marie stared me down. Didn't nod, didn't say a word. Her gaze moved to Nolan, with his bandage and his bloodstained hair. And to Jeffrey, his lip swollen, his eyes ghoulish from lack of sleep.

"This young lady narrated quite a story." Evan frowned. "I keep telling her that maybe she wants to rethink what she told me. That maybe her recollection isn't exactly right. But she insists that it is."

"I know it must sound crazy," I said, "but I swear, we never meant—"

Evan held up his hand like a stop sign. "She says that you, Will, first met her several weeks ago at the convenience store where she works. That you heard her singing along to the radio one day and complimented her voice. Said it was the best voice you'd heard in ages. Then, last week you invited her to record some demos at your studio while your friends were in town. You began to fill her head with talk of how you all would make her a star."

Marie stood beside him, nodding right along.

"On Friday," he continued, "you all came here to begin recording, but little by little it became clear you didn't like what she was doing. You didn't like her voice as much as you'd first thought. You told her to try harder. You all worked late into the night." He spoke dispassionately, as if he'd memorized a set of lines but was bored by them. "She thought she could prove to you all that she had what it takes. But now you're telling her you were wrong. Now you're telling her she has no talent. You've crushed her dreams and wasted her time, and for that she wants compensation." He turned to Marie. "Do I have it right?"

She nodded. "They made a promise, and now they're backing out."

I started to ask what the hell the two of them were talking about, but Evan cut me off again.

"I've suggested to her," he said, "that maybe her story isn't entirely accurate. But she insists that it is. So I'm asking all of you, is that the way it happened?"

So this, I thought, was how Evan would be able to wake up in the morning. How he'd decided to square his felon friends with his professional obligations. Evidently, he was willing to get his hands dirty, but only if his sensitive ears remained ignorant.

I looked at Nolan, at Jeffrey. Nobody said a word.

"Very well," Evan said. "Then shall we move on from here?"

Move on from *where*? I was thinking, when Evan said to Marie, "Go on. Tell them what you want."

Marie looked at me and shrugged. "Two million."

Sleepy, confused, I asked her what she meant.

"That's how much I want." She looked at each of us. "Two million dollars, for my time. And for keeping quiet about . . . everything."

Nolan let out a short, mean laugh.

"You're the victim here," I reminded her. "Don't become the criminal."

"But I want two million dollars."

"Shut up," Nolan said.

"You shut up," she shot back. "I'm not sure any of you people should be giving advice, okay? You aren't exactly role models."

"We're trying to help you," I said.

She waved me aside with the back of her hand. "I don't need your help. Me and your friend Evan had a nice talk, and now I know what needs to happen. You guys are going to pay me two million dollars. Otherwise, I change my story. I walk into the police station and I tell them that you've done something horrible and dirty. That the three of you kidnapped me and locked me up and threatened to kill me. And *you*"—she nodded to Nolan—"I'll tell them that you *tried* to kill me."

He shook his head. "I didn't."

"Well, you could've fooled me. And now you're going to pay. All of you. Any questions?"

I had two million of them but was shocked into silence. We all were.

"Evan," I said, "help us out here."

"You have some fucking nerve." Evan's face looked reddened and hard. "Let me remind you that you called me. Not some local attorney, not the police. You called me, your friend Evan. Well, first of all, I'm not your friend anymore, and after today I don't ever want to hear from any of you again. Second, I'm a deal maker. That's my job. I make deals. And you knew that when you tracked me down and demanded I fly across the whole goddamn country through a goddamn snowstorm to be here." He looked around the studio and shook his head in disgust. "The truth is, I think you're a coward, Will. I think you're all cowards. And I think this young lady is being terribly foolish. You said it right—she's

194

the victim. So do I think she's doing the right thing? Fuck, no. But she's made you an offer. She's willing to deal. So you should all consider yourself damn lucky, and either put up or shut up."

We were all quiet for a while. It was Jeffrey who finally spoke. "To begin with," he said calmly, politely, "we don't have anywhere close to that kind of money."

And suddenly we were considering it.

Marie shrugged again. "I don't care. Come up with it."

She was fearless. I had to give her that. "You don't understand," I said. "You're asking something of us that we can't give." I had ironic visions of robbing banks. Of kidnapping some other girl for ransom in order to pay for this one.

She sighed. "I thought maybe you all didn't want to spend your lives in prison. Your friend Evan thought so, too. But I guess we were wrong." And with that, she walked quickly to the exit.

She was halfway out the door when Nolan said: "Wait."

CHAPTER 23

AFTER NOLAN'S MOTHER DIED, his father had sued her original doctor, the one who'd failed to diagnose her cancer. The suit settled out of court for $1.5 million. Nolan had never mentioned this to me before now. Or that when his father had died last year from a massive heart attack, all the money had gone to him. He'd invested half a million for his retirement. The other million he had just begun to spend on his senatorial campaign.

"See that?" Marie said. "We're almost there already."

And the rest of us? Cynthia and I had close to eight thousand in a savings account, plus another two thousand in a checking account.

Jeffrey's investments, once worth a fortune, now totaled slightly under a hundred thousand dollars.

"And I'm sure you can all sell some stuff if you need to," Marie said. "I'll give you until Friday."

"No," Nolan said. "I don't like this. How do we know you won't take the money and then go to the police anyway?"

"You don't," she said. "That's a chance you'll have to take."

"No, it isn't. Get the fuck out of here," Nolan said. "Go on. Turn us in."

Did he mean it? Was he ready to lose everything now, when all that stood in our way was money?

Marie didn't leave. She stood there a minute watching Nolan, and then she clenched and unclenched her fists, and her face seemed to relax a little. I thought she might be about to lower her demand to something halfway reasonable.

She said, "Sixteen fifteen." We waited for her to explain. "My nana's assisted living facility. Timber Cove. That's her room number."

"I don't know what you're telling us," Nolan said.

"Her name is Emily Cole," she went on, as if that clarified everything.

"Again," Nolan said, "I don't know—"

"Yes, you do. You know exactly. If I ever blab, you have my permission to visit her. In room one six one five." She said the numbers slowly, so we'd remember. And in case there was any doubt what we were talking about, she added, "She's on oxygen."

Before writing up the agreement, Evan insisted that Marie leave the studio in case she felt under any duress or threat.

"If you really mean to go through with this," he instructed her, "then come back in a half hour. We'll be waiting for you."

Next he was walking her to the recording room door, and then he was opening it for her, and this time the door closed behind her and she was gone.

Evan returned alone. "This is the sleaziest thing I've ever heard of. The whole thing fills me with unhappiness."

Although I respected Evan, I couldn't help thinking, *You weren't there.* So easy to judge when he wasn't there, in that car, with Jeffrey yelling at me to drive. I really had thought somebody was dying. Had Evan been behind the wheel, what would he have done? Sat there in the Milk-n-Bread parking lot and sorted out the confusion?

No. When your friend shouts at you to drive, you drive. You step on the gas. And what about the moment he figured out there was no injury? Would he have stopped then? Maybe. Or maybe he'd have hesitated for just an instant with the knowledge that somehow his entire life had become wrapped up in what he did in those next few seconds. The thought would be unavoidable. So he thinks. He hesitates—just for an instant. But when you're behind the wheel, a couple of seconds is a very long time. Long enough to be down a road you never imagined taking.

You weren't there, I wanted to say again. Instead, I looked at my watch and prepared for the longest half hour of my life.

Less than five minutes later, she was back.

"So can we pretend a half hour has passed?" she asked. "I'd really like to get this show on the road."

In addition to drawing up a contract, Evan wanted a recorded statement from Marie. I set up a microphone and fed a roll of blank tape into the reel. Marie stood in front of the microphone and began to read what Evan had written for her:

My name is Marie Craft, and today is Sunday, April 25, 2004. Nolan Albright, Will Walker, and Jeffrey Hocks have been working with me to record music at Snakepit Recording Studio. They promised me a recording contract. However, I am now told that such contract will not be forthcoming. As compensation for my time, and for termination of the verbal agreement that we would be making a record together, I am accepting their payment of two million dollars. This payment is contingent upon my remaining forever silent about everything having to do with the recording contract, its termination, my whereabouts this past weekend, the source of the two million dollars, and this agreement itself. This agreement has been signed by all parties, and this statement has been made by me voluntarily, under no duress or threat.

198

She could always change her story, of course. She could go to the police, or claim she was pressured into signing something that wasn't true. But if she did any of those things, it would be hard for her to explain away the two-million-dollar wire into her checking account.

We listened back to the tape. Then each of us signed one of the four copies of the contract that Evan had handwritten. We each were to take a copy and deposit it in a safety-deposit box that nobody else had access to. Marie folded up her copy and stuck it in her back pocket like it was a grocery list.

Monday morning, she would call me at the studio with her checking-account number and wiring instructions. Evan told me to tape-record that call—additional evidence of our mutual agreement—and put it into my safety-deposit box along with the contract. Nolan and Jeffrey would wire their shares of the money to me by the end of day on Thursday. By noon on Friday, I would wire the entire two million to Marie.

We actually shook hands like business partners. And without another word, she left.

The sound of her fading footfalls filled me with relief, but new anxieties were already building. Like being not only a felon but also flat broke. We all were. And I sensed that in spite of the agreement we'd all reached, or maybe because of it, I'd never sleep soundly again for fear of being awakened in the night by a heavy fist on my front door.

Her footfalls continued to diminish, and then all trace of her was gone. We waited for the second hand on my watch to circle five times. I rewound the tape, put it back in its case, and shut off the console and studio lights. Then we walked down that same hallway and outside to the world from which we'd removed ourselves some forty hours earlier.

Outside, the sun shone obscenely. I made a visor with my hand

and looked left and right down Lincoln Avenue. Cars passed, a few pedestrians were out for a Sunday stroll, but she was nowhere in sight. Was she in some nearby building calling for a cab? Calling the cops? Had she already flagged down a passing squad car?

Squinting under the hot light, we walked to my car. A piece of paper flapped underneath the windshield wiper. An advertisement for a new dry cleaner. I pocketed the flyer. Jeffrey and Nolan got in. Evan went to his rental car. He'd follow us home.

I started the engine and drove. Nolan sat beside me; on his lap was the tape container that on Monday I would put into my safety-deposit box.

We were silent the whole way, each of us thinking about the cars we'd sell this week, the credit cards we'd max out, the various means by which we would raise, before Friday, the few hundred thousand dollars that we were short. We looked out our windows as if we were lifelong prisoners who'd sprung free to find that the outside was only a larger version of the inside.

We played golf.

First, though, we ate most of the food in my refrigerator. Then we changed into shorts and collared shirts, loaded our clubs into my car, and headed out to the course. Should it ever come to our needing an alibi, at least some people would have seen us out there playing. And while the timing wasn't exactly right—Marie was free by then, obviously—we hoped that our golfing might imply innocence. Would kidnappers hit the links so soon after committing their crime?

But also, we didn't know what else to do with ourselves.

The drive out to the Kittatinny Mountains took us into the less populated part of New Jersey. The peaceful part. There, the afternoon air felt soft and summery, and the sun cast sharp shadows as we bounced our carts along the narrow fairways, contemplating our next shot. The course was as advertised— completely secluded, with beautiful sloping fairways and speedy greens. We spent the next four hours discussing club selection, the prior hole, the next hole. I shared a cart with Jeffrey, and when the girl came around on her beverage cart, we bought sodas and hot dogs.

I wasn't too surprised that Evan decided to join us. He might have despised us now, but we had been friends for thirteen years— a long time—and I supposed he preferred his last image of us to be on the golf course, where we were at our least complicated, our most innocent.

Jeffrey sipped his soda and said it tasted better than the sodas in California.

"I think the carbonation's different," he speculated.

Evan asked, "Are we playing 'winter rules'?" when his ball got stuck in a fairway's soggy spot.

I was struck by how easy it was for us to play this game to- gether, to act as if nothing were any different from the last time we were all together.

Only Nolan was quiet. Contemplative. I wasn't sure how he'd play at all with his injury, but he did, for a while. Rather than ride in Evan's cart, he preferred to walk the fairways alone. After the ninth hole he bought a soda and sat by himself on a bench, away from us. Somehow I knew it wasn't his ear that made him stop. I imagined he must be thinking about his return to Missouri in the morning, to whatever was left of his campaign.

He walked the second nine holes with us, hitting only the oc- casional shot, sometimes just looking out into the woods. For the rest of us, though, it could've been any Sunday of golf.

My short game was off, but my drives were better than usual.

When Evan sank a twenty-foot putt, he couldn't stop his mouth from curling into a smile.

A passing shower dropped warm, light rain on us for ten minutes and then stopped.

A beaver scrambled across the fairway. Later on, two deer stood and looked at us before loping off into the woods.

And while we were standing at the tee box on the eighteenth hole, the afternoon winds having picked up a little, we saw not one but three eagles overhead, riding the currents of spring air. We stopped what we were doing to watch them climb and dip and climb again, until finally they flew over the mountain ridge and were out of sight.

After putting the last hole, we all shook hands and said, "Good round."

Back at the cart return, the kid wiping down our clubs with a towel smiled and asked, "Did you gentlemen have fun today?"

CHAPTER 24

E VAN LEFT MY HOUSE at six thirty with Jeffrey in the rental car. He would drop Jeffrey at Newark Airport and return the car there, then take a cab back to Manhattan. Nolan's flight wasn't until noon the next day, so I suggested he spend the night at the house. He'd said very little since we left the studio hours earlier. I didn't know if he'd want to stay over, and I wasn't sure I wanted him to. But Cynthia wasn't due back until midmorning tomorrow, and the thought of spending the night in the house alone with my thoughts seemed almost unbearable.

"Sure," he said. "I'll stay."

The afternoon breeze had stilled, and it was becoming a pleasant evening. Nolan decided to go for a run while I showered. "I can't remember the last time I skipped two days," he said.

"What about your head?" I asked.

He shrugged. "It'll be a good test. See if it stays attached."

I started a pot of coffee and went into the bathroom. A half hour later, I emerged clean and shaved and feeling half alive. And ravenous. I put on a pair of jeans and a T-shirt and ordered a large pizza for delivery.

I poured myself a cup of coffee, flopped onto the sofa in the living room, and turned on the television. I flipped the channels, looking for special news segments, interrupted programs. This is how I'll watch TV from now on, I thought. But soon I settled on a baseball game, and for a while I watched it, until Nolan came through the front door covered in sweat.

"Good run?" I asked.

"I'm getting too old to skip days," he said. "This was exactly what I needed." He wiped his face with his T-shirt. "Except, now I'm starving."

"Pizza's already on the way—sausage and peppers."

"Pizza?" He shook his head. "We can do better than pizza. Call them back. Cancel the order."

"You have something better in mind?"

"As a matter of fact, I do." He smiled. "What's the best restaurant in town?"

"Why?"

"Because we're going there. My treat." He went into the kitchen and returned a minute later with a glass of water. "I think you and I need to have a first-class dinner."

"You sure about that?"

"Cancel the damn pizza, Will." He chugged the rest of the water and went to put the glass in the sink. "I'm going to take a shower. Afterward, maybe you can help me change this damn bandage. In the meantime, make reservations. And don't be cheap about it."

While Nolan took a shower, I called the pizzeria, and then went online to see if La Cachette was open on Sundays. I'd never eaten there before—way too pricey—but it wasn't far away, and I'd read somewhere that it was the governor's favorite restaurant.

• • •

204

Our table was by the window of the converted Victorian mansion. When we were seated, and had ordered a bottle of wine and the special fruit and aged-cheese appetizer, Nolan said, "So that sound board, in the studio. You said it's getting replaced?"

"In a couple of months. That's the plan, anyway."

"So what'll make the new one better than the old one?"

He really seemed interested. Maybe this was a politician's trick, but I didn't think so. More likely, the trick was that for some people, being interested in the details of others' lives wasn't a trick.

"Well," I said, "for one thing, the old console is just plain busted. Certain tracks don't work at all, or they're noisy, or unpredictable. But the main difference is that the new one will be digital."

"Everything's going digital now, it seems."

"Just about. It used to be that digital recording didn't sound very good. But now the sampling rates are so high, it's nearly impossible to tell the difference between digital and analog."

"So why do it?"

"Easier editing, easier backup . . . basically, a lot more flexibility because you're dealing with files of data rather than tape."

"But you'll have to learn the new console. Will that be hard?"

"Not too hard," I said. "The basic principles are the same."

"I'll bet you're good at your job," he said.

I thought about it a minute. "I am. It isn't glamorous work. But I think I make the bands I work with sound better."

A basket of bread had come, and we each took a piece.

"I really like this restaurant," he said, looking around. "Good choice. You don't find many French restaurants in Missouri."

I'd nearly finished my glass of wine. I felt soothed by it, and by the clink of silverware against fine dishes and the quiet conversations going on at the other tables. People around us seemed to be enjoying their meals, their wine, one another's company. Checks lay unpaid on tables while cups of coffee got refilled and wide slices of pie were slowly chipped away at. A world of worry and hurt waited outside, beyond the valet-parked lot, and nobody seemed in a rush to get there. Nolan had been right. We needed this. I refilled my glass.

"Do you remember," he was saying, "when you tried to speak French to that girl in our dorm freshman year?"

Of course I remembered. Just as I remembered Nolan—or Evan or Jeffrey—reminding me about it any number of times over the years. Three evenings ago this would have bothered me, but now I felt glad for this ready-made role I could step into, this simpler version of myself that I could inhabit.

"Sandy," I said.

"*Sandy*, of course." He laughed. "The girl whose goat you loved. Tell me again what it was in French?"

I sighed. "*J'aime votre chèvre.*"

He laughed some more. "*Sandy, I love your goat.* How can you beat that?"

I'd thought *chèvre* meant hair. I'd only taken a few weeks of French.

He finished his glass of wine and poured another. "Well, nobody could blame you for trying. You weren't the only nineteen-year-old in love with Sandy and her long blonde goat."

"I was only eighteen," I said.

Youth. The ultimate excuse. Let me be eighteen again! I hadn't much liked it at the time. But never mind. Let me try again—eighteen, or fifteen, or five—so I could learn everything all over and maybe this time get it right.

We ate, and we drank, and we were funny and charming. Except for the extraordinary bill, it felt almost like old times.

The waiter cleared off the table, brushed the crumbs from the tablecloth, and returned with menus for dessert and after-dinner drinks.

I was full from all the courses that seemed to keep coming and waved off the dessert menu. "Just coffee for me."

"Have you ever tried vintage port?" Nolan asked me. And before I could answer, he had ordered a glass for each of us. Then we both ordered dessert to go with it.

We didn't leave the restaurant until after ten. By then I was fairly drunk. By the time the check came, I was having trouble keeping my eyes open. The port had gone down easy, and the coffee was warm and soothing.

Nolan offered to drive us home, and I gladly handed over the keys. Several times I felt myself nodding off in the car. Walking into the house, my limbs felt unimaginably heavy. There was a message from Cynthia on the machine. *Just checking in. Looking forward to seeing you tomorrow. Call if it's not too late.*

I helped Nolan open the futon in the living room and got some sheets and pillows from the linen closet.

"I can take it from here, chief," he said. "You look beat."

"Yep," I said, already imagining how good the bed would feel.

"You'd mentioned on Friday a bottle of Scotch. Do you mind if I . . ."

"In the cabinet over the refrigerator. Help yourself."

"You're probably too tired for one more."

"You could say that." I was heading toward the bathroom to brush my teeth, but on the way I stopped. "I want to thank you for dinner. I really enjoyed it."

He smiled. "So did I."

"I don't know what's going to happen to us. You know, tomorrow or whenever. But I want you to know that this was really . . . good. It was a good thing to do."

"I feel the same way," he said. "It really was a perfect dinner."

I yawned, and hoped that when I lay in bed, the room wouldn't spin. "Well, it's getting late. So I think I'm going to turn in. If you need any extra blankets or anything—"

"I'll be fine. Go to bed. I might just have one more drink. Watch a little TV. Let me know if the volume's too loud."

"I'm sure it won't be. I'm really tired. Well, good night."

"Good night," he said.

I lay in bed, glad to see that the walls and ceiling were holding in place, and from the phone on my bedside table I dialed Cynthia's cell. Trying to sound reasonably sober, I left a message on her voicemail: *It's me, golf was fun, I'm going to bed, can't wait to see you tomorrow. Oh, and if you need me, call the house—my cell still isn't working.*

I had her sister's home number memorized, but they all went to sleep early and I didn't want to wake anybody.

I shut off the light and lay on my back. It was almost eleven. Cynthia was probably in bed right now, too. Reading a book, maybe. Or more likely, the kids had worn her out and she was asleep.

I was fairly certain that when she came home tomorrow, I'd tell her exactly how I'd spent the last three days. I didn't see how we could live the rest of our lives with such a profound secret between us. So I knew I ought to have felt dread lying there, staring into the darkness. But I didn't. While I didn't expect Cynthia ever to understand the things I had done, I had the feeling that she'd find a way to forgive me and to accept what had happened. Our marriage would survive.

I couldn't account, exactly, for my optimism. Yet I felt it. Maybe it was that hastily drawn-up contract with Marie. I didn't want my friends to lose all their money—and I didn't want to lose all mine, either—but I couldn't help feeling relieved by

Marie's reckless, greedy demand. It showed tremendous nerve, and it meant that maybe we hadn't traumatized her quite as badly as I'd thought.

But ultimately all that mattered was that we had let her go, just as we said we would. Two days too late? Of course. But I'd protected her. I'd kept my word, and now she was free—to collect the money, to move her grandmother into a better nursing home, or not. Free to turn us in, if that's what she decided to do. Free to do whatever the hell she wanted.

And I felt optimistic about that, too. Because I was pretty sure that she'd decide to live up to her end of the bargain. It was just like Nolan had said. She was one of us. She'd take the money and leave us alone. She'd keep her word, same as we would.

A train rumbled quietly several miles off in the distance. Ever since childhood, this had been a peaceful sound to me. I'd lie in bed and hear that deep rumble and imagine all the people on the train heading off to follow their dreams.

I took a sip of water from the glass on the bedside table, turned my pillow over to the cool side, and settled back down.

This was what I concluded: I had acted badly, but not so badly that I felt like a stranger to myself. Not so badly, I hoped, that I wouldn't be able to sleep at night.

And to prove it, I closed my eyes and went to sleep.

CHAPTER 25

M OVEMENT IN THE DARK bedroom. Something coming quickly toward me.

I gasped.

"Relax, it's only me," Nolan whispered. My heart whacked against my ribs.

"What's wrong? What time is it?"

"Put on some clothes and meet me by the front door. Dark clothes. And don't turn on any lights." Before I could ask him more, he left the bedroom.

I looked at the digital clock on my nightstand: 2:13 AM. I put on sweatpants and a T-shirt, used the restroom, and went to the front hallway. Nolan was waiting for me. He had on jeans and a black T-shirt. His shoes were the black loafers he'd been wearing all weekend.

"I need you," he said, "to run an errand with me. We won't be gone long. Leave all the lights off. Come on, we're wasting time." He opened the front door and waved me ahead of him.

"Wait." I was still feeling disoriented from being awakened so suddenly. "What's this about?"

"There isn't time. Just come on."

"I need to lock up."

He held up a set of keys—mine—and handed them over. I locked the front door behind us and stepped down onto the front walkway.

The air had cooled considerably since dinner. My car was in the driveway, where Nolan had parked it earlier. He motioned me toward the driver's seat.

"You drive," he whispered.

"Where?"

"I'll tell you when we're in the car."

When we were seated, doors closed, he said, "You were telling me the other day about that place you used to hike. Up in the mountains. Back in high school."

"What?" I realized that I was probably still a little intoxicated. "Yeah, that's right. So . . ."

"So that's where I need you to take me."

"Now?"

"Yes, now. Up in the mountains. Can you find it?"

"It's been years. I don't even know if those trails still exist."

"But you'd know where it is."

"Nolan, it's two in the morning. What's going on?"

He shook his head. "Sorry, Will. For your own good, I'm going to have to decline."

"Well, if you aren't going to tell me . . ." I reached for the door handle.

"*Please.*" He put a hand on my arm. Despite the cold, he was sweating. "I know it's a strange request. But I spent almost two million dollars today. I think I'm entitled to a favor. So please—do me this simple favor. Take me to the hiking trail."

I started the engine and backed out of the driveway. Nolan apologized for ruining my night's sleep. When I didn't respond, he had nothing else to say.

Every so often, a session at the studio would run late into the night, and I always found it peaceful driving the streets that, any other time of day, were jammed with angry motorists. We drove these local roads that I'd come to know so well, then took the highway northwest through rolling hills. The sky darkened, the hills grew larger. After thirty miles or so the car's engine began to work hard as we rose more steeply into the Kittatinny Mountains, well past the turnoff for the golf course we'd played earlier that day.

At the town of Colesville, I exited the highway and, not having made this drive in over a decade, hoped that my instincts would push me in the right direction. We wound round the narrow road that cut through dense woods, the headlights revealing sharp curves seconds before we reached them. It seemed likely that where there had once been forest there would now be a shopping mall or a multiplex. But no. These hills were still remote, still populated only by trees and rocks and dirt. When I'd first left the city for the suburbs, I'd been amazed by the dark night sky. I had forgotten about this. This was real darkness.

The road curved sharply back and forth up one side of a mountain, then along a ridge and down again. At this time of night, no other cars were on the road. Nor were there buildings, road signs, or even mile markers. I wasn't sure how far to go. But then without even remembering which landmark to look for, we came upon the small green sign telling us we'd just entered the town of Grafton. I began to look for the next left turn, which, if I remembered correctly, would take us close to the trail.

After turning left, the road cut steeply downhill, narrowed, and after about a mile turned to gravel. Then, abruptly, it ended. No cars, no streetlights, no houses. Not even a sign for the trail. The trailhead was still eight or ten miles down the road from where we'd turned off. But my friends and I had liked to enter

212

here, because the Boy Scouts and day hikers never made it this far along the trail.

"Cut the lights and the engine," Nolan said.

"Tell me first what's going on."

"Cut the engine and I'll show you."

We got out of the car. Clouds had moved in since dinner, and there were no stars. Just a dull reminder of the moon behind a canvas of clouds. The elevation of these mountains wasn't much, fifteen hundred feet maybe, but the wind was strong here, the air cold. It was a raw night best spent indoors, not out here. Not when you've run out of the house without even a jacket or sweatshirt. I shivered.

"I want you to know," Nolan said, "that I'd have done this alone if I thought there was any way that I could. Okay, open the trunk."

The word "trunk" snapped me awake and sobered me up. Something was in the trunk. And I had driven it here.

I shook my head no.

"Open it, Will." When I didn't move, he said, "Then give me the keys." He took them from me.

A moment later, the trunk was open, and I was looking in. I don't know exactly what I expected to see, but I was surprised at first. And, for a moment, relieved.

"That's from the studio," I said.

"I know."

I was trying to piece together a coherent story as to why Nolan would sneak out of the house while I slept, let himself into the studio with my keys, and steal the canvas sack filled with drum hardware.

As I thought about this, he opened the back door and removed the shovel. It was mine, from the garage. The one I used to dig our garden plot. That was when my surprise turned to understanding, and then to revulsion.

213

While I'd been sleeping, Nolan had been busy.

My legs nearly gave out from under me. "You killed her."

After everything we'd been through, he'd gone and killed her anyway. It made no sense.

Nolan shook his head. "No—is that what you . . . no. Will, I didn't."

"You did."

"I swear, I didn't."

"Then what—"

"How about you don't ask me that, okay? Let me do you that favor. Just shut up, take an end, help me carry this awhile, and don't ask me a single thing. We'll do this, then we'll drive home, you'll go back to bed, and when you wake up it'll be tomorrow. Let's do it exactly like that, okay?"

"So you didn't . . . hurt her?"

"It isn't a body, Will. I promise. Now take an end."

I looked into the trunk again. It was just a bag from my recording studio. Drum hardware. Cymbal stands and snare-drum stands and the metal legs of floor toms. It didn't need to make sense.

I began to lift an end of the bag out of the trunk.

It was very heavy, no surprise. But silent. Metal drum equipment would rattle.

Although we were alone, I wanted to be safely in the woods before saying another word. We hauled the bag out of the car. I gripped the handle at one end of the bag with both my hands. Nolan needed only one hand. With the other, he carried the shovel. We walked sideways, the bag swaying between us. Once I could no longer see the car or the road, I told Nolan to set the bag down.

We'd barely gone a hundred feet, but I was down on my haunches sucking wind.

"You're lying." Frigid air stung my throat. "How could you? We had an agreement. You didn't even give her a chance."

"Listen to me. Marie is perfectly fine. Now please, I'm begging you—"

"No. Not until you explain."

"Goddamn it, Will . . ." He threw down the shovel. "Can't you see I'm trying to do you a favor?" He stared at me. I stared back. We waited while the tops of trees bent in the wind. And when he saw that I wasn't going to budge or even blink until hearing the truth, he knelt down beside me and his voice softened. "He saw us. He saw *her*."

At first I thought he was talking about Joey, but then I understood.

"He was only a panhandler," I said. "He wouldn't have put anything together."

"He *saw* her, Will. There was no choice."

"There's always a choice."

"It was our only loose end. I had to do it. For all of us. Because nobody else would have."

He'd come to this decision, no doubt, during his late afternoon run. While I'd been showering, working to scrub every bit of the weekend's filth from my body, Nolan had been planning a murder. And then he'd dined with me, and gotten himself drunk, and then he'd gone and done it.

"Good lord," I said.

"Don't 'good lord' me. I understand your horror. It's horrible. Don't you think I know that? But we created the horror. The moment we drove away with that girl in your car, somebody was going to die. All we're doing now is seeing it through. This"—he looked down at the bag—"is the endgame."

"Don't call it a game," I said.

215

He watched me, maybe waiting to see if I'd bolt back to the car. "Nobody saw me do it. And nobody's going to miss him. It's done." He stood up, brushed dirt off his jeans. Picked up the shovel from the ground. "So I'll ask you again. Please, Will, take an end, and let's finish this already so that we can leave here and go home to bed and pretend this was all a nightmare."

We walked. But it wasn't easy.

The spot where we'd parked the car was a tenth of a mile from the trail. As seventeen-year-olds lugging a case of beer, we'd had no problem. Now, shrubs and vines and lack of light, as well as the weight of our load, kept us moving slowly, the bag's handle carving into my tightly gripped palms. We stepped uneasily over the hilly ground. Several times we almost walked right off the trail, which was hidden underneath a layer of wet, decaying leaves.

We took breaks every few hundred feet, and we massaged our palms, and then we walked again.

I wondered what the man's name was. I'd never asked. And I wondered other things: where Nolan had done it. And how. And what he'd felt at the exact moment it was happening. But I wasn't going to ask, because I didn't really want to know. Nor was there any need to satisfy my morbid curiosity, because I was certain that Nolan had covered his tracks. His epitaph someday would read: *Nolan Albright. He covered his tracks.*

We followed the trail deeper into the woods. It was very difficult going. The trail was too narrow for us to walk side by side. So we had to walk practically sideways, single file, Nolan ahead of me, the bag between us. The only sound was the uneven rhythm of our footfalls on the trail, punctuated by the snapping of a twig or the rolling of a rock kicked accidentally.

After about thirty minutes, Nolan stopped walking and looked around. By then our eyes had adjusted somewhat. We'd been walking so slowly, we probably hadn't gone more than a mile. But this section of the forest looked untouched and particularly dense.

"This will do," he said. "Let's head off the trail now."

"Not yet," I said.

Yes, we were about as far from civilization as one could get in New Jersey. Yes, my hands and arms were burning, and I wanted nothing more than to stop. I was desperate for it. But by now I had a destination in mind, and I was pretty sure we could find it if we kept walking.

CHAPTER 26

T HE CAVE WAS FARTHER than I'd remembered.
For nearly another hour we traveled at a glacial pace through the unchanging, leafless forest. Trees were beginning to bud. Soon they would distinguish themselves. At this time of night, though, everything about the landscape looked dead and endlessly repetitive. Up a slope. Down a slope. More trees. More walking. Hands burning. Muscles straining. My thigh ached from where the bag rubbed against it with each step. An ankle nearly twisted from a carelessly placed shoe.

After several thousand steps the hill to the left of the trail began to rise—first gradually, then steeply—and became rocky. The trail ran along the base of the hillside for maybe another tenth of a mile, and then curved away from it.

"This way," I said, when the trail began to curve. We carried the bag off the trail and then away from it for several hundred feet, and when we reached the rocky wall we set it down.

We had first found the small cave, a couple of friends and I, back in high school. The entrance was behind several large boulders and not visible from the trail, but we'd been horsing around, trying to climb the rocky wall, and had stumbled upon it. We'd only ever gone inside that one time. We'd been disappointed. It wasn't a real cave so much as a small chamber caused by the way several large boulders jutted out slightly from the rest of the wall, forming a sort of triangle.

It didn't take me long to find the entrance. I ran back to Nolan, and we carried the bag inside.

The chamber was no larger than a small bedroom. About half of it was covered by rock, and the other half looked up into the sky. It wasn't much darker than the rest of the woods. But if we were looking for a secluded place, somewhere nobody would ever find, this was it.

"You're right," Nolan said. "This is a better spot." He looked around some more, inspecting the place. "Still, one of us should gather up some rocks and branches to cover the hole when we're done. Otherwise the ground is going to look freshly dug up."

"You do it," I found myself saying, despite my aching body. "I want to dig."

"Okay," he said, and handed me the shovel. "Let me know when it's my turn."

When he left the chamber, I tried to read my watch, tilting it until the face was readable. Four fifteen. During the last part of our walk I could see increasingly well. Probably just my eyes adjusting. And the moonlight glowing stronger through the thinning clouds. But morning was coming, and sooner than we'd like. By the time the sun came up, we had better be home.

I heaved the shovel into the ground, and my wrists nearly exploded from the vibration.

Stone! I cursed my stupidity. I hadn't considered that the ground at the base of a rock wall might well be composed of rock.

"Nolan!" I whispered.

No response.

219

I thought about going to find him. But first I tried another spot in the ground, and, to my relief, the blade cut solidly into dirt. A few more tests, and I concluded that, no, the floor wasn't mainly rock. At least not near the surface. I'd been unlucky the first time. And so I began to dig. It did me some good, the physical labor. I didn't pace myself at all and was out of breath almost immediately. Good. Throwing myself into the hard job of moving earth, I was able to keep myself from thinking too hard about the reason I was here.

Each time I rammed the shovel into the ground, I prepared myself for the inevitable layer of rock. But each time I came up with dirt, I felt a little closer to going home.

I heard Nolan return a few times, dropping branches and rocks outside the cave. Then he came inside and asked if he could take a turn. By then a hole was already taking shape at my feet, and a heap of wet dirt was growing beside me.

"No," I said. My face felt gritty from sweat and dirt. "I'll keep going."

"You sure?" he asked.

My answer was another shovelful of dirt. He left me alone without another word.

My back began to ache like it did whenever I shoveled snow. I acknowledged the pain with indifference, but I didn't quit or even slow down. The hole was growing. Soon this would be over. The only thing that could stop me, I believed, was a layer of rock. Or maybe a thick, thick root.

First, what I see in dreams: the bag beside me moving almost imperceptibly in the moonlight. So slightly, I wonder if it's only shadows paying tricks. Or the defective vision of someone who's been shoveling dirt too long. I resume my digging, but then I hear a slow zippering sound. Fascinated, I watch as the bag unzips an inch, then two, then three. First I'm hit with the rotting stench of a thousand corpses. Then a finger slides out. Sometimes it's the stiff, hairy finger of an aging panhandler. Other times it's a young, feminine finger, the nail carefully polished, and I know right away that it's Cynthia in the bag—badly hurt, but not dead. Sometimes it's one finger; sometimes it's two or three. When that happens, the diamond in her engagement ring reflects the moonlight.

And then the nearly deceased speak to me. They ask simple questions, the only ones that matter.

What have I done wrong?

I tell them they've done nothing wrong. I try to explain that I never meant for any of this to happen. I just kept believing we could fix our mistakes without anyone getting hurt.

Must I die?

Yes. You must.

But you can change your mind.

I'm sorry. There's nothing to be done.

But you could if you wanted to.

What makes you think I can be a hero now, when I couldn't do it two days ago when all I had to do was stop a car?

Not a hero. Just a human being.

I'm sorry.

Then you must be the devil.

I don't think I am. But I suppose it's possible.

Every so often, in the dream, I'll surprise myself. Yes, I see your point, I'll say, and unzip the bag. And whoever it is inside will emerge as if from a cocoon, whole again, and I'll feel a joy unlike anything I've ever felt in waking life. But when the dream takes this course, eventually I realize that I'm dreaming, and that this dream, as beautiful as it is, hasn't been worth it, because now I'll have to wake up. But I don't wake up. When the dream shoots off in this joyous direction, it always repeats and repeats until eventually it gets back on track and the worst thing happens.

I don't know why these dreams always include the sound of the bag unzipping. It isn't what happened out in the woods that night. The sound I heard was different.

Soft, breathy, lasting about three seconds. A sound like the last moments of an air mattress deflating. Then it stopped.

I froze. Wondered if I'd imagined it. Or heard a gust of wind, made strange by the acoustics in this rocky chamber.

It hadn't sounded like the wind, though. It sounded like a sigh of resignation, an animal's last gasp. Maybe even a blissful utterance, an unconscious response to a final dream of shimmering light. But one thing was sure: It was a sign of life.

Sometimes the dream will begin much earlier, back at the house in Newfield. Sitting on the back deck with Cynthia on a sunny late afternoon drinking iced tea. Or it will begin at a gig. I'm a drummer again, living in New York City and playing with High Noon, and Gwen is playing the bass, and everyone I've ever loved is there in the audience watching, cheering me on, and I feel so glad to be making music again that I can't help myself from sobbing.

But no matter where the dream starts, or how often it repeats, it always ends exactly the same way: in the cave, with the bag slowly opening.

And then—always—the shovel.

This is where my nightmare and my waking world collide.

I held perfectly still, staring at the bag and listening. I stared and listened and prayed that my ears had played a trick on me. Then I heard it again. Unmistakable. A human breath. My eyes widened, and my skin crawled, and my heart—already racing—lurched crazily. For an instant my whole life nearly forked differently as I imagined the cold days of my future warmed by the knowledge of this one decent thing I'd done. But I hadn't done it—not yet, not ever—and then the instant was over, and what I saw was how this canvas bag in front of me was all that lay between me and the rest of my life, and I raised the shovel and brought it down and began to smash the bag as hard as I could. Again and again and again. I couldn't begin to count the number of times. And I wasn't only hitting the bag, I was stabbing it with the shovel's sharp point. I was massacring it. I was no longer Will Walker—I was an animal in the woods and I was making this other animal go away. Nothing would be left when I was done. I was going to turn the contents of that bag to soup.

I don't know how much time passed, but when Nolan returned I was sitting on the ground, hands tucked into my armpits, shivering because my sweat had turned cold, the shovel lying beside me in the dirt.

I let him dig awhile.

CHAPTER 27

THREE YEARS PASSED BEFORE I saw any of them again.
Nolan lost the election. Would the extra money for his campaign have made a difference? It's anyone's guess. The 2004 election was more a referendum on George W. Bush than anything else, and Nolan was a Democrat running in a Republican state with gay marriage on the ballot. From the news stories I read online, he seemed to have fought a good fight. But how could his heart have been in it? He lost by eight percentage points and, following his concession speech, dropped out of the news, relegated by an unforgiving political machine to the status of burned-out firecracker. Not a has-been, but an almost-was. I don't know what he's doing now. I haven't asked.

Evan made partner. I read this in the "Class Notes" section of the *Princeton Alumni Weekly*. I assume his life now is much as it was before he made partner, except there is more of everything: more money, more hours, more responsibility, more anxiety. I thought briefly about sending him a congratulatory e-mail, but then thought better of it. There was no way he'd want to hear from me.

Nor did I correspond with Jeffrey. A couple of times he e-mailed me—short, polite messages hoping that Cynthia and I were well. I never replied, and in time his messages stopped. Despite the kidnapping, I didn't resent him. In fact, I felt bad for him. He'd come to my town battered and bruised, and left with nothing. That saddened me, but not enough to communicate with him ever again.

Without my money or anyone else's—the two million got wired exactly as we'd all agreed—Long-Shot Records got put on indefinite hold. To avoid thinking too hard about what had happened, I started spending long hours in the studio. And gradually the unexpected happened: I stopped thinking of the studio as the place where we'd kidnapped a girl and started thinking of it as a place for music again. Joey began to take more notice of my work and to see the studio's full potential. He invested money to refurbish. With digital recording technology exploding, he was able to modernize the place without spending a fortune. Word spread about the studio and the work I did there. We weren't a record label, and we didn't plan to become one, but several indie labels started sending their bands to us to record their albums. My name started appearing on liner notes under *engineer* and, occasionally, *producer*. I started to pull in better money for the studio and some for myself, too—enough that Cynthia and I began to talk about moving out of Newfield and buying a place of our own.

I told Cynthia about the kidnapping. Monday morning I'd called and canceled my session with The Fixtures, telling them I had the flu. When Cynthia came home from Philadelphia late that afternoon, I sat her down at the kitchen table and recounted every detail of the weekend, except that in my rendition, the story ended when Nolan and I came home from dinner and went to sleep. She cried, and I cried, and it would be a lie to say that the next couple of days weren't excruciating. I'd catch her glancing at me, watching me differently from how she'd ever watched me before—struggling, I'm sure, to square these new, unsavory facts with the man she thought she'd always known.

She didn't leave me, though. Didn't call the police. Little by little we discussed what all of this meant in terms of our future, which I hoped to mean our future together. The second evening, I remember, we spoke softly in bed all night, and by the time the morning birds were piercing the darkness, we were all talked out and I felt that we'd be okay. Two years later, eating our first breakfast together in our small fixer-upper in nearby South Orange, our daughter, Kim, running in the grass, I felt surer of it.

And yet nighttime always came. After television or a chapter in a book, after the lights went out and Cynthia rolled onto her side and pulled the blanket up to her chin, and it was just me looking up into the dark, despite my best effort not to, I'd find myself listening for police sirens. For that knock on the front door. It felt as if a radioactive rock were sitting on my nightstand, with a long yet unmistakable half-life. Every month that passed without hearing those sirens or that knock seemed to decrease the likelihood, down the road, of ever hearing them. But the half-life was long, very long.

There was no half-life, however, to my dreams. Each night, I fought sleep for as long as possible. And when I felt myself losing my hold on consciousness, I did so with undiminished terror, because I knew I was about to enter the woods again.

A month ago I got roped into seeing a community theater production of *My Fair Lady*. This was what happened when you bought a house and became a member-of-your-community. You supported the local arts. Our babysitter, a local college student, was singing in the chorus. Cynthia and I went closing weekend (after struggling to find an alternate babysitter). The performance was forgettable, though the woman who played Eliza Doolittle was terrific—she had a belting soprano voice and was a believable actress and strong dancer. It was midway through the second act—when she walked to the front of the stage and the spotlight hit her just right—before I recognized who it was underneath all that theatrical makeup. Of course there was also the cockney accent and the fact that she was now three years older. But at one point she seemed to look right at me, and I nearly bolted out of the theater.

The only thing that kept me in my chair was the knowledge that this wasn't the first time I thought I'd spotted Marie. Far too often she'd be in my periphery, crossing a street or entering an elevator. My head would snap in her direction and she'd be gone or have turned into somebody else, a stranger. The eyes play tricks. I quickly paged through the playbill, and the name of the lead actress—Gloria Diamond—brought me a measure of relief.

After the show, Cynthia went to congratulate our babysitter. I lagged behind, watchful. And just as my wife was chatting with our sitter, Eliza Doolittle emerged from the dressing room. She hadn't seen me, and I quickly ducked behind a door. I peered around it to see her hugging friends and cast members. A tall middle-aged woman approached her and, beaming, said, "You were *won*derful!" They hugged.

Marie's teeth looked huge, framed by the thick, dark lipstick. Her blue eyes blazed, and it only then occurred to me that Gloria Diamond was exactly the sort of stage name that she'd have chosen for herself.

"Thanks, Mom!" she said. The two separated, and when her mother turned toward me, I got a good look at her. An attractive woman. Gorgeous blue eyes. Although the mother was a blonde, the resemblance to Marie was striking. And suddenly the pieces snapped together to a puzzle that I didn't even know existed.

I ran for the parking lot, hid in the car, and waited for Cynthia.

"Why'd you do that?" she asked several minutes later, clearly annoyed. "I had no idea where you were."

"I started to feel really ill," I told her, and was a mile down the road before she even had her seat belt on.

After not sleeping at all, early the next morning I drove to the Timber Cove assisted living facility in Elizabeth to see who, exactly, occupied room 1615. Since I wasn't a relative, doctor, or cop, I assumed that getting an answer might not be easy.

It was, though.

"There is no room sixteen fifteen," said the friendly lady in the white uniform. She was behind the counter in the lobby. Beside the Danish and Styrofoam cup of coffee was a clipboard. She looked at it, flipped to the second page. "Maybe you mean room fifteen sixteen?"

I said that maybe I did. She probably wasn't supposed to give me a name. "That'd be Len Burnham," she said.

I asked how long he'd been living in that room.

"Mr. Burnham has been here for as long as *I've* been here."

"And how long is that?" I asked.

Eleven years.

That afternoon I asked Joey for a few days off so that I could travel to San Francisco. He agreed to split the ticket with me if I set up meetings with a couple of record labels while I was there. Then I e-mailed Jeffrey, telling him I was visiting on business and wanted to see him.

His reply—*It'll be nice to get together after all this time*—seemed innocent enough, but in its terse politeness I read guilt.

It was early evening, just a few days later, when I arrived in San Francisco, and as soon as I'd checked into my hotel I called his cell phone. "I'm glad to hear your voice," he said, and asked if I'd like to come over to the house later that night for a drink. No, I told him, that wouldn't work. We agreed to meet up at the Starbucks near my hotel the next day at noon.

The fog lifted in the morning to reveal a bright California day. When I arrived at the café, Jeffrey was already seated at a table with a drink. I noticed that he was clean shaven and had cut his hair short. The short-sleeved oxford shirt he had on was an olive color that showed off his tan. He looked healthy—way more fit than the last time I'd seen him.

He rose to shake my hand, and so I shook it. Then, while he waited at the table, I stood in line for the largest coffee in the place. It'd become a compulsion to ingest as much caffeine as possible in order to limit my sleeping to light, dreamless naps between recording sessions and during the commercials of TV shows. Most days, I went through at least a dozen cups of coffee in my ongoing struggle to avoid the terrors of deep sleep.

I set down my drink and sat across the table from Jeffrey. He hadn't asked why I wanted to see him, and I hadn't told him. But he knew. I could tell from the way he avoided my gaze, the way he seemed to be interested in the bags of coffee beans on display, in the people waiting for their drinks, in the words printed on his paper cup. I let him ask me a couple of polite questions—"How's the family? How's the house?"—and then we sat in uncomfortable silence, his eyes still looking around the café for anything that was not my face, until I said, "So who was she?"

Jeffrey looked at me and frowned. "I beg your pardon?"

"Was she Sara's niece? Younger sister?" He shook his head slightly, still pretending not to understand. "I saw the girl's mother," I said. "She could be Sara's twin." And then to be as clear as possible, I added, "Don't fuck with me, Jeffrey. I *know*. That's why I'm here."

He sighed, took a sip from his drink, then set it down again. Drummed his fingers on the tabletop. There was music being pumped into the café, soft jazz, but Jeffrey's drumming had nothing to do with the beat. Finally, he said, "The mother is Sara's first cousin. That makes Marie—I'm not actually sure. Her cousin once removed?"

I'd had little doubt about my suspicions, but hearing Jeffrey confirm them made me want to climb over the table and hurt him, witnesses be damned.

"Did you even lose your money?" I asked. "Or was that a lie, too?"

"Of course I did—I lost all of it, just like I said." Now he stared straight at me, looking offended, as if I were being unkind to doubt him.

"So I guess the two million dollars came in pretty handy."

"It wasn't quite that much."

"What are you talking about?"

"Well, a hundred thousand of it was already mine." He bit his lip, as if trying to balance his need for secrecy against his need to show me how clever he'd been. "And then there was the cost of two years of living expenses in New York City." I must have given him a confused look, because he added, "For Marie. She wanted to be an actress. This way she didn't have to wait tables." So that was their deal. "But yes, the money was extremely helpful. Sara and I live a lot more modestly now. I prefer it, actually."

"You're still together, then."

He shrugged. "What do you want me to tell you?"

"Your marital problems . . . the guy she was cheating with at work . . . you made all that up?"

"Sara and I are peas in a pod, Will. Same as you and Cynthia." He saw me shaking my head. "Look—I needed money. Nolan had it. So I took it."

"That simple, huh?"

"I didn't say it was simple. Come on, you were there—you know it wasn't simple. It was probably the hardest thing I ever did. But he had it coming."

"Bullshit," I said. "College was a long time ago. People make mistakes."

He was about to take a drink, and he slammed his cup down on the table, spilling some of his hot coffee. "We were in love! And he *knew* it. And he slept with her anyway and didn't even have the balls to tell me."

"Then who did tell you? Was it Sara?"

"She didn't have to." He looked at me as if I were being obtuse. "It was all in her *story*. Look, you read it, too. You know exactly what I'm talking about."

"So you planned this for, what, ten years?"

"Of course not. I had no idea Nolan inherited all that money. But I was online one day, reading about his campaign, and all the information was right there in the article. I knew right away what I had to do. I knew what he deserved."

Jeffrey looked better than he had in a long time. Even his teeth looked whiter. He was definitely feeling clever, and I hadn't counted on that. He seemed almost to be enjoying himself, revealing to me how wise and cunning he thought he was. But he didn't know anything. I sat there looking at him, thinking about how easy it would be to change him forever. Reduce him to dust.

"Honestly, Will—I wasn't sure I could pull it off," he was saying, "and I was so fucking scared the whole time. But it worked. She's a good little performer, isn't she?"

Yes, I thought. She was a true triple threat. "You robbed me, too, you asshole. And Evan."

"Oh, come on. Evan made partner. He's probably pulling in a million a year. I'd say that dwarfs his contribution to the cause."

"And what about me?" I asked.

"Now *that* I felt bad about from the beginning, honest to God. Hell, I almost called the whole thing off the week before. But you know all about that."

231

The late-night phone call.

I shook my head. "And I talked you into coming."

"Oh, don't beat yourself up over it. I probably would've come regardless of what you said—because there's something you don't know about yourself that I know."

I stared coldly at him.

"Well, don't you want to know what it is?" he asked.

I didn't want to take the bait. I really didn't. But I'd flown all the way to California for this. "Why don't you enlighten me."

He actually grinned. "You're a winner."

"Fuck you."

"You are. You're ambitious, same as the rest of us. Even though you won't admit it to yourself. Hell, if I know you, I'll bet you never even lost a beat. I'll bet you're doing better now than ever before."

I looked away, because I did know this about myself. I hadn't known it before the kidnapping. But I knew it now. I was one of us. I was my own nightmare, a monster hiding in the woods, waiting for me.

"I hope you aren't planning to tell anyone about this," he said. "The publicity would kill Evan's career. He'd lose his license. And it wouldn't be good for you, either. Or Cynthia."

And there was a dead man in the ground. There was nothing to say except for what couldn't get said.

"Don't look at me like that," he said, and his mouth curved into a tentative smile. "And don't pretend you aren't a little impressed. Admit it. You'd have done it, too, if you were me."

"You're wrong," I said. "There are things I wouldn't do." But my words rang hollow, even to me. "I've got to go."

"Do you want your money back?" he asked. "Is that it? Because I'd be happy to pay you back. I could write you a check."

"Good-bye, Jeffrey," I said.

I was about to stand up when he said the most peculiar thing. "You know, we can still be friends. I hope you know that. I mean, we've been through some crazy shit together, and now we have kids the same age." He leaned forward and put a hand on my shoulder. "Come on, man, why don't you come over to the house tonight for dinner, and I'll write you that check."

All around us, people traded stories of their lives in the pungent meeting place of a new millennium. An espresso machine whirred like an alarm clock telling me it was time to rise and shine. Get a move on.

I stood up, grabbed my coffee, and left him sitting there. From my rental car, I confirmed my next appointment with Bay Area Records. They were interested in using our studio for one of their Pennsylvania bands. "Yes," I said, unfolding my directions. "I'll see you soon." I hung up my cell and lit a cigarette. And before pulling away from the curb, I looked in my rearview mirror and happened to catch a glimpse of myself. I saw a thirty-three-year-old man with sleep-deprived eyes tinged with horror, but hope, too—hope for his wife, for his child, and, above all, for the day when the radioactive rock on his bedside table might cease to glow.

I took a long swallow of coffee and secured the cup in the car's cup holder. As I pulled into traffic and slowly coasted down the steep San Francisco street, I began to rehearse my presentation out loud, so that once the meeting started I would say everything right. I would be perfect.

CHAPTER 28

A LONG TIME AGO, JEFFREY told me that were he to write Sara into a story, he'd never demean her.

What would he have written? How would he have begun? How would I?

Maybe I'd begin with the tiny mole, the dark speck so easy to miss in the tan sky of her inner thigh. Or maybe I'd describe the curve of her hip.

Or the face she made when the take-out Szechuan shrimp was too spicy, or the Riesling too sweet.

I could describe the sight of Sara wet from the shower, beads of water clinging to her body, as she stood brushing her blonde hair, which darkened to luminous gold when wet.

I could describe how, when she made love, she became deadly serious and she gritted her teeth and locked her eyes on yours. Or the downy hairs on her smooth face that could only be seen from inches away under a pink late-afternoon light.

I could describe the sound coming from deep in her throat, the low moan that she herself had failed to present on the page in all its textured sensuality.

These things I could describe easily.

Romantic drivel? Maybe. So sue this second-rate sound engineer.

I could describe how Sara took your hand before falling asleep and kissed it lightly, or how in the morning she'd lie in bed only so long before becoming impatient and poking your ribs until you awoke.

I could describe the abrupt sound, almost like a delighted laugh, when she came, and the sound of her catching her breath as you caught yours, and then how, just when you thought it was over, she'd snuggle close, bite your shoulder, and whisper: *Do it again.*

Had I known how often I'd find myself carrying my drums in and out of the trunks of cars, up and down staircases, down city streets, on and off stages, into and out of basements and attics, across restaurants and bars, through doorways and around drunken dancing revelers . . . had I known all of this when I was twelve years old and choosing an instrument, I might have chosen something smaller. Anything, really. Sometimes I'd even say it to myself—*The harmonica, Will. A nice, little stick-it-in-your-pocket in-strument*—hauling gear to my car after a show when everybody else had already packed up and gone home.

One Wednesday afternoon in the April of my senior year of college, I was carrying my drums from my dormitory room, down a flight of stairs, and into my car. Ordinarily this took me five trips. I had just finished the third trip when I saw Sara coming back to the dormitory. Last week had been cold, but today was warm and breezy, and Sara was a snapshot of spring: short-sleeved pink shirt and blue jeans, hair blowing behind her as she walked along the flagstone path, knapsack slung over one shoulder.

When she got close, I noticed that she'd been crying. I'd seen Jeffrey cry twice before, the first time after accidentally driving

235

over a cat, and recently—though he denied it afterward—during the closing minutes of the film *Sleepless in Seattle*. But never Sara.

"Do you need any help with that?" she asked.

"Are you all right?" I asked.

For a moment she looked surprised, as if unaware that her puffy red eyes had given her away. "Yeah, I'm okay." She looked away. "How much do you have left?"

"I think we can get the rest in one trip." I wasn't going to pass up an offer that came along so rarely.

My gig that evening was in New York. All year I'd been going there fairly often to see bands and meet musicians. Back in the fall, I'd seen Fred McPhee play a couple of times and introduced myself after a show. When I ran into him again more recently, he'd told me that he needed a drummer to substitute with his band, High Noon, over the summer. Their regular drummer had accepted a two-month engagement to tour with another band.

So tonight's gig was really an audition. They played every Wednesday night at Donny's Den, in the West Village. If I did well, the summer gigs were mine. I could imagine no better way to transition from college student to New York musician than having a summer's worth of performances lined up.

Sara and I went up to my room and came downstairs again with the last of my equipment.

"So tonight's the big night," she said.

"Yep." I shoved the last of my gear into the backseat and shut the door. "But seriously, what's wrong?"

I wondered if she'd had an argument with Jeffrey before he left for the airport. He'd been on edge all week. The other morning, when I went by his room for some book I'd lent him, he opened the door in his interview suit. He was trying it on, making sure it fit. He handed me my book and said, "I guess I won't be needing *these* any longer. You know—books?"

"This is only a temporary job," I reminded him. "One year—that's all it is."

"Assuming I'm lucky enough to get it."

He made several sad attempts to put on the tie. Too long, too short, too long again. He muttered profanities each time. Finally, he crumpled up the tie, threw it in a corner of the room, and asked if I'd join him for a tequila shot or three.

It was a time of transparent emotions for all of us. Except for Evan, who was headed to law school at the University of Virginia in the fall, none of us knew what we'd be doing after graduation. And while we knew that we'd garner no sympathy from people facing real hardship, such knowledge didn't lessen our anxieties.

Now it looked as if Sara could use a tequila shot. She leaned against the car and crossed her arms. "I just met with Tanya Mahoney in her office. She offered to help me find a job in publishing. Editorial assistant, or some job like that."

The chance to study with Tanya Mahoney was one of the reasons why Sara had come to Princeton. Now her teacher, a renowned author and Pulitzer Prize winner, was offering to help her find work. I couldn't see why this was anything but incredibly good news.

A Frisbee whumped into the side of my car. On warm days, campus became a battlefield for mad disk hurlers. I'd spent all spring ducking and dodging.

I picked up the Frisbee and threw it to the guy running toward me from the quad, who waved an apology.

Once he'd run off again, I asked Sara, "What am I missing?"

"I don't want to be an editor. I want to be a writer."

"Ah." I didn't know the ins and outs of publishing. "She must like your writing, though, if she's willing to help you out."

"As a matter of fact, she doesn't. As a matter of fact, she thinks my writing is, quote, *young*. She said that to me today. And do you know what else she said? She said, 'While you show promise, you are not yet ready for publication.'"

As she recalled her meeting, fresh tears came to her eyes. She wiped them away with her fingers.

Not being ready—that was my own biggest fear. I imagined Fred McPhee shaking my hand later that night, after our set, and saying, *Thanks, Will. But don't call us, we'll call you.* These were New York musicians, professionals, and I worried whether I'd be able to play at their level. All week I'd been having nightmares where I show up to the gig and my drums are set up all wrong, so that I can barely reach them. Or they're set up correctly but my arms move in slow motion, as if I'm underwater.

"And now," Sara was saying, "as a reward, I get to go to the writing lab and work all night on my Shakespeare paper. How fun for me."

"When's it due?" I asked.

"Monday."

The solution seemed obvious. "Put it off," I said. "Come with me to the city and hang out."

"I don't know . . ."

"Come on, it'll be good for you."

She bit her lip. "You really wouldn't mind?"

I assured her that I could use a friendly face. "Anyway, our set's only an hour long. I'll have you home by midnight."

But at midnight we were still at the bar, still part of the electric cloud of urgent talk and meaningful glances and cigarette haze and sweaty bodies dancing to a jukebox strained to the limit, all of which came together in a great surge of energy that seemed to power this large city. I imagined that right now, a quiet home in some Jersey suburb was experiencing an unexpected burst of light and heat because of what was being generated in this small music club way down in Greenwich Village.

Sara and I were at a table in the corner with Fred and his girlfriend, Eve. Fred had just invited us for a drink at their apartment a few blocks away.

I looked over at Sara, who for several hours now had been on a steady diet of rum and Cokes. She looked back at me and shrugged. "It's your night, big guy. Whatever you want."

"You sure Shakespeare can wait?" I asked.

She cocked an eyebrow.

"Because scholars everywhere are probably on pins and needles waiting to hear what you have to say."

She lifted her hand and shared with me the international sign for *I'm not amused.*

"Okay," I said to Fred. "Maybe for just a little while."

A half hour later, my drums were moving up flight after flight of stairs, carried by the three members of High Noon, Fred's girlfriend, three other friends, Sara, and myself. Drums left in a car are asking to be stolen, so we carried and climbed our way up four stories to Fred's apartment, one of many old buildings lining Sixth Street like a smile of dirty crooked teeth.

We collapsed on the floor. Fred put on a couple of dim lamps and went to change his shirt.

The apartment was old and worn-out, a typical rattrap, yet not without the charm that comes from old construction. High ceilings, wood floors. Eve pointed out the view of a small brick church through the bay window. "You can't see it now," she said, "but there's some grass behind the church where they have outdoor weddings. It's nice."

A frantic beagle came running out of the bedroom, followed by Fred. "Ignore Garfunkel—I don't want him pissing in here."

He handed Pete, the rhythm guitarist, a bowl and lighter and then clipped a leash on the dog and left the apartment.

Eve put on a CD. Jimi Hendrix began quietly playing as the bowl and lighter got passed around the room.

The gig had gone well. Grunge music had been infiltrating nearly every nook and cranny of America, but in the West Village alternative rock still mattered. I'd have been happy to play the gig under any circumstances, but I found myself truly liking High Noon's songs. This, I couldn't help thinking, was a band with a future. After the first song, once it became clear to the other guys that they didn't need to worry about me missing cues or rushing tempos, everyone seemed to relax.

"There's a chance," Fred said to me afterward, amid the hand-shaking and back-slapping, "that Ian will stay in California permanently. So if things work out for all of us this summer . . ."

"That'd be great," I said.

"No guarantee, though."

"Sure," I'd said. "I understand."

When Fred returned to the apartment, he carried the dog back to his bedroom, explaining that Pete was deathly afraid of small dogs.

"Dude, I'm *allergic*," Pete said.

For the next hour we talked, the nine of us. We smoked, and we drank the beer that was in the refrigerator, and we ate slices of the pizza that I don't recall anybody ordering, and Mark, the bassist, his face freckled and hair in dreadlocks, made an impassioned defense of pineapple as a topping until someone pelted him with a napkin.

Our conversations involved the whole group but also smaller numbers, and we talked not like strangers but with the warm, easy feeling of old friends.

Sara exhaled a stream of smoke, her body shrinking into a deep sigh. As far as Jeffrey knew, she was in the computer lab working on her Shakespeare paper. She caught my eye and winked. One of her Texas gestures. Before leaving for the city, she had changed into a tighter pair of blue jeans and a black tank top, cut just low enough. She had stood at the rear of the bar at first and watched us play a couple of songs. But eventually she merged with a group dancing closer to the stage, the day's annoyances appearing to have slid away.

She sat on the floor now, leaning against the sofa, boots kicked off, her hands clasped around her legs and her eyes closed. I took a good look at her and wondered if after three years, Jeffrey still felt the pleasure of arriving someplace with a woman who lit up a room. Like looking at an optical illusion, I could still see the Dallas Cowboys cheerleader, but I could also see the young woman I'd come to know. Somebody who wasn't larger than life. Just a friend with a red bug bite on her ankle and fingernails bitten down to the quick.

I asked her if I might make an observation.

"Shoot," she said, without opening her eyes.

"I don't think that anything your teacher said means that she doesn't think you'll be a great writer someday."

"Thanks, Will," she said.

"Maybe you just need more experience. And in the meantime, she's offered to help you make some contacts. I'll bet you she doesn't make that offer to too many of her students."

"Maybe."

"I'm guessing like one or two a year, if that."

The hint of a grin. "Possibly."

"So she probably thinks you're talented, and she's doing what she thinks is best for your career."

She opened one eye and looked at me. "I've always liked you, Will."

I assured her that the feeling was mutual.

Our numbers dwindled as the Hendrix CD ended and a Black Crowes CD began. The pizza was gone, and yawning became contagious. Gradually, people peeled themselves off the floor, bade farewell, and descended the stairs to whichever part of Manhattan or Brooklyn they called home. "See you soon," they all said. I liked that.

Then it was just the four of us: Fred, Eve, Sara, and I. Fred let Garfunkel out of the bedroom. The dog clicked its way over to us and flopped onto its back so we could scratch its belly. We fussed over the dog for a while, and I looked at my watch.

"You two should stay," Fred said. "I've got plenty of room." His sister shared the two-bedroom apartment, but she was in DC visiting her boyfriend.

I thanked him but declined.

"We can at least help you carry your drums downstairs," Eve said, and yawned.

"Go to bed," Sara said. "We'll just stay for a couple more songs, sober up a little, and get going."

"All right," Fred said. "But feel free to change your mind." He stood up. "Will, great job tonight. We'll talk next week. And Sara, pleasure to meet you." He slung an arm around his girlfriend. "Okay, it's bedtime." He slapped his thigh, and Garfunkel, tail wagging, followed them into their bedroom.

My sobriety was in question; my wish to prolong the evening was not. I went over to the stereo and made the music quieter, which had the effect of releasing the sounds from outside: a police siren wailing, then fading in a Doppler decrescendo. A horn. Another. I sat beside Sara again, and we got to talking about her writing—the sort of things she wrote about, and why. The authors she loved (Woolf, Márquez, and, of course, Mahoney) and those she didn't (Hemingway, London, "all those tough-guy macho assholes"). She spoke of her multiple drafts, all the rewriting, and I came to see my own naïveté about how literature got made. It seemed natural to me that mastering a musical instrument would take years of practice, yet I had never really questioned my assumption that writers were more or less born with their talents fully formed.

"Sometimes I'll read the stories I wrote a year or two ago," she said. "I thought they were good at the time, but . . . yikes."

I began to sense that when I'd seen Sara earlier in the afternoon, she already understood that her teacher knew best. That was why she'd been so upset—not because she'd been told she had no talent, but because her own suspicions about all the work that still lay ahead had been confirmed.

She wasn't upset now, though. Hadn't been since we left campus on our small adventure. A number of guys I knew seemed to prefer women who were perpetually gloomy. Those men believed in the stereotype of the brooding romantic, forgetting that it also meant you had to be with that person. I preferred happiness and took it on faith that such preference made neither me nor the object of my affection shallow or boring. I liked making Sara happy tonight, and felt a stab of jealousy—not the first time—toward Jeffrey for having that role full-time.

We listened to a couple of songs—an Elvis Costello album was playing—and then she said, "It's my turn to make an observation."

"Shoot," I said.

"It's actually a secret I feel like telling you."

"Why me?" I asked.

"Because you don't seem to have any of your own."

"You're right. I don't." Most of the time my uncomplicated life suited me well, but sometimes I envied those whose lives made secrecy necessary.

"That's probably a good thing," she said. "Secrets are hard to keep. Seems like they're always getting out, one way or the other."

"I can keep a secret," I said.

"I know you can." She scrunched up her nose. "I'm drunk, though. And a little high. Maybe I shouldn't be saying stuff right now."

"It's up to you."

"How about you tell me something first. A secret of your own."

"You just said I don't have any secrets."

"Oh, right. Well, think of one anyway," she said. "Or make it up."

"I'm actually next in line for the British throne."

"No, don't make it up. Tell me something real."

My heart rate quickened. I, too, was drunk and a little high. I feared my own confession.

"I'm not sure you want that," I said.

She looked at me severely, studying me, and I was forced to look away.

"Wow," she said.

"What?"

Her face softened. "I think you just told me everything."

The bedroom was small and simply furnished: bed, dresser, mirror, night table. A few framed photographs of Fred's sister and her boyfriend on what appeared to be various vacations. Hiking amid pine trees. Standing on a beach.

The bed was soft and comfortable. I could smell the smoke from Sara's hair and a trace of scented soap or maybe shampoo. And sweat, too. She had danced hard, and I had drummed harder. Underneath the covers and with the lights off, we had stripped to our underwear. I pretended this was no big deal. We were adults, and friends, and therefore supposedly above adolescent titillation. I lay on my side, facing the window, for what seemed like a long time, and had assumed from Sara's steady breathing that she had already fallen asleep.

"Can I spell a word on your back?" she asked.

A radiator rattled somewhere else in the apartment.

"Um, okay," I said. Then I felt a fingernail. A straight line, down the center. Then another. Then a horizontal line. An *H*.

Then an *I*.

"Hi," I said.

Then she wrote, "I had fun tonight."

"So did I," I said.

She wrote, "You are a good drummer."

"Thanks," I said, to the compliment as well as to her method of communication. The delicate tracing of letters felt wonderful on my back, soothing and sensual, and yet it was also putting me to sleep. I was already seeing the outlines of dreams, and then the fingernail stopped its work and her hand came to rest on the bed, just barely grazing my back, or perhaps I was only imagining this.

"We should go to sleep," she said. "I hope you don't mind that."

"No," I said. "I don't mind."

"We're both drunk," she said. "I don't want to go to sleep." She sighed deeply. "But we're drunk. We need to be good."

"I know," I said.

"We're good people, aren't we, Will?"

I agreed that we were.

"I'm glad to hear it," she said.

"I just remembered something," I said.

"What's that?"

"You never told me your secret."

She sighed. "Yeah, I did."

My heartbeat quickened, and I lay there in silence, fighting the urge to say: *Passion isn't always bad, you know.* Finally, I said, "Can I make one more observation?"

"I don't know. Okay."

"I'm sure you already know this, but there's no better place in the world for publishing than New York City."

Her hand, against my back, pulled away.

"Sorry," I said. "I just meant . . ."

She shushed me. "Good night, Will," she whispered.

"Really?"

"Really." Another sigh. "Good night."

"Spell it."

She waited a moment, then spelled it on my back, thirteen perfect letters.

"Thank you," I said.

"Now go to sleep."

"Okay."

One of the songs we'd played tonight was in my head. It was called "Renegade" and had a ska rhythm that I'd worked all week trying to master. But I had, in the end, mastered it, and the song had gone over well. It was the song that'd gotten Sara and others up and dancing. I listened to it in my head for a while.

"Will?" she whispered.

Once again, I'd assumed she had fallen asleep. "Hmm?"

"Thanks."

She shifted in bed, pulling covers, resettling. Four stories below, a motorcycle went by. A few cars. I looked over at Sara, at her beautiful form, and in that instant I felt a deep longing and yet, simultaneously, an overwhelming sense of peace. Like I was exactly where I belonged. *This*, I thought, *is how it could be*. But I knew it couldn't. And so I turned my pillow over to the cool side, closed my eyes, and dreamed this night again.

Sometime after sunrise, only a few hours after we'd gone to sleep, there were church bells and a bright slant of sunlight filling the room from the large east-facing window. Only a sheet covered us. The blanket had been kicked to the foot of the bed. I got up, shut the shades, pulled up the blanket a little, and went back to bed. I awoke again sometime later to the steady stream of traffic sounds four stories below.

I looked at the clock on the nightstand: 8:15. Sara lay on her stomach. Her shoulders were exposed, and part of her back. I put on my clothes and then touched her lightly on the shoulder, waking her, and went into the bathroom so she could get dressed in private. We carried my drums out of the quiet apartment and downstairs to the car. Three endless trips. Then we drove home, saying little to each other, listening to the sound of the New Jersey Turnpike rushing underneath my tires. When we arrived at the dorm at ten o'clock, it felt as if we'd been away longer than a single night. We found street parking by the dorm, and she helped me unload the car.

Standing in my doorway, wearing yesterday's clothes, she said, "That was fun." She said it sadly.

I nodded. "Listen, Sara—"

"Don't. I mean it."

"But you don't know what—"

"Just don't say anything. Say good night."

"It's morning."

"Then say good morning."

"Good morning, Sara," I said.

"Good morning, Will," she said, and left me alone with my drums.

I sat on the bed a minute, then changed into shorts and a T-shirt. Went down the hall to the bathroom to brush my teeth and wash my face. I was behind in my senior thesis. There was plenty to do, here at Princeton, in the few weeks until graduation. The gig was done, my night with Sara was now in the past. Shake it off. A couple more hours of sleep in my own bed, so the day wouldn't be wasted. Then I'd get to work.

When I returned from the bathroom, she was sitting in the hallway, on the carpet outside my door.

"This'll all be okay, you know," she said. "There's absolutely nothing to worry about."

Her smile was a question.

I opened the door, my answer.

We went inside and spent the next two days there.

ACKNOWLEDGMENTS

M ANY THANKS TO Catherine Pierce, Felice Kardos, Christopher Coake, Michael Piafsky, Becky Hagenston, Josh Kutchai, and James Mardock for discussing this book with me at its conception, reading parts or all of it while in manuscript form, and helping me to make it better. Thanks to Jody Klein for her generosity and wisdom, and to Otto Penzler for making the new guy feel welcome. Finally, one more thanks to Katie, and to Sam, too. You both make me happy.